Jeans hung low on his hips and he was bare-chested.

"Trouble sleeping?" he murmured.

His voice slid across her skin like the best sex she'd ever imagined. "Uh, yeah. I've never been this close to an ocean. I'm not used to the sound of it."

"You get used to it after a while. I find it soothing."

Sophie raised her arms to chase away the goose bumps raised by his centrefold sex appeal. Her palms itched to glide over every inch of that chest. To hook her fingers in the waistband of his jeans and tug them lower. To see if he wanted her half as badly as she wanted him.

His eyes were black pits in his shadowed face.

Unfathomable. Unreadable.

Dear Reader,

Welcome to installment number six of THE MEDUSA PROJECT! This story was inspired by a bet and a treadmill. The bet came from a friend who challenged me to run in a 10K race supporting breast cancer research. It was such a worthy cause, how could I say no? Small problem – I hadn't exercised seriously in a number of years, not since I had become a mummy and life went crazy.

So I jumped on a treadmill and started jogging. And swearing under my breath. And sweating. A lot. Somewhere in that morass of pain, it occurred to me to wonder if a regular woman leading a normal life could ever be transformed into a Medusa. And Sophie Giovanni was born.

Clearly, it would take a very special trainer to coax, bully or bribe her into the sort of fitness required of a Special Forces operative, and yummy Brian Riley took shape. I have to confess, he was a lot more fun to imagine while I jogged than Sophie was.

The 10K race went fine. I managed to run the whole distance at a not-humiliating pace, and we raised a lot of money for a great cause. Whenever I got tired and wanted to quit, I thought about Sophie and Brian, and they spurred me onwards. Like Brian says to Sophie in the story, nothing's impossible if you really put your mind to it.

Happy reading and may Sophie and Brian inspire you to try something new!

Warmly,

Cindy Dees

The Medusa Seduction

CINDY DEES

MILLS & BOON®
Pure reading pleasure™

*First published in Great Britain 2008
by Harlequin Mills & Boon Limited,
Eton House, 18-24 Paradise Road, Richmond, Surrey TW9 1SR*

© Cynthia M Dees 2007

ISBN: 978 0 263 86003 0

46-1008

*Harlequin Mills & Boon policy is to use papers that are
natural, renewable and recyclable products and made from
wood grown in sustainable forests. The logging and
manufacturing processes conform to the legal environmental
regulations of the country of origin.*

*Printed and bound in Spain
by Litografía Rosés S.A., Barcelona*

ABOUT THE AUTHOR

Cindy Dees started flying aeroplanes while sitting in her dad's lap at the age of three and got a pilot's licence before she got a driver's licence. At age fifteen, she dropped out of school and left the horse farm in Michigan where she grew up to attend the University of Michigan.

After earning a degree in Russian and East European Studies, she joined the US Air Force and became the youngest female pilot in its history. She flew supersonic jets, VIP airlift and the C-5 Galaxy, the world's largest aeroplane. She also worked part-time gathering intelligence. During her military career, she travelled to forty countries on five continents, was detained by the KGB and East German secret police, got shot at, flew in the first Gulf War, met her husband and amassed a lifetime's worth of war stories.

Her hobbies include professional Middle Eastern dancing, Japanese gardening and medieval re-enacting. She started writing on a one-dollar bet with her mother and was thrilled to win that bet with the publication of her first book in 2001. She loves to hear from readers and can be contacted at www.cindydees.com.

This book is dedicated to my daughter, who has known all along that nothing is impossible. Thanks for reminding me of that fact, sweetheart.

Chapter 1

Sophie Giovanni walked down the sidewalk, swinging her arms freely, breathing deeply and relishing scuffing the aspen leaves. It was a perfect fall day, cool and crisp and dry. The Wasatch mountain range ahead wore the first dusting of snow of the season, harbinger of the winter to come. Maybe this year would be the one when she'd get up the nerve to strap on skis again and fly down those mountains like she used to. The idea made her gut clench in raw terror.

Maybe this winter.

But not today.

Back at Sophie's apartment complex, the tall man in the khaki pants and black polo shirt, who'd been working on his car for the past hour, watched her cross the street and head for the city park. She was the one in the tennis shoes, baggy sweat pants and a University of Utah sweatshirt. *Show time.*

After waiting long enough to be sure the Giovanni woman wasn't coming right back, he approached her door, looked both ways, and deftly inserted a locksmith's gun in her lock. It popped open in a matter of seconds. He slipped inside, closing the door quickly and silently behind him.

He moved around the apartment, pulling the shades and closing curtains to keep out prying eyes that might identify him later. Then he slipped into her bedroom and unfolded the collapsible duffel bag he'd brought with him. He checked his watch. She'd been gone ten minutes. He probably had ten safe minutes to get what he'd come for. He gave himself seven.

Sophie tilted her face up to the gentle rays of the sun. She really ought to get out like this more often. The doctor said exercise was good for her knee. But after the skiing accident, she'd been leery of doing anything that might aggravate the joint. She'd worked her way up to jogging, but anything that might twist the joint like tennis or basketball—both sports she used to enjoy—forget it.

Maybe she should take up one of her old sports on her lunch hours. To date, she'd made excuses to herself about the volume of work stacked up on her desk. But she really could stand to lose a few pounds. Ever since she'd turned thirty, she'd been getting a little rounder and softer.

She couldn't do the exercise thing this coming week, though. The Morton case was going to trial Thursday, and she had a boatload of last-minute motions to type up for her boss.

Maybe next week.

He started in her closet, pulling out random shirts and slacks and stuffing them quickly into his bag. He moved on to her dresser drawers, snagging shorts, socks and a new exercise suit with the tags still on it. He opened yet another drawer. Stared down at the array of underthings and swore under his breath.

Bypassing the colorful, lacy stuff, he grabbed a fistful of cotton briefs and the one sports bra in the drawer. But his fingers hesitated. Yearned toward the sleek satin and sheer lace. Aww, what the hell? He grabbed the slinky stuff and tossed it in the bag, too.

He stepped into her bathroom and paused, inhaling in surprise. It smelled like a woman. A girlie one. He sniffed again, trying to place the scent. Peaches. Yup, entirely *edible*. Into his bag went toothbrush, hairbrush, hair dryer and the entire contents of her makeup drawer. He poked at a couple bottles of perfume. Took off the lids and sniffed them. The first one was too flowery. But the second one sent a shiver of delight down his spine. It was sexy and subtle. Naughty. Oh yeah. Into the bag with that. Shampoo, conditioner and deodorant rounded out his haul in her bathroom.

A glance at his watch. Three minutes before he had to be out of here.

He retreated to her bedroom and looked around. What else? He grabbed a picture of his target with an older woman whom she looked like—her mother probably—and tossed it in the bag. Her alarm clock and the book from her bedside table. A romance novel about a Scottish rogue of some kind. Into the bag with both. He spied a basket of yarn and knitting needles on the floor beside her bed. Not that she'd have time for a hobby, but it might make her feel a little more comfortable. Although he planned on making her damned uncomfortable before it was all said and done. The knitting basket was bulky, but he stuffed it in.

Next, he headed for her desk in the living room. Into his bag went her checkbook, a box of blank checks, address book, cell phone charger—no sign of the phone. Must have it with her. Her spare keys and—bingo!—wallet. He rooted through the drawers and came up with another gem. Her passport. *Perfect.* He tossed it in with his loot.

Sophie paused at the edge of the park, across the street from her apartment complex, steadying herself on the back of a bench while she caught her breath. That was the thing about living in the mountains. When you ran out of air, there wasn't a whole lot of oxygen readily available to replenish your body. Dizzy and winded, she breathed deeply and tried to relax. When she got home, she was going to take a nap until any more errant urges to exercise left her completely.

Two minutes left.

And now to clean up. Pulling out a microfiber cloth, he retraced his steps quickly through the apartment, wiping down every surface he'd come into contact with. There. Good to go. He picked up his haul and slung the duffel bag's wide strap over his shoulder.

Sophie waited while a city bus rolled past. Holding her breath to avoid the noxious diesel fumes, she stepped off the curb and hurried across the street. Her apartment complex loomed in front of her, and she headed toward her building.

A quick peek out the door into the breezeway. All clear. He locked her door from the inside, slipped out and pulled it shut behind him. He hurried down the concrete steps to his car, tossed the bag in the trunk and closed the lid.

Now to collect the woman herself.

He slid into the breezeway once more and not a moment too soon. Here she came. Damn. He'd cut that a little too close for comfort. He blended in with the dim shadows as if he were part of them. But then, maybe he *was* part shadow. Expectant patience flowed into every part of his body.

Sophie walked between the last two cars and headed wearily for her apartment. Yep, a hot shower and a nap were just what the doctor ordered.

When the tall, athletic man stepped out of the shadows, her first reaction was not alarm or even surprise. It was rather more visceral than that—an immediate and instinctive reaction to the sheer physical presence of him. It wasn't that he was movie-star handsome. Although he was. Charismatic didn't cover it, either. He struck her more like a…force of nature. He was one of those perfectly turned out men—perfect physique, perfect creases in his slacks, short hair, perfectly combed from a side part.

In the millisecond it took her to register all of that, he was in front of her—almost, but not quite, invading her personal space.

"Uhh, can I help you?" she mumbled, startled.

"Miss Giovanni?"

He knew her name? "Who are you?" she blurted, surprised.

His left hand came up out of his pants pocket, palming a flash of silver. "Federal agent. I need you to come with me."

Another man started to round the corner, but caught one glimpse of the two and ducked back into the shadows, swearing silently to himself. He spun and strode quickly across an adjacent parking lot. *Damn.* He climbed quickly into a car with black-tinted windows and punched out a number on his cell phone, agitated.

"Patch me through to Mother," he muttered tersely.

A male voice, Arabic accented, responded, "One moment."

A series of clicks, and then a female voice picked up the phone. *"Allo?"*

He switched to French. "I need to speak to him." No need to identify *him*. Everyone in the house he'd just been connected to knew who *he* was. Fouad Sollem ruled with an iron fist over not only his global network of operatives, but also his home.

"Un moment."

A familiar voice came on the line and said merely, *"Oui?"*

He replied in English, "It's me. I found her."

Sollem responded in quick, flawless English, "You're sure it's her?"

"Yes. But there's a problem. She was just arrested."

"Arrested! For what?"

"I have no idea."

"Find out." A pause while Sollem's formidable mind no doubt considered the possibilities. Then, "The police will let her out on bail soon enough. When they do, kill her."

"As you command."

The flash of silver went away and his right hand wrapped around Sophie's upper arm. She'd glimpsed his badge just long enough to know she was looking at a real one. In her work at the law firm, she'd seen plenty of them. He turned her away from her door and propelled her forward all in one smooth movement.

"What's going on?" she gathered herself enough to ask.

"You're not in trouble. Into the car, please. I need to speak with you. In private." He reached out with his free hand, opened the car door and guided her into the vehicle.

She frowned. Her law firm wasn't involved in any federal investigations that she was aware of. And she was aware of pretty much everything the firm did. "What is this in regard to?"

"I'll give you the details when we get where we're going."

"And where's that?"

No answer.

"Who are you? Where are you taking me?"

"I told you. I'm a federal agent. And I need to talk to you. In a private location."

He started the car, backed out of the parking space and accelerated away from her apartment. If she didn't buy his story, her window of opportunity to get away from the guy was closing rapidly. She weighed her chances of jumping out of the car without hurting herself. Not good.

She announced, "Federal agents don't run around snatching private citizens off the sidewalk for random interrogations."

"This isn't a random interrogation, and we detain anybody we have to when a matter of national security is involved."

National security? "What's your name?" she demanded. "Exactly which government agency do you work for?"

The car sped up a ramp and onto the highway. Crud. No chance of jumping out of the car now.

"My name's Brian Riley. I work for the Department of Defense and Homeland Security."

"For the record, I'm not at all certain this snatch-and-drag act is legal. If you've violated my civil rights, you can expect to hear from my lawyer about it."

"I've merely taken you into temporary custody for questioning. You're under no suspicion of having committed any crime. Like I've already stated, I merely need to ask you a few questions."

"Don't split hairs with me. I work for a law firm. You grabbed me, all but pushed me into a car and are now whisking me off to God knows where to interrogate me or worse."

Unaccountably, he glanced over at her and grinned. A movie-star, megawatt smile that would knock most girls on their behinds. Heck, under normal circumstances, it would knock her over. But these were *not* normal circumstances.

"What are you so bloody amused at?" she demanded.

"You've got spunk. That's good."

"Spunk? You make me sound like a puppy."

He laughed aloud. "You and I are going to get along just fine."

"With all due respect, what the hell is going on here?"

Infuriatingly, he smiled and continued to drive. Patience never had been her strong suit. Huffing, she crossed her arms over her chest and glared out the window at the traffic whizzing by.

Before long, he exited the highway. She blinked in surprise at the signs. "Luke Air Force Base?"

Still no reply. A military matter then. She reviewed the law firm's clients. No military members came to mind.

Riley drove up to the front gate and the guard waved the car through without stopping him to ask for ID. Her companion threw a snappy salute at the security policeman and breezed past the guard shack. He was known at this base, then.

When he drove past another guard shack and right out onto the flight line, her general irritation was replaced by surprise. Who *was* this guy? He stopped the car and she eyed the narrow, low-slung business jet in front of her. She asked suspiciously, "Where are we going for this interrogation of yours?"

"California. San Diego to be precise."

California? Holy cow! This is what she did every Saturday afternoon…jet off to California with a hunky federal agent to have a chat. *Not.* "I'll ask you one more time. What's this about, Mr. Riley?"

"Captain Riley," he corrected absently as he climbed out of the car. He pulled a briefcase and a black duffel bag out of the trunk, then came around and opened her door for her. "I'll tell you more once we're airborne. Trust me."

"Trust you? Sure. No problem."

"Have I hurt you? Threatened you? Been anything other than polite with you? You've been detained for questioning. You haven't been arrested, nor are you being charged with any crime. You have information vital to national security, and I merely need to talk with you about it."

"What guarantee do I have that you won't tromp all over my civil rights or throw me in jail for no good reason?"

"None." A pause. "Except my word of honor."

He looked her squarely in the eyes. No hesitation, no evasion, no overly sincere effort to look honest. After years of sitting in on depositions and trials, she had a finely honed sense of when she was hearing lies or truth, and she was hearing truth now.

"Look around you, Miss Giovanni. You're standing in the middle of an air-force base. I had to pass multiple sets of armed guards who know me on sight to get out here on the ramp. Nobody's worried about me or your presence with me."

He had a point. She sighed.

A pilot poked his head out the plane's hatch. "We're ready to go when you are, Cap'n Riley. All we have to do is button up and crank the engines."

She murmured, "San Diego, huh? I've never been there."

Relief flickered through his gaze. "You're gonna love it."

Settling into a state somewhere between shock and disbelief, she ducked onto the jet, which the pilot called a C-21. Riley told her it was a military version of a Learjet 35, which didn't mean much to her, either. As soon as she'd buckled her seat belt, the whine of jet engines wound up outside. They taxied out to the runway and were airborne in a matter of minutes. The wheels thunked up into the gear well and the plane banked left, climbing steeply.

"Okay, Captain Riley. We're airborne. Start talking."

He startled her by reaching into his pants pocket and holding out a cell phone to her. "Here. I'd like you to make a phone call first. I want you to verify my identity."

"You're not supposed to use cell phones on airplanes!"

He grinned. "We get to break the rules. Call information for the 202 area code."

She punched in the number, and as the phone started to ring at the other end, she murmured, "202. Washington D.C.?"

He nodded. "Ask for the Pentagon operator."

In a moment, she was connected to the Pentagon. She nodded at Riley.

"Now ask for jay-sock headquarters. Then ask someone to verify my identity."

She did as he directed…whatever the heck a jay-sock was.

"Jay-sock headquarters," a female voice said in her ear.

Sophie frowned. "Excuse me, but what's a jay-sock?"

"J…S…O…C, dear. Joint Special Operations Command. How may I direct your call?"

"I'm with a man who says his name is Captain Brian Riley. Is there someone in your office who can identify him for me?"

"Standby for General Wittenauer, ma'am," the secretary replied smoothly.

A man came on the line and barked a single word. "Go."

"Uhh, my name's Sophia Giovanni, and I have a man here with me."

"Ahh yes. Riley. May I assume then, that you're going to take us up on our offer, Miss Giovanni? That's excellent news!"

Offer? What offer? "Actually, I'm calling to verify that he's not an axe murderer. Could you tell me what he looks like?"

"He's about six foot two. Fit as a fiddle. Brown hair. Handsome lad..." The general paused and Sophie heard him shout, "Mary, what color are Captain Riley's eyes?"

Sophie heard a faint female reply. "Blue, sir. Turquoise blue."

"He has blue eyes, ma'am. Didn't he show you his military ID or Homeland Security badge?"

"Those can be faked easily enough."

"I suppose." A pause. "Have him show you his concealed-weapons permit. Or his official passport if he's got it on him. Those are pretty hard to fake. And if neither of those convince you, have him show you his scars. He took a bullet through the right shoulder a couple years back. There was an entry wound in the front and an exit wound in the back, as I recall. He should have a large, horizontal scar on his stomach, too. Knife wound he picked up in Israel. Oh, and on his right hand, at the base of his thumb, you'll find a patch of tough skin. Comes from shooting guns. A lot."

Knife wounds? Shooting? "General, if you're trying to inspire confidence in me about the man, you're not doing a very good job of it."

"Ma'am, Brian Riley is as fine a soldier as I've ever had the privilege to work with. Hear him out. And please. Give his request serious consideration. We did our level best to spare you—looked high and low for someone else we could bring into this operation. But you're it."

What in blue blazes was Wittenauer talking about? Doubtfully, she said, "Thank you for confirming his identity at any rate, General."

"My pleasure. I'll look forward to hearing from you again, Miss Giovanni."

Riigghht.

She hung up the phone, roundly confused. She looked over at her companion.

"He said to ask for your concealed-weapons permit or your official passport."

Riley reached for his wallet.

"Just pass me the whole thing." That made him look up hard. The way his eyes glittered made it clear he didn't like the idea of her pawing through his wallet. Nonetheless, she held out her hand. His jaw muscles rippling, he handed her the leather billfold.

No pictures of kids. No women, either. North Carolina driver's license naming him Brian T. Riley. A couple of credit cards. Hundreds of dollars in cash caught her attention, though. "It's not safe to carry that much money on you, you know."

He stretched out, lounging across the chair with the casual power of a lion. "Who's going to take it from me and live?"

She gulped and tore her gaze away from all that muscle.

"The concealed-weapons permit is in the pocket behind the credit cards. You'll have to dig it out. Not something I flash around often."

She wedged out the laminated card. The picture on it made him look like a cover model. She looked up at him. "Take off your shirt, please."

"What?"

"General Wittenauer said I should check out your scars. They can't be faked."

She thought she heard him curse under his breath, but he leaned forward and peeled off the soft, black cotton polo shirt.

Sweet merciful Heaven. She was not one of those women who swooned at the sight of a half-naked man, but this one made her come close. Suddenly the cover model sat across from her in the flesh. She glanced up from acres of ripped muscles at his face. He was smirking at her, darn him! She scowled back. "How'd you get that scar on your shoulder?"

"AK-47 in Afghanistan."

"And that scar on your stomach?"

"Which one?" he drawled. "I got the little one over here when I had my appendix out. I got this one—" Using his index finger, he traced a long, puckered white line wrapping from his left side almost all the way to his belly button. "—in a knife fight in Tel Aviv."

Her eyes widened, following the mesmerizing path of that tanned finger across the washboard muscles of his stomach. She practically had to shake herself to get her brain in gear again. "Would you mind showing me your right hand?"

He held it out silently, palm down.

She leaned forward across the narrow aisle separating them. Her fingers touched his and the world stopped spinning. His gaze jerked up to hers in surprise, and all of a sudden, she was drowning in the lazy, warm, tropical ocean that was Brian Riley's turquoise eyes. Such power in that gaze.

Such power in those long fingers lying still within hers. The pinkie was crooked near the base. His nails were short. Neat. Pale against his bronze skin. Slowly, she turned his hand over. And gasped at the angry red scar slashing across his palm. Only peripherally did she notice the heavy callous at the base of his thumb as advertised.

"Hell of a life line, isn't it?" he rasped.

"Does it hurt?" she breathed. She couldn't stop herself from running her fingertip lightly over the wound. A fine shudder passed through him. "What happened?"

He shifted uncomfortably but didn't remove his hand from her grasp. "A guy pointed a semi-automatic machine gun at me. He'd been firing it for a while and the barrel was hot. When I grabbed the gun to dissuade him from shooting me, I burned my hand."

Her stomach tightened at the thought of how painful that must have been. "I'm sorry," she murmured.

He forced a laugh and extracted his hand from her grasp. "You're sorry I got burned, or that he didn't shoot me?"

She gave him a reproachful look and didn't bother to answer. She leaned back in her seat. But it wasn't anywhere near far enough from him to dampen the sexy vibes pouring off him—or her reaction to them. He shrugged back into his shirt. But the close atmosphere of the jet remained charged.

"Okay, I believe you. You're Captain Brian Riley. Now what?"

He sighed. "I'm afraid this conversation hasn't gotten off to a good start. You look like you're planning to put my eye out any second, and we haven't even gotten to the part that's going to make you mad, ma'am."

"You can stop calling me ma'am. It makes me feel older and dowdier than I already am."

He opened his mouth like he wanted to protest. Closed it. Opened it again and said, "I'm involved with a very important investigation. You're here because I need your help."

"What sort of help?"

"The information I'm about to share with you is highly classified. It actually is a matter of national security. Before I tell all, though, I need to inform you that a background check has been performed on you and a top-secret clearance was issued for you yesterday."

Sophie stared. "You're kidding."

"I have a form I need you to read and sign that explains the legalities of such a clearance."

She checked his eyes for signs of humor. But he was one-hundred-percent serious. She shamelessly watched the way his taupe dress slacks hugged his muscular thighs and juicy tush as he climbed into the cargo area in the back of the jet and fetched his briefcase. *My, my, my.*

Perching it on his knees, he opened the case, reached

inside and pulled out a government document with attached carbon copies.

"If you could read and sign this…"

She took the document and scanned it quickly. The dry legalese didn't faze her. She dealt with this sort of stuff all day long. It did indeed appear that she was now the proud owner of her very own top-secret clearance.

"Don't these things take a long time to do?" Even in the heat of a high-profile criminal trial, a decent background check took several days and a whole lot of man-hours.

"My investigation is high priority."

"Tell me about it."

"Please sign the clearance paperwork first."

He held out a pen. Her fingertips brushed his as she took it, and the same thing that had happened last time happened again. The moment froze, suspended in time while sexual energy buzzed all around them, shivering across her skin. She gave herself a mental shake and signed the document. "Any other hoops you want me jump through before you tell me what the heck is going on?"

"No ma'am—sorry, uhh, no."

A vague sense of foreboding wedged her shoulders deep into the leather upholstery as he began to speak. She folded her arms across her chest, hugging herself protectively.

"Everything I'm about to tell you is top secret and falls under those rules you just signed off on."

She nodded her understanding. Don't reveal anything she was about to hear to anybody else or he'd have to shoot her— or something like that.

He continued, "Several weeks ago a team of military observers intercepted signal intelligence that led them to believe a major terrorist attack was being planned against the United States."

She snorted. "What's new?"

"True. But this is a specific attack on a nuclear facility in the United States. And from what our surveillance team has been able to gather, it's well-planned and stands a reasonable chance of succeeding."

"I assume you've put said nuclear plant on high alert?"

He snorted back at her. "Are you kidding? It's already off-line. It'll stay that way until we resolve this problem."

"I'm sorry, I interrupted. You were saying?"

"We know practically nothing about the leader of this terrorist cell. However, we know enough about him that a decision has been made to neutralize him in the name of national security."

Her sense of foreboding deepened. "Neutralize him? Are we talking about putting him in jail here? Or something else?"

He replied smoothly, "We're talking about whatever it takes to stop him, up to and including killing him."

Dread crept up her arms like a cold chill. She rubbed them to ward it off, but it didn't help. He said that so calmly. "I fail to see how I can be of any help in…eliminating…a terrorist."

"Ahh, but you see, you're the key to killing him."

Chapter 2

Watching closely for Sophie's reaction, Brian asked casually, "Ever heard of a guy named Freddie Sollem?"

Immediate recognition lit her face. She answered readily, "I grew up next door to him and his family. His grandmother babysat me when I was little so my mom could work. When I got older, Grandma Sollem watched me after school. Heck, I spent more time at the Sollem house than I spent at my own. Freddie and I were in the same grade. We were good friends—as good as a boy and a girl under the age of ten can be."

Brian knew all that. It was why he was here. "What language did the Sollems speak at home?"

"Bhoukari. They're from Bhoukar. It's a little place tucked in between Oman and Yemen."

He knew all that, too. "Did you learn any Bhoukari hanging out with them?"

Sophia laughed. "I spoke it better than English when I was tiny. When I got mad at my mom, I used to yell at her in Bhoukari."

"Still speak it?"

"Good grief, no. It's a pretty obscure dialect. It's not like I ever got any chance to use it after the Sollems moved away."

"Where'd they move to?"

"Back to Bhoukar as far as I know. Freddie's dad thought the kids were being corrupted by living in America. He hauled them all back home to live in their own culture."

"What did Freddie think of that?"

"Why all these questions about Freddie? Are you telling me he's become a terrorist?"

"Do you think he's capable of it?"

She leaned back and crossed her arms under her chest again. "What's going on?"

He studiously kept his gaze off of the breathtaking cleavage her pose created above the edge of her shirt. Not that the impression of it hadn't already burned itself hopelessly into his brain. "You are correct, Miss Giovanni—"

"Call me Sophie."

"All right. You are correct, Sophie. Young Freddie appears to have crossed over to the dark side of the Force."

Her eyebrows lifted. "Why do you want to talk to me? You've obviously done your homework if you know about Freddie's fascination with *Star Wars*."

"Nonetheless, we'd like to talk to you about him and his family. Perhaps you can provide some vital tidbit we've missed." That, of course, was only a fraction of what he hoped to talk her into doing, but after meeting her and seeing how cautious she was, instinct told him he'd better ease her into the proposition rather than hit her with it all at once.

"What sort of tidbit are you looking for?"

He shrugged. "We won't know until we find it. Are you willing to help us?"

"I'm an American citizen. Of course I'm willing to help. What do you need me to do?"

Triumph surged for a moment, but he reined it in hard. They were a long way from her agreeing to the whole proposition. "I'm taking you to a private location where we can talk at length about Freddie."

"To interrogate me."

"Debrief you."

"You want to pick my brains by whatever name you choose to call it."

"Close enough."

"How long is this going to take?"

He shrugged. "As long as it takes. Days. Weeks."

That alarmed her. "I have a job. I can't just up and leave for weeks."

"I spoke with your boss. The government has hired a temporary replacement and will pay all of that person's expenses until you return to work."

"You called my boss without even talking to me?"

He gazed deep into her eyes, doing his damnedest to convey how much he needed her help. "Time is of the essence. The situation is unfolding very rapidly, ma'am. Lives are on the line."

She murmured absently, "I told you not to call me ma'am."

He leaned fractionally closer to her. "Sophie—" The word felt like melting caramel in his mouth, all sweet and smooth and languorous. "—Please. I need your help."

She sighed. "That's the second time you've said please. And darned if I'm not a sucker for polite men."

He allowed a tiny smile to reach his eyes.

"But I don't have anything to wear. Not even a change of clean under—"

She broke off. *Didn't want to talk about underwear with him, huh?* Wait till she found out he'd already pawed through hers *and* packed it for her.

"I took the liberty of packing a few things for you."

"Of packing?" She repeated blankly.

"Yes. Packing. Putting clothes and toiletries into a suitcase to take with you on a journey."

Startled, she laughed. She had a great laugh. It was warm and fun and invited a person to laugh with her. "I've got that part. But…how…" she demanded all of a sudden, "did you break into my apartment?"

Ahh. Time to make the lady well and truly mad. "I let myself in and packed a few things I thought you might need."

"You broke in…that's illegal! Of all the—"

He gently interrupted her sputtering. "For what it's worth, I'm sorry. I did what was necessary. And I had permission from a judge."

That made her start. "You mean a warrant?"

He flinched slightly. He'd avoided the word because of its criminal implications. The last thing he wanted to do was make her defensive or uncooperative. "Technically, yes. A warrant. But I repeat, you're not under suspicion for anything. We just need to talk to you."

"What kind of warrant? A bench warrant?"

He sighed. "I'm not a lawyer. All I know is someone way above my pay grade got permission from someone else way above my pay grade for me to enter your residence and pack a few things for you. You have to understand, it's very tricky for military members to take any kind of direct action against a civilian citizen of the United States."

She replied dryly, "Pesky little document, that Constitution."

He smiled. "Exactly."

"Why would your superiors go to all that trouble so I could have a change of underwear and my toothbrush?"

"You're very important to us."

She hmmphed and subsided into silence, turning her head to stare out the window, obviously thinking hard. He watched closely to gauge her reaction to his explanation. Did she have the moral flexibility to do what they needed her to? Could she accept that she was a pawn in a greater game? That the government was willing and able—and in this case without any choice in the matter—to do something unsavory in the name of a greater good?

It was clear she didn't like the fact that he'd broken in to her place. That was good. She'd need a steady moral compass to succeed at what Uncle Sam had in mind for her. Finally, she turned her head. Made solid eye contact with him. Another good sign. Not shying away from the issue.

She said wryly, "I tremble to think what you packed for me to wear."

He released his breath carefully. She'd passed the test. She'd accepted that necessity sometimes dictated unpalatable action. Not to mention that she'd resorted to humor to break the tension of the moment. A perfect reaction all the way around.

"Anything I forgot to grab, Uncle Sam will be glad to purchase for you."

"Why didn't you just knock on my door, introduce yourself and let me pack my own bag?"

"I couldn't take a chance on you saying no. And besides," he added lightly, "I'm a helpful guy."

Her shoulders relaxed as if she'd made her peace with what he'd done. Another good sign. She wasn't the type the hold grudges. Better and better. Maybe his task wasn't entirely impossible after all.

Although, her general softness was going to be a hell of a

hurdle to overcome. Particularly in the limited time they would have together. Not only were her plentiful curves distracting as hell, but he doubted she was a serious athlete if she was shaped like that. She was by no means unhealthy, but the women special operators he'd worked with didn't carry an ounce of fat to give their bodies Sophie's womanly hourglass.

She opened her bag and grabbed a skirt and blouse off the top of the pile of clothes he'd stuffed in it. She excused herself and moved to the back row of seats where she changed clothes quickly. He resolutely kept his gaze glued on the rusty hues of the high desert stretching away outside his window. Not that he saw a lick of it. In his mind's eye danced images of a curvaceous woman, with a come-hither smile and smelling of peaches, peeling off her clothes inch by inch to reveal a tempting landscape of satin-smooth skin, a garden of delights to beggar the senses.

She returned to her seat on a whiff of peach that all but made him lunge across the aisle and devour her whole. It had been too long since he'd had a woman. Suddenly, the idea of the beer-and-pretzels groupies who hung out in Coronado looking to pick up SEALs curdled on his tongue. It was peaches he craved. Ripe, sweet, sassy peaches.

He turned away from Sophie as much as he could within the confines of the Lear's tight seats. Definitely not designed for a man his size. Uncomfortable on several levels, he stared out the window, disturbingly aware that she was studying him intently. He did his best to ignore the attention. He failed, but he faked it.

They landed in San Diego, barely three hours after he'd first snagged her. Even by his standards, things were moving fast. Poor Sophie must feel like she'd been caught up in a tornado. The Learjet taxied to a stop. Out his window he spied a car driving out onto the tarmac. He caught sight of the driver and swore under his breath. Crash Kazinsky. A surge of possessiveness roared through Brian's gut.

Crash was a certified ladies' man, and completely without scruples when it came to chasing skirts. His theory was that if he could lure a woman away from another man, then the other guy wasn't taking proper care of her anyway. The last thing Brian needed right now was Crash hitting on Sophie and distracting her. Brian needed her attention focused solely on him. Hell, he *wanted* her attention focused solely on him.

"Let's go, Hollywood."

Sophie's comment startled him. He blurted, "I beg your pardon?"

"Surely you know you look like a movie star."

Heat rushed to his face. He mumbled, "Uhh, thanks," and reached for the black duffel. "I'll get your bag."

She reached for it. "I can get it."

"I'm sure you can. But I'll carry it anyway." He was being more surly than the moment required, dammit. He shifted the bag to his other shoulder, out of her reach. "Let's go. Our ride's waiting for us."

Thankfully, Crash—Kyle was his real name, but Crash was his field handle—caught Brian's hand signal to be silent and nodded, an eyebrow cocked questioningly. Unfortunately, there wasn't a hand signal for "keep your paws off my woman and don't even think about making time with her." Maybe he ought to invent one. Crash sat up front, grinning like a damned crocodile in the rearview mirror the whole way out to North Island and through the city of Coronado.

Finally, they pulled up at a beach house on the Pacific Ocean. Literally. Out the living room window was nothing but an expanse of silver sand and blue water glittering in the late-afternoon sun. The starkly beautiful view lent the place a deceptive sense of isolation.

"Wow," Sophie breathed.

Brian paused in the act of carrying her gear through the main room and upstairs to one of the two loft bedrooms. "Calls to a soul, doesn't it?"

She shot him a surprised look over her shoulder. *Whoops. Didn't mean to say something so revealing, there.* He turned his back and jogged up the stairs with her bag.

When he came down, she'd gone onto the deck and was leaning over the railing, gazing out to sea. The wind blew her cotton skirt against her body, and what the contours of the thin fabric didn't reveal, the sun's backlighting did. He cursed under his breath. Thank God, Scottie and Stoner were due here soon to keep him from doing something stupid like making a pass at her. At least both of them had some scruples when it came to messing with their teammates' women.

Speaking of which, Scottie would be hungry as a horse when they got here. The boy was always hungry. Brian picked up the phone and, without dialing, spoke directly into the dial tone. "Riley here."

The dial tone disappeared. "Go ahead."

He recognized the no-nonsense voice of his boss, Major John Hollister. "Sir. The subject is in the safe house. How's the audio?"

"All the microphones are five by five. Only one we haven't gotten a sound check on is in the kitchen. If you could hop in there and give me a quick test count, we're good to go."

"Will do. Any chance you could send over some food?"

"Name your poison."

"She looks like the type to go for Chinese."

"I'll have Scottie and Stoner bring some with them."

"ETA on Fric and Frac?"

"Estimated time of arrival, thirty minutes plus however long it takes them to pick up supper. How's she warming up to the plan?"

"Haven't popped it on her yet. She still thinks she's here just for a debrief. I'm easing her into it."

"You know what you have to do."

"Yes, sir."

Brian hung up. Sighed. Went outside, leaned his elbows on the redwood rail and joined Sophie in her silent contemplation of the ocean. It was calm, with practically no waves. Just quiet ripples depositing momentary foam on the sand before retreating.

"How dangerous is Freddie?" she asked.

"He's one of the scariest dudes on the planet. He's killed dozens of people and masterminded who knows how many terrorist attacks around the world. It's taken us years to get close enough to him figure out who he is."

"It's hard to imagine the sweet kid I knew turning into that. What happened to him?"

Brian shrugged. "Brainwashing, probably."

"Must've been pretty intense to change him so completely."

"The *madrahsa*—that's a private religious school—he went to in Bhoukar is infamous for turning out fanatics."

"That's a shame. He was a really bright kid."

"Yeah, well now he's a really bright killer."

They fell silent.

"Two of my teammates are going to be here soon. They're bringing take-out. I figured nobody would feel like cooking tonight. As soon as they get here, we'll begin."

"Where is Freddie now?" she asked.

"Hiding in Bhoukar."

"How do you know that?"

"Because a team of operatives called the Medusas are watching him around the clock."

"If you've got a team that close to him, why don't *they* just…neutralize…him?"

"He's inside a large, partially underground compound. Unless he comes out, they can't get a shot at him. Because he's underground, we can't just drop a bomb on his head. Plus, he's surrounded by dozens of women and children. And contrary to popular belief, we military types do our best not to kill innocents."

"What am I supposed to do to help?"

"All in good time."

"Why isn't now a good time to tell me everything?"

He frowned. She wasn't ready to hear the real reason she was here, yet. Fortunately, a faint sound of bass voices drifted down the beach just then. He turned his head toward it automatically.

Sophie asked, "What's that?"

"SEALs."

"I didn't know there were seals on these beaches. I'd have thought there were too many people for them to come ashore around here."

He couldn't help it. He laughed.

"What?" she demanded.

"Navy SEALs. As in Special Forces soldiers."

"Oh." Her cheeks turned pink.

What must it be like to be so completely ignorant of the world he lived in? The real world, as he usually thought of it—politically charged, violent and dangerous. Full of SEALs and men like him who dealt with it by meeting violence with violence. Regret stabbed him. He was the bastard who'd get to strip away her innocence. He swore under his breath.

The rhythmic song became a little louder. He recognized the tune as one of the filthier running songs the SEALs trained to. Singing helped regulate their breathing and keep them in step with one another. A grin twitched at the corners of his mouth. "You might want to go inside if you're easily offended. The ditty they're bellowing isn't exactly fit for a lady's ears."

"Thanks for the warning, but I promise not to swoon."

The formation came into view—two dozen men in camouflage pants, combat boots and olive-green T-shirts running through the surf at the edge of the ocean. The black T-shirted BUDs instructor running alongside the trainees raised a hand in greeting to Brian as they ran past. He waved back.

"Friend of yours?" Sophie murmured.

"Yeah. We go back a ways."

"Ever work together?"

He looked over at her sharply. She did have a knack for asking questions with a buried edge. "Yeah. We've worked together."

"Are you a SEAL?"

"Hell—pardon me—heck, no. I'm a ground pounder. Army all the way."

"So how did you end up working with a SEAL?"

One corner of his mouth turned up. "Us Army guys would say it was a piece of extremely bad luck."

"A little inter-service rivalry?"

He shrugged. "Lucas Stone is in the Navy. He's one of the men joining us tonight. And I gotta say, he's one of the sharpest guys I've ever worked with. But don't tell him I said that."

She smiled. "What about the other one who's joining us?"

"Scott Cash. He's Army like me."

She turned to face him more fully, leaning a hip on the railing. "I'm not under arrest, right?"

Foreboding slammed into him. He answered cautiously, "No."

"Are you planning to arrest me at some point?"

"Of course not."

"So I'm here purely voluntarily. Doing my civic duty."

"Correct." He was starting to get an inkling of where she was going. *Dammit.*

"Here's the deal. You want me to tell you everything I know about Freddie Sollem. I'm not under any obligation to do so, however. I'm thinking that if you don't tell me the rest of whatever it is you're not telling me, I may suddenly develop big trouble with my memory. I mean, it was all a very long time ago and I was just a kid."

He exhaled slowly. Straightened to his full height. Stared down at her piercingly. Then said grimly, "And there we were, getting along so well. I never have taken real well to threats, veiled or otherwise."

To her credit, she stared back up at him defiantly and didn't back down. Reluctant admiration for her guts flickered through him. Many a brave man had wilted under the stare he was leveling at her right now.

"And I never have taken real well to people not being square with me. What gives, Riley?"

Chapter 3

Sophie stared up expectantly at Riley. She had him over a barrel and they both knew it.

"Tell me about your knee injury," he said abruptly.

She started. Now how in the world did he know about that? An unnerving sense of this man having invaded the most personal and private corners of her life crept over her. He'd already broken into her home. Handled her clothes. Her toothbrush, for goodness' sake. A shade defensively, she retorted, "You're the guys who did the top-secret background check on me. You tell me about it."

Unaccountably, he grinned. More often than not, this guy reacted exactly the opposite of how she expected him to.

He said, "We know you crashed at the U.S. Junior National Ski Championships. Tore your left ACL and had surgery to repair it. Six months of physical therapy, but no sign of any attempt at a comeback to downhill skiing after that. From which we inferred you suffered a…" He paused, searching for a word.

"The phrase you're looking for is 'career-ending injury.'"

"Were we correct?"

"That I wrecked my knee skiing? Yes. That it was career-ending? I don't know. I never went back to the slopes to find out."

"Why not?" he demanded.

"Because I didn't want to," she shot back.

"Why not?"

Why not, indeed? Because the thought of standing at the top of a three-thousand-foot nearly vertical drop to a valley so far below that the people were mere specks made her break out in a cold sweat. Because the thought of seeing trees and moguls and icy downhill courses flying past her at seventy miles per hour made her want to throw up. Because the memory of hot needles of pain shooting through her knee from twenty different directions and the months of agonizing recovery had never really faded. *Because she was afraid, dammit.*

"What does my decision not to return to skiing have to do with Freddie Sollem?" she challenged. Even she heard the truculent edge in her voice, warning him off this subject.

He was dense and didn't catch the hint, however. Or maybe he just ignored it. He plowed onward. "It actually has a great deal to do with Sollem. Please answer my question."

"I thought you said you weren't going to begin the interrogation until after supper."

"Consider this your warm-up."

She glared at him.

He stared back implacably.

The quiet, rhythmic whooshing of the ocean filled the silence between them, ebbing and flowing like the battle of wills ongoing between them.

"Your knee." He finally prodded. "What's its status now?"

"Why do you want to know?"

"Look. I'm not your enemy. I need to know, okay?"

"Not okay. Tell me why."

"Because you may have occasion to do some exercising while you're here, and I need to know how much it can take so you don't hurt yourself."

Sophie started violently as laughter erupted from the doorway behind them. A muscular African-American man stood there with several white, trapezoidal, take-out cartons in hand.

"She may have occasion to do some exercising, eh? Ripper, you crack me up."

Riley spun, his shoulders hunched up in what looked like irritation. "Sophie, this is Lucas Stone. Stoner, say hello to Ms. Sophie Giovanni."

"Pleased to meet you, ma'am."

She smiled back at Lucas. Her first impression was that this man was sharp, sharp, sharp. Self-contained. Professional from the top of his head to the tips of his toes. If he were an opposing prosecutor in a trial, she'd quake in her boots. Juries would love this guy. He oozed integrity and charm.

Riley interjected a tad hastily, "I was just starting to explain things to Sophie. She and I agreed not to start the formal debriefing or go over any details of what's going to happen while she's here until after supper."

"No," she contradicted. "You were trying to cheat and find out how banged up my knee, before supper—and refusing to tell me why you want to know."

Stoner looked back and forth between them, an amused glint in his eyes. "Sorry, man. My money's on the lady."

"Thanks for the support," Riley retorted wryly.

Stone smiled at Sophie, sharing the joke with her companionably. "The chow mein's getting cold. Shall we repair to the dining room and partake of the repast?"

She smiled back at his gallantry. "I'd love to. Hey, this porch is big enough to hold a table and chairs. Why don't we eat out here?"

The two men exchanged quick glances, engaging in a silent conversation that took no more than a fraction of a second. Riley spoke up regretfully. "The sun'll go down soon and it gets chilly fast in the evening. We'd better eat indoors."

She frowned. His insistence on eating inside had nothing to do with the weather. Of that, she was sure. And then it hit her. Not only did her law firm always have a legal typist at depositions, but it also videotaped them. Tone of voice, a significant pause, uncomfortable or guilty body language, all could be critical to making or breaking a case. A transcript couldn't capture those nuances. But a videotape could. There was a camera somewhere inside the house and they needed to keep her in front of it.

Without protest, she followed the two men inside. A third man was in the kitchen, scrounging up plates and utensils, and pouring glasses of iced tea.

Riley murmured from behind her, "Scottie, this is Sophie. Sophie, Scott Cash."

She nodded. The red-haired man looked a few years younger than Brian and Lucas but every bit as buff physically. He looked over his shoulder. Paused. Turned around fully to give her a blatant up-and-down with dancing emerald eyes. And then broadly smiled his approval. Wow. He really knew how to make a girl feel good.

"Pleazhuh to meet you," he said laughingly. His voice was thick with the round vowels and absent Rs of South Boston. His gaze drifted over her shoulder toward Riley behind her. "Looks like you nabbed yourself a spirited lass, bro."

"Stuff it," Riley bit out.

Sophie's head whipped around and she studied her host closely. What had his knickers in such a twist? He scowled, grabbed the plates and forks and stomped out of the kitchen. She and the other men followed him to the dining table, which happened to sit beside a floor-to-ceiling picture window that looked out upon the ocean.

The four of them dug into the cartons of food, and only desultory conversation broke the silence for a few minutes. The formation of SEALs ran back down the beach, still singing, as the sun hung low in the west.

"Have those guys been out running all this time?" she asked surprised. "It's been over an hour since they went past the first time."

The three men grinned at her. Riley answered, "Yeah, they were only out for a short jog today."

"How far did they go?" she replied.

"Six or seven miles, I imagine."

"In the sand?" she blurted. *Ouch.*

Riley glanced over at Stone, the Navy man. "Yeah. Those SEALs are pretty soft. Rangers would've run that far knee-deep in the ocean."

A round of Army and Navy bashing ensued, and Sophie sat back, entertained by the easy camaraderie these men obviously shared. But trepidation built like a brick in her stomach as the food on the table steadily disappeared, marking the end of her reprieve. As much as she dreaded what was to come, the moment arrived when she couldn't eat another bite. She pushed back her plate.

"Are you done?" Scottie asked her.

"Yes."

Riley interjected, "If you want seconds, get them now, Sophie. Once Scottie goes on clean-up detail, there won't be a single grain of rice left."

The redhead shrugged, not denying the accusation. "I have a high metabolism."

Brian retorted, "If that means you burn crazy amounts of calories chasing girls, I guess you're right."

A flurry of quick hand signals flashed back and forth between the men, followed by uproarious laughter. What the heck was that all about? Must be some guy-soldier thing. She shrugged and stood up to clear the plates.

"Sit," Lucas told her firmly. "I'll get those."

"A man after my own heart. Great biceps *and* he does dishes. Do you fold laundry, too?"

He grinned. "Not if I can help it."

"Me, neither," she confessed.

Brian cleared his throat with just enough emphasis to demand her attention. Why didn't she feel at ease with him like the others? He made her tense. Nervous. Edgy. Was it that he was simply an uncomfortable man? Or was it something else? Some undefined tension between them?

He broke into her train of thought, announcing, "We have work to do, and time's critical. The Medusas are stuck out in the middle of the desert with their necks on the line, waiting for us to give them something to help them complete their mission."

"Where do you want to do this?" she asked in resignation.

"Here at the table's fine if you're comfortable."

She glanced around. "Don't you want to video this? At least tape-record it?"

Brian didn't exactly lurch. In fact, he didn't actually move at all. But she'd definitely startled him. "Uhh, that's okay. We just want to talk with you. Nothing so formal as all that."

Stoner and Scottie came back in from the kitchen and sat down again. She caught the infinitesimal nod Stoner shot Brian. The recording equipment must all be in working order. Brian Riley was easy to look at, but what met the eye was most definitely only the surface of this secretive man.

She took a deep breath. Let it out. "Okay, gentlemen. Uncle Sam went to a lot of expense and trouble to get me here. What can I do for you?"

"Ahh, if only they all said that," Brian quipped.

She tossed him a quelling look.

"Sorry." He was almost boyishly cute with that contrite look on his face. Then he said more seriously, "How about we start at the beginning? Where were you born?"

Sophie answered their rapid fire questions without pause for the next hour. The sheer volume of information they extracted from her was astounding. And the amount of it they retained was even more impressive. Often one of them would refer back to something she'd said earlier, an off-hand comment or minor detail, with unerring accuracy. For all their flirting and inane banter, these were three highly intelligent men.

After they'd filled in the details of her childhood, notably minus her contact with the Sollem family, they took a short break. Sophie went to the restroom, and when she came back, Brian was just setting a cup of hot tea and a plate of lemon wedges down on the table in front of her chair. He looked up guiltily as she stepped up behind him.

"I didn't want your voice to give out," he mumbled.

"Thanks. That's kind of you."

He grimaced. "Now there's a word I don't hear applied to me very often."

"What? *Kind?*"

He shrugged.

Darned if she didn't suffer a momentary attack of shyness as he pulled out her chair and held it for her in silence.

"Sugar?" he asked.

"Honey if you've got it. But I'll take sugar in a pinch."

"I think I saw some in a cupboard."

He was back in a minute with a plastic honey bear that looked ridiculous in his powerful grip.

Scottie returned just then. "Dude. Less than one day and she's already domesticating you!"

"Nobody's domesticating me," Brian snapped back. Then his gaze flashed to her, alarmed.

Hmm. Was he actually worried about what she thought of him? He seemed intent upon maintaining his macho image for her. But he kept slipping up and showing flashes of the nice guy within. Must not get out around women too often.

She asked abruptly, "You don't date much, do you?"

His gaze widened in shock, then narrowed into a scowl. "Not much time for it in my line of work," he finally muttered. He avoided eye contact with her and glanced over at the tall palm tree in the corner.

Ahh. That must be where the video camera or one of the concealed microphones was hidden. No way were they conducting this interview without making a complete record of it. She leaned back in satisfaction. The other two men joined them in a few moments.

Brian picked up where they'd left off. "That brings us to Freddie Sollem. Tell us about your earliest memory of him."

She complied, spending the next hour describing a fairly routine upbringing in a traditional Middle Eastern family ensconced in America. Her brain was starting to feel distinctly like mush when Brian looked over at Scottie and asked quietly, "Would you bring us the pictures?"

His teammate left the table and came back in a moment with a thin folder. Brian opened it to reveal a stack of eight-by-ten photographs, some clear, some grainy and blurred, all of Middle Eastern men in their early-to mid-thirties.

"Look at these, Sophie. Do you recognize any of them as Freddie Sollem?"

She picked up the first one. Stared at it in dismay. "I haven't seen Freddie since he was ten years old! How am I supposed to recognize him fully grown, with a beard and turban?"

"It's called a *keffiyah*," Brian replied. "Don't worry if you don't recognize him. Take your time. Study each picture. See if there's anything in one of them you recognize. A look about the eyes or an expression."

She put aside the first picture. "I'm pretty sure that's not him." She picked up another photo. Studied it carefully. "This one might be him."

Brian nodded and started a second pile.

Carefully, she sorted the pictures into those she was certain were not him and a half-dozen pictures that could be Freddie. Brian took notes as to why she thought each of those pictures might be the terrorist.

She handed Brian the last picture to be added to the definitely-not pile. "I'm sorry I couldn't be of more help."

He smiled at her. "You did fine. And these will help us more than you know. We'll analyze your comments and the features common to all the pictures to develop a hypothetical composite. And, you've eliminated nearly two-dozen men from being mistaken for Sollem and killed."

Her gaze snapped to the pile of pictures now in his left hand. Life and *death* had hung in the balance while she was looking at those pictures? Nausea rumbled ominously under her ribs.

"You shouldn't take my word for all this," she said quickly. "Get someone else to look at those pictures. I'd hate to have something so important ride on my opinion. I could be wrong—"

He interrupted her gently. "There is no one else, Sophie. To our knowledge, you're the only Westerner alive in the world today who knows Sollem well enough to identify him."

"That's not possible! We went to school with dozens of kids. Freddie had three or four good buddies he hung out with all the time. They were all American."

"And they're all dead. Tommy Thompson, Ethan Cassopolis, Larry Macintyre, Eddie Delgado. All four have died of other-than-natural causes."

"Are you accusing Freddie of killing them all?" She gasped in horror. She hadn't heard those names in years, but every one conjured up a laughing boy running around the playground at school and being a general pain. And they were *all* dead? At Freddie's hand? "It can't be!"

"It can and probably is. You have to admit it would be a hell of a coincidence otherwise."

"Then why am *I* still alive? I knew him better than any of the rest of them."

"That's an excellent question, Sophie. One to which we were hoping you could give us the answer."

She blinked rapidly, absorbing the myriad implications of that. Did they think she was a terrorist after all? In cahoots with Freddie somehow? After all, here she was, all alone in the middle of a Navy base, surrounded by at least three commandos and a bunch of SEALs. Was she under arrest after all? Was this all a giant ruse to trick her into talking to them without them having to reveal their real motives to her?

Why *hadn't* Freddie killed her? They'd shared a fairly innocent crush on one another as kids. Was that enough to stay his hand? Or was it simply a matter of the adult Freddie— apparently a thoroughly ultraconservative Muslim these days—discounting her as a threat because she was female?

Very belatedly, she commented, "I have no idea why he didn't kill me."

"Has he ever contacted you since he and his family moved away?"

She was aware of the intent looks all three men were giving her. A great deal rode on her answer to this question, apparently. If they didn't believe her, she suspected all semblance of a pleasant debrief would evaporate instantly. She looked across the table at Brian and said as calmly and openly as she could, "No. I've never seen or heard from Freddie or anyone in his family since they moved away. We moved away from Virginia not long after they did. I doubt he'd know how to find me."

Brian studied her for a long time, obviously weighing her answer. Why was this so important to him? As long as he got the information he wanted about his terrorist from her, who cared if Freddie had left her alive by accident or otherwise? He was holding out on her. No doubt about it. There was something huge about this whole trip to California that he wasn't telling her.

She leaned forward and looked him square in the eye. "I've answered all your questions so far, and I'm prepared to keep doing so. But it's time for a show of good faith from you. What aren't you telling me? Why all the secrecy? What's really going on here?"

Scottie and Stoner both leaned back, crossing their arms and, for all the world, settling in to enjoy the show.

Brian looked out the window at the night without. Exhaled heavily. Looked back at her. "Freddie Sollem isn't just any terrorist. We think he's the mastermind behind a global network of terrorists. I won't spell out all the attacks we think he planned and engineered unless you want to hear about them, but take my word for it, the list is impressive. Your boy

Freddie isn't just smart. He's brilliant. In our estimation, he's one of the most dangerous men alive on the planet today."

"And?" she prompted.

"His intelligence extends to his personal security. He's highly disciplined and doesn't make mistakes. We've had round-the-clock satellite and ground surveillance on this guy for months, and we haven't gotten a single break. Not only have we had no chance to kill him, we've had no chance to even *see* him. We know where he is. But that's all we've got.

"And then we found out that you exist. For some unknown reason, Freddie either neglected to or chose not to kill you. I must emphasize, you're the *only* person alive on this side of the war on terror who's ever seen him and might be able to identify him today."

She just knew she wasn't going to like what came next.

"We were hoping you could look at this stack of pictures and immediately spot Sollem and make a positive ID on him. But you couldn't. So that means we have to move on to Plan B."

"Which is?"

Brian startled her by standing up. Pacing a lap around the open living room. Finally, he stopped and stared down at her, tall and imposing. Dang, he was good looking.

"I've racked my brains to find the right way to break this to you. And I've come up empty." He paused. He'd been fretting over this ever since he'd picked her up. What could wrap a man like him—a soldier, a commando, for goodness' sake—so tightly around an axle?

She spoke quietly. "I've sat in on client-attorney meetings for years. And in my experience, everyone feels better if they just blurt out what's bothering them. Even axe murderers feel better once they've confessed. You've got me anticipating the very worst, so unless you hurt small children or torture puppies, I'm bound to be relieved when you finally just come out with it."

His troubled gaze met hers. The man clearly felt truly bad about whatever was coming next. Inexplicably, a wave of emotion swelled up within her. Maybe it was nothing more than misplaced attraction to him. Maybe it was appreciation for his finally being honest with her. Or maybe she was just a sucker for a big, strong man showing a vulnerable side. Compassion, forgiveness, flowed into her eyes, and his gaze widened fractionally in response. Gratitude flashed back in his stormy gray gaze. And then the corners of his eyes crinkled in a smile. A private one from somewhere deep inside. And her heart melted a little.

He nodded resolutely. "Okay, then. Here goes."

Chapter 4

"The police do not have her, my Leader."

The man cringed as Fouad exploded in a spate of furious Arabic on the other end of the phone. His Leader's tendency toward violence when he lost his temper was famous, and he quailed at this display of it directed at him.

"Then find her! And *kill* her!"

"It shall be as you decree."

"Just do it. Now!" Fouad roared.

The man disconnected the call and took a nervous, reflexive look over his shoulder. If he didn't find the Giovanni woman soon and eliminate her, he hadn't the slightest doubt that more of Sollem's men would come, but this time with him in their sights.

He'd called his contacts in every police agency in the state of Utah, and not one of them had a thing on the Giovanni woman. She'd never even had a parking ticket; she certainly had never been arrested. So who had that tall man been? The one with the badge.

If not a local or state law-enforcement agency, that left only Federal agencies.

And it couldn't be good if the woman who knew Sollem's face had fallen into the hands of the United States government.

He had to find her. Had to. Soon. He must protect one of the Cause's greatest warriors. Plus, he really didn't want to die. At least not without the glory of a martyr and the commensurate rewards to follow in Paradise.

He sighed. His informants within the United States government were few and were hard to contact. The favors they owed were limited and must be cashed in sparingly. But if this was not a worthy cause, he didn't know what was. He took a deep breath and dialed his phone.

Brian took a deep breath. She was an extraordinary woman. And he hated to do this. "So here's the thing. We can't just go around killing people who might look like Freddie. When we do the deed, we have to be sure. Not only for moral reasons, but also because if we miss him, he'll go so deep into hiding we'll never get a shot at him again."

Sophie nodded.

"We need someone to get close to Freddie. To positively identify him. To tell us which man is Sollem, without a shadow of a doubt."

Sophie's big brown eyes widened in dawning horror. Yup, she saw it coming now. He forged on relentlessly.

"We need you to find Freddie."

"And finger him for you?"

He flinched at her choice of words, but nodded reluctantly.

"Forgive me for my ignorance of things military, but won't

that be incredibly dangerous? Suicidal, even? You yourself said Freddie has already killed all the other kids who knew him well."

He met her frightened gaze head on. "You're correct. However, we don't intend to send you on this mission without a safety net. We have a plan."

"Which is?"

Her voice sounded more than a little wobbly. It wasn't often that some random woman going about her business got pulled off the street one afternoon and asked to risk her life for her country. He had to give her credit. She wasn't falling apart completely. At least not yet.

He said gently, "Promise me you won't say no right away. Hear me out. And then think about it for a while before you give me your answer."

"You're scaring me, Brian."

It was the first time she'd used his name. And the sound of it on her lips all but brought him to his knees. He couldn't believe he was doing this to her. To a woman who knitted, kept a picture of her mother beside her bed, and smelled of peaches.

"We'd like to train you. In covert operations. Special Forces procedures. Armed and unarmed combat. And then we'd like to send you inside the Sollem family compound to locate and mark Freddie for us."

"Mark?" Her voice was thin. Fragile. Hell, he didn't blame her.

"We'll provide a nanoburr—a tiny microtransmitter nearly invisible to the naked eye—for you to attach to his clothes. We'll have receivers nearby to track the burr. Once you activate it our people will move in, acquire the target and take him out."

Sophie sat unnaturally still. Said nothing. An uncomprehending look blanked out all expression on her face. He flashed Stoner and Scottie a hand signal to retreat. The two men arose quietly and left the room without a word.

And still she said nothing. The file he'd read on her said she was highly intelligent. That she was an orderly and logical thinker, capable of making intuitive leaps of logic. He could almost hear her mind working its way through the unspoken implications of what he'd just said. He sensed that she needed a little while to process the bomb he'd just dropped on her. He opted to retreat, too, and turned on silent feet to head for the deck.

He leaned against the railing, staring out to sea and calling himself a dozen kinds of bastard for several minutes. The door behind him slid open. He felt her join him at the railing.

"Go for a walk with me?" she asked quietly.

"Sure."

They paused at the base of the bleached wood steps to kick off their shoes. The sand was cold and damp between his toes. It sent a quick chill through his normally oblivious body. He followed Sophie down to the water's edge. The tide was all the way out and she crossed the wide stretch of flat, hard sand to dip a foot in the water. She jerked it back fast and he smiled reluctantly.

"Welcome to the Pacific Ocean. It's that cold year-round."

"And people swim in this?" she exclaimed.

He grinned. "If you want me to take you down to the BUDs training facility in the morning, you can see a whole bunch of guys jump in at five o'clock."

She shook her head and took off walking—beyond the reach of the shallow sheet of surf rolling up on the sand. He caught up to her and fell in beside her. They strolled in silence for a couple of minutes.

Then she asked, "Am I correct that you said you're a Ranger?"

"Yes."

"They're commandos or something, aren't they?"

He smiled. "Or something. We're Special Forces soldiers if that's what you're driving at."

"But you do dangerous stuff. Scary stuff."

"Yes."

"Do you get frightened?"

He frowned. "We're trained to manage our physical and psychological reactions to high-stress situations. To channel them effectively. We acknowledge that the body reacts autonomically to dangerous or threatening situations, but with proper training and mindset, the hormone bursts and disrupted thought patterns can be contained and controlled."

She stopped. Turned to stare up at him incredulously. "What the heck did you just say?"

He froze. Felt an odd bubbling sensation rise up in his gut. Was that laughter? Tamping it down with some of the same control he'd just referenced, he replied, "I said we're taught not to feel fear. Or, if we do feel it, to ignore it."

"I don't think I could do that."

"Sure you could. It's all a matter of the right training and some self-discipline."

She spun away and resumed walking, shaking her head in the negative. "Not for me."

He frowned for a moment at her retreating back then hustled to catch up with her. "What frightens you?" he asked gently. For as sure as God made little green apples, some phobia lurked in her gut that had her convinced she'd never conquer fear.

She whirled to stare up at him. "Don't you think that's a little personal?"

A wave rolled in higher than the others, drenching their ankles in icy water. The tide was turning. Neither of them budged as they stared at one another. A zephyr of night breeze teased a strand of hair out of her ponytail and across her face. He reached up and tucked it behind her ear, his fingertip running lightly around the sensitive shell of her ear. The shudder that ran through her also ripped through him. Now *that* was personal.

"If you agree to do this mission with us, I've been assigned to be your personal trainer. And trust me, I'll invade your privacy a whole lot more than that before we're through. I'll know more about what makes you tick than you do. I'll know everything about you…."

He stopped abruptly. His nostrils flared and his body roared to full attention at the arresting thought. A need to absorb her into him, to become one with her slammed into him like a tsunami.

Crap.

He'd just said it himself. He was supposed to be her instructor. No way in hell was he about to take advantage of her while in a position of power. But to learn everything about her—No! His ethics were ironclad. He would never compromise those. He'd watched more than one guy tank a promising career all for the sake of a female. And the hell of it was that the relationships didn't work out as often as not. No way was he going down that road. Not even for this woman.

Sophie's sharp intake of breath yanked him back to the moment.

He tried to mask his flash of irritation over her apparent horror at the idea of him training her, but probably wasn't entirely successful. "What?" he ground out.

"What would this training entail?"

Aww, hell. Did she have to sound so breathless all of a sudden? Like maybe she was actually aflutter over the idea of him working so closely with her?

He shrugged. "We'd do a fair bit of fitness training to

make sure you're strong enough to handle anything that comes along. You'd have to learn about weapons—firearms, knives, a few other useful gadgets. You'd need to pick up miscellaneous skills like lock picking and offensive driving. Then there'd be the covert-ops stuff. Insertion. Extraction…" Damned if images of inserting and extracting himself from Sophie's lush, welcoming body didn't flash through his head. His voice caught. He cleared his throat and plowed on grimly. "Surveillance techniques. I'd have to teach you those. And of course, we'd have to get your Bhoukari back up to speed."

"That's an awful lot of stuff. What sort of time frame are we looking at here?"

"I don't know. At least a few weeks. Ideally, several months. But we don't know if young Freddie will give us that kind of time. It will mostly depend on him."

"What are the odds of my succeeding?"

"Reasonable, I should think. Particularly if we can exploit your closeness to Grandma Sollem. I think Freddie won't immediately freak out if you enter the compound ostensibly to see Grandma and not Freddie directly."

He held his breath. Please let her not ask the other question. The obvious one. The one where she questioned her chances of getting out of this mission alive. She turned around to head back for the beach house. He let out a careful breath. Thank God. She didn't go there. Not yet. But soon. She was too smart not to.

"Where would we do this training?"

"Right here. All the facilities and equipment we'll need are here. Time permitting at the very end of your training, we'll take a field trip out into the desert to give you some practical experience."

"Then what?"

"Then you and I will fly over to Bhoukar and join the surveillance team that's already on the ground. And you'll do your thing."

The beach house came into view, its welcoming lights glowing golden and warm across the sand. In the far distance, a cluster of green lights winked on suddenly in the ocean, bobbing in the waves not far from shore.

"What're those?" Sophie asked, startled.

He grinned. "The SEALs are swimming."

"At night?"

"They do their best work in the dark."

"The possible comebacks to that line beggar the mind," she retorted dryly.

He chuckled. "And the SEALs would relish every one. But don't tell Lucas I said that. He'd kick my butt."

"Are you admitting he's tougher than you?" she replied jokingly.

Brian grinned. "I'm just a pretty boy. All looks and no substance."

She snorted. "You forget I've seen you with your shirt off."

The observation hung heavy between them. Intimate. Suddenly sexual. Memory rocked him of how turned on he'd been when she demanded that he strip off his shirt. She'd drunk in the sight of him unabashedly. Greedily. Like a starving woman at a feast. It had been all he could do to sit there and just let her look. He'd wanted her to taste, to touch—hell, to inhale him. To pleasure them both, to rub her body against his, to purr like he knew she wanted to.

She asked another question and it took him a moment to replay and process the words in his lust-fogged brain. What had she said? *"That's why you wanted to know about my knee, isn't it? You wanted to know if it would hold up for that sort of training."*

He nodded belatedly. No use denying it.

She sounded a little embarrassed when she answered, "I don't know what it will take. I haven't ever really tested it."

"We can take care of that. I'll have one of our docs look at it tomorrow. We've got some of the best orthopedic guys in the business here. Knees and backs are what always give out on S.F. guys."

"S.F.—Special Forces, right?"

He grinned. "I give it two weeks before you'll be talking in acronyms with the best of us. Wait till you're FUBARed because you got a little too FIGMOed and a SNAFU blew your ROEs."

She laughed. "I have no idea what you just said."

"Just as well. Most of it's not fit for a lady's ears anyway."

"For the record, I don't faint at the occasional swear word. When I smash my thumb with a hammer, I don't let out a hearty *gee whiz*."

He laughed. "Good to know. Still. My mother taught me to mind my mouth in front of ladies. Old habits are hard to break."

"Far be it from me to undo your mother's training."

His mother had nothing to do with the improper thoughts that crossed his mind as Sophie bent over to brush the sand off her feet. Her derriere was a curvaceous affair that looked imminently suited to his hands. Perfect for gripping tight and rocking back and forth on top of him—

Jeez. He was losing his mind.

He held the sliding glass door for her and surreptitiously breathed in her fragrance as she brushed past. Oh yeah. Sultry Southern summers and heated nights. Crickets singing and honeysuckle sweetness hanging in the air.

Stop. That.

She paused, staring at him with those big, dark eyes of hers in something akin to shock. It was as if she'd plucked the thoughts directly out of his head. Slowly, slowly, her shock gave way to something alluring, something that invited him to come hither. He started to step forward, started to wrap his arms around her, to seek and find the very soul of her.

He had to get away from her. Except the two of them were trapped in this tiny damned house together until she made her decision. With his subtle nudging to get her to make the right choice, of course.

He cleared his throat and tried to think sober thoughts. Something intellectual. Distracting. Anything not to watch the way her sweater stretched taut across her breasts as she waved her arms around to release tension in her shoulder blades. With every passing second, his shorts got tighter and he was abjectly grateful for the Lycra sports briefs he'd happened to don that morning. No boxers for him with this lady around, thank you very much. Not unless he wanted to embarrass the hell out of both of them. As it was, he wasn't entirely sure he'd be able to walk upright across the room.

"Uhh, I'm gonna turn in," he mumbled. "It's been a long day."

Sophie nodded absently, her thoughts elsewhere. "Is there more tea in the kitchen?"

"Yeah."

"I think I'll brew myself a cup before I come up to bed."

The loft was split into two bedrooms, each with its own attached bathroom. "I'm in the room on the left. You're on the right." Although if she wanted to walk on the wild side, she could feel free to join him. He sure as hell wouldn't say no.

Except, if she said yes to the mission, he'd have to keep his hands strictly off her. How he was going to manage that, he didn't want to even think about. Cold showers. Long swims in the frigid ocean. And self-discipline. Buckets of it, dammit.

He limped up the stairs and prayed she didn't notice the

stilted way he was walking. Hell, he almost wished she'd turn
down the op so he could pay her a late-night visit and ease
this ache tearing him in two. Too uncomfortable to even think
about sleep, he headed for his shower and opted for enlightened self-relief rather than the ubiquitous cold shower. The
physical release wasn't the least bit satisfying, however, and
within minutes of stretching out across his bed, he was in
nearly as bad a shape as he had been before. The woman was
a fire in his blood.

Please God, let her say no. He couldn't do this for the next
couple of *months*. She'd kill him for sure.

Chapter 5

Sophie couldn't sleep. But that was no surprise. It wasn't everyday a hunky commando swept a girl onto a private jet, whisked her off to a hideaway and invited her on a secret mission with him. She had no illusions about what Brian and company were asking her to do. Finding and marking Freddie Sollem would be dangerous at best and suicidal at worst. She didn't want to become a soldier! But to spend weeks on end with Brian Riley—it was almost enough to make a girl consider the proposal.

It had all happened so fast her head was awhirl. Images of six-pack abs, jogging SEALs and grainy photos of terrorists swam in her mind. And then there was Brian himself. So much sex appeal poured off him she all but drowned in it. One look into those bright blue eyes and she was lost, adrift in a sea of sexual promise without any anchor to call her back. He was the only solid object in the vast expanse of pounding blood and throbbing need that yawned between them.

There was always a chance she was imagining it all. But she thought not. Okay, she hoped not. If she was feeling all this rampaging lust and he didn't reciprocate at least a little, she stood in grave danger of making a complete and utter fool of herself. As it was, she was far too restless to even think about going to sleep.

Brian had asked her to think about her decision, but not for too long. Was she willing to attempt a secret mission that sounded insanely risky, that she didn't see any possible way to adequately prepare for and which stood a more than decent chance of getting her killed? And for what? Vague assurances that she was the only one who could do it? That her country needed her? We the people and liberty and justice for all?

She paced the living room for a while. Stood out on the deck until she was so cold her teeth chattered. Came back inside and paced some more. And all the while, the question and the man who'd asked it tangled in her head until she was so confused she could hardly recall her own name.

It must have been three o'clock when yet again, she came inside, chilled to the bone, and stood staring out the living room's big picture window. The tide was coming in and the wind—and waves—had picked up. The breakers were several feet tall now, curling over with muffled crashes onto the beach, sending up silver spray in the moonlight. The rhythmic pounding was mesmerizing. Something deep within her responded to the primal sound, aching with need.

All of a sudden, she got a feeling she wasn't alone. She whirled around, her hands flying up defensively.

Brian.

Looming no more than three feet behind her. And she'd

never heard him coming. How did he do that? Was that predatory silence part of the training he was offering her? Jeans hung low on his hips and he was bare-chested. His hair was just messy enough to make him look like a male poster model in the faint moonlight.

"Trouble sleeping?" he murmured, his voice husky.

Oh, my. His voice slid across her skin like the best sex she'd ever imagined. "Uhh, yeah. I've never been this close to an ocean. I'm not used to the sound of it."

"You get used to it after a while. I find it soothing."

She rubbed her arms to chase away the goose bumps raised by the sight of his brawny, centerfold sex appeal. Her palms itched to glide over every inch of that yummy chest. To hook her fingers in the waistband of his jeans and tug them lower. Her breathing hitched.

His eyes were black pits in his shadowed face. Unfathomable. Unreadable.

"Been thinking?" he queried.

Yes. About you. About rolling around in a tangle of sheets with him. About straddling him and riding him until they both exploded. About him picking her up in those strong arms and driving into her until she was too weak and sated to stand. About breathing him in, becoming part of him.

She shrugged, her throat too tight to speak.

"Do you have any more questions for me or the guys?"

Crud. He wanted to talk about the mission. He didn't return her interest in the least. And what kind of a head case did that make her? A lonely legal secretary entering her thirties without any prospects of finding a man. She'd latched on to the first decent-looking guy who'd come along who gave her the time of day. She'd managed in approximately twelve hours to become completely obsessed with him. Sheesh.

The mission. Right. She dragged her sluggish brain away from improper thoughts of Brian Riley.

"Do you seriously think I can do this job? That I can find Freddie and mark him for you?"

"I think you can do anything you put your mind to."

A warm tingle whispered up her spine, but a cold wash of dread traveled back down it. She couldn't possibly live up to his expectations. "I think you're delusional."

He laughed softly. "I've seen the most unlikely people do the most amazing things. Mothers really do pick up two-ton cars off their kids. Nothing's impossible if you put your mind to it."

"How impossible is this situation?"

"Freddie Sollem has the potential to kill thousands or even millions of innocent people if he's not stopped. Case in point, his recent plan to attack nuclear power plants. Had we not gotten wind of it, and had he actually managed to breach an operating reactor, there's no telling how much radiation he could have released. Or what if he gets his hands on a nuclear device—which we have intel that he's trying to do? What if he explodes it in New York City or London?"

Even the cold chill of Brian's words wasn't enough to entirely extinguish the heat low in her belly. The idea that this man was willing to stand in the gap, to fight a man like Freddie on Sollem's own terms was incredible. And sexy as heck. Lord, she was a mess! A shiver rattled through her.

Brian stepped forward as fast and silent as a cougar. "Are you cold?"

"I'm okay."

"No, you're not. I see the goose bumps on your arms." He whirled away and headed for the big sofa, returning in a moment with an afghan. He draped it around her from behind, his big hands gentle. They lingered on her shoulders, need-lessly tucking the blanket higher about her, the backs of his fingers brushing against her neck just below her ears. A tremor raced through her in response, fizzling out somewhere below her knees, leaving them wobbly.

He took a step closer behind her. "Are you sure you're okay? I threw a bunch at you today. It's a lot to take in."

His tenderness was almost more than she could stand. Her eyes started to burn suspiciously. "It's not that…."

"Then what?"

His voice was barely a murmur, a baritone caress that promised power and glory that would sweep her completely away.

"I…" She turned to face him in frustration. There were no words for it. And even if she did have the words, she wasn't brave enough to tell him what he did to her. The things he made her think of. The images her brain conjured when he stood this close.

His chest was no more than six inches from hers. Her nipples budded up tight and hard, straining against her bra, irritated by the lace rubbing against them.

The mission, darn it! Business! The $64,000 question.

In desperation she blurted, "Answer me this. If I do this, am I going to die?"

Something intense built behind his eyes. Tightly leashed, but wild. Straining to get out. It reached out between them and wrapped around her almost violently. He ground out between gritted teeth, "It's a possibility."

Terror twisted her stomach tight. It was the only logical conclusion based on the information she had, but hearing it said aloud—by an expert—made it a great deal more real. A great deal more frightening. She took a deep breath and asked the next logical question. "How big a possibility?"

His voice was practically a growl. The beast within him was winning. "I don't know."

"Give me a ballpark figure. Do I have a fifty-fifty chance of making it out alive?"

"Jeez, Sophie. Don't ask me that. There are so many variables…so many possible scenarios for how this could go down."

Was he actually willing to send her on a no-kidding suicide mission? Tears burned her eyes. "If you're asking me to die, I have a right to know, don't you think?"

The beast broke through, bursting its restraints with an almost audible roar of fury. Brian stepped forward, desperation distorting his face into a grimace of physical pain. He swept her up in his arms, dragging her against his body in a grip so tight she could barely breathe.

"Aww, Sophie. Don't cry. I can't stand tears."

The dam within her broke and she pulled in a sobbing breath. His mouth swooped down to capture hers and stole the breath completely away.

"You even taste like peaches," he mumbled, nipping at her lower lip, plucking at strings of desire running straight down to her core.

"Huh?"

"Peaches and woman."

She whimpered against his mouth, her hands plunging into his hair, tugging him closer for more. He kissed her voraciously, his tongue plunging inside her mouth in a blatant and carnal imitation of sex that left her panting. Absolute certainty flooded her that he didn't want her to take the mission. That he was scared stiff about what could happen to her. That he wanted her to stay alive. For him.

And her heart melted.

He tore his mouth away from hers. "Please, please, don't cry. If I'm crazy out of line, tell me. If you want this to stop, you're going to have to do it, because I want you so bad I can't think straight."

The rest of her turned to molten lust then and there. *He wanted her. As bad as she wanted him.* The realization blew every last vestige of rational thought out of her brain. She mumbled between kisses, "Thank heaven. I was worried I was the only one who felt like this."

He laughed into her mouth, backing her across the room toward the couch, his hands everywhere, pushing up her sweater and pulling down her bra to reveal her aching flesh. His mouth closed on her sensitized nipple and she about jumped out of her skin. Her skirt bunched up around her waist all of a sudden and clever fingers found her core, stroking deep into her heat.

He groaned, and with one knee on the couch, lowered her to her back on the cushions. He followed her down, kissing her stomach as he pulled the sweater all the way over her head. "I can't get enough of the smell of you."

She reached for his zipper, dying to feel the hard, velvety length of him. To know the measure of his desire for her. His jeans sagged open and she pushed them down over his hips. His buns were muscular and taut, flexing under hands, all eager male.

He lifted away long enough to pull off her skirt and panties, and cold air hit her naked flesh…a quick jolt of what-the-hell-was-she-doing? She heard the quick snap of a condom, and then he was back.

"Miss me?"

His tongue plunged into her mouth while his finger matched the motion lower, massaging her slick, swollen flesh into betraying her last shred of common sense. It worked.

"Brian—" she gasped, her tears and terror evaporating by the second.

"That's it. Ride the wave for me."

She arched up into him, bucking against his hand. She cried aloud and his mouth was there to drink the sound in, to soothe her lips for a moment with wordless murmurs. And then he was inside her, a stretching fullness that sent her oversensitized nerves into a paroxysm of release.

"Holy Mike, you feel good when you do that," he groaned.

Her internal muscles clenched around him and he groaned again, pushing even deeper into her. "Am I hurting you?" He began to retreat and she wrapped her legs assertively around his waist.

He laughed and plunged home. They found the pounding rhythm of the ocean, their breathing harsh as they strained against each other. It was wild and raw and completely uncivilized, and she didn't think she was ever going to get enough of him. The fury built within her once again. Together they clawed higher and higher, a wire stretching tighter and tighter between them until, with a shout, Brian made one last shuddering plunge and pushed them both over the edge.

The fall was spectacular; entire galaxies of stars burned up within her.

Wow.

Double wow.

Holy—holy what the heck was she thinking, Batman? If she accepted his offer, she was going to have to work with this man for the next several months! And then a truly horrifying thought slammed into her. *Holy smokes, those cameras better be turned off, Batman.*

"Brian?" she murmured in dawning dismay.

"Hmm?"

"Are your surveillance cameras still going?"

His forehead sagged against hers and he swore under his breath. "They're sound or motion activated."

"I think we're in trouble on both scores."

A reluctant laugh escaped him. "I'm in trouble. Not you." He pulled away from her and sat up, tugging the forgotten afghan over her. He swore some more under his breath. Then turned to her and said dead seriously, "I'm really sorry. I'll ask Stoner or one of the other guys to take over handling you. I'll be out of here before morning."

Panic ripped into her. *He was leaving?* She asked in a small voice, "Are you running away from me?"

"Hell no. You're amazing. I'm running away from me."

In a smaller voice she whispered, "But I don't want you to go. I'm scared."

"Aww, hell." He speared his hand through his hair and glanced over at her, his gaze as bleak as the cold moonlight filtering into the room.

And then he leaned over, wrapping her up in his big, warm, safe embrace. He lifted her into his lap and she snuggled close, soaking up the comfort he offered.

Finally she murmured against his chest, her mouth a sleepy caress on his skin, "I hate good-byes."

"So do I," he mumbled.

"But you're good at them, aren't you? Another mission is always out there, beckoning, isn't it?"

He sighed with what she prayed was genuine regret. "Yeah. There's always another crisis around the corner. I suppose it's an addiction after a fashion. But I just have to be at the middle of the action."

She heard between the lines, loud and clear. He might not like good-byes, but he sure as heck was good at them. He was warning her: he said good-bye to every woman, sooner or later.

He muttered into her hair, his breath an achingly soothing caress. "Honey, you've got more strength in you than you have any idea of. I'm the royal bastard here. I took advantage of you in a vulnerable moment." He added in an almost bewildered tone, "But damned if I could keep my hands off you."

And in that moment, as he tore himself up with remorse over not treating her right, her decision crystallized. She didn't stop to question it too hard. No telling if her logic would hold up under scrutiny or not. But she knew deep in her gut, with utter certainty, what she was going to say.

Chapter 6

"I'll do it."

Shocked to the core of his being, Brian pulled back enough to stare down at her. Incredulous, he exclaimed, "Are you sure?" He surged up over her, tipping her onto her back and covering her, afghan and all with his body in almost instinctive need to protect her. From the mission, from him…hell, from herself.

She gazed up at him, her dark eyes limpid and calm. Calmer than his, in fact. He could drown in them happily. "I'm sure."

"Don't do it." The words burst out of him before he could stop them. What the hell was he thinking? This is exactly what he wanted. What he'd spent all day working toward. What the mission required of him—of them both!

She blinked up at him, startled. "Why not?"

"I—You—Oh, hell. Never mind. Don't do this on account of us, though."

"I'm not."

Bull. He ought to call her on it. Not let her do this thing. She was stepping into a suicide trap for all the wrong reasons. For him, for God's sake! How could he possibly stand by and let her do it? In losing control of himself, he'd inadvertently manipulated her into her decision. *Hey, baby. Volunteer for the stupidly dangerous mission, and in return, I'll give you really great sex up until the part where you die.* What kind of bastard did that make him? The very worst kind. One who'd take advantage of a vulnerable woman's feelings to get what he wanted. Disgust tasted bitter on his tongue.

He couldn't help it. The words just came out, a desperate whisper. "Promise me you're not doing this because of what just happened between us."

She reached up and placed her soft palm against his rough cheek. "Yes, Brian. I promise. I have one condition, though."

Quick dread stabbed his gut. "What?"

"Don't leave. Stay with me. I want you to train me."

He groaned aloud. "No way will my boss agree to that after—Well, after."

"He's got no choice. It's the only way I'm agreeing to do this. I trust you. You'll keep me safe."

"I haven't done a hell of a good job of protecting you so far."

"Stop beating yourself up. We're two consenting adults. Nobody forced me onto this couch or out of my clo—" she broke off.

She probably just remembered the ubiquitous camera in the corner. He cursed mentally. What were the odds he could get a hold of that tape and destroy it before anyone else saw it? Nil, no doubt. This op was too important to run the surveillance equipment on remote feed. There'd be a live operator at the other end of the damned camera. Copies of the tape were probably already being distributed through the Ops

Center. The guys were probably popping the popcorn and getting ready to enjoy the show this very minute. He swore under his breath and pushed up away from her.

"I have to make a phone call," he declared grimly.

He headed for the scant privacy of the kitchen and picked up the phone there. Hollister was already on the line, waiting for him.

"What in the *hell* were you thinking?" his boss demanded without preface.

Brian closed his eyes. If he was lucky, the upcoming butt chewing would only hurt like crazy. If he wasn't lucky, he'd just blown his career to hell. "I wasn't thinking, sir. I absolutely deserve everything you're about to shout at me."

Hollister was silent for a long, heavy moment. Brian held his breath while the guy gathered himself to deliver the mother of all ass whuppings.

Finally, his boss bit out, "We picked up the audio of her agreeing to do the mission."

No doubt about it, Hollister was mad as hell. But the guy had formidable self-control. Brian let out a careful breath.

Hollister continued in a tight growl. "I'm going to assume you seduced the subject because in your professional judgment that was the only way to get the job done. Otherwise, you would be guilty of a…gross…breach of professionalism. And I would be extremely disappointed in you."

Ouch. Disappointed? That was a low blow. Brian winced. He almost wished the guy would scream and holler at him.

Hollister said grimly, "We picked up her condition, too."

"Yeah," Brian mumbled glumly.

"I'm prepared to agree to her condition. But I have a condition of my own."

Brian's eyebrows shot up in surprise. Hollister was willing to let him continue to run this op…even after what he'd just done with Sophie? Frankly, he was stunned. But then his brows slammed together. The other shoe had to drop, here. Hollister might maintain control of his temper, but he also didn't hesitate to let the hammer fall when it was called for. Brian's shoulders hunched up, preparatory to the blow he felt coming.

Hollister ground out, "If you lay a hand on her again, I'll kick your ass back into the Stone Age, Riley. I'll bury your career so deep you'll never climb out of the hole I toss you in. I'm talking court-martial here. Conduct unbecoming an officer. A long career breaking rocks at Fort Leavenworth. You got that, Captain?"

"Yes, sir."

"We'll talk more in the morning. My office. 6:00 a.m. Sharp."

"Yes, sir."

The phone disconnected abruptly. So much for professionally and diplomatically getting the reluctant civilian to agree to the incredibly risky mission. Man, he'd messed this one up bad. Brian set the receiver down gently. All of a sudden, the prospect of spending the next few weeks, day and night, with Sophie—under the watchful eye of his boss— made his blood run cold. He was going to have to keep his hands off her. Way off her. Completely and totally off her. Not only for his sake, but for hers, too.

He was a dead man.

When Sophie woke up, the smells of coffee and cooking bacon drifted to her nose. Ahh. Gotta love a man who could take you to the moon and back and then cook breakfast for you the next morning.

She jumped into the shower, got dressed and headed downstairs in a delicious, dreamy haze of memory of last night. It had been incredible. Brian had been incredible. And he'd been crazy for her. Her! Twenty-four hours ago she didn't even know Brian Riley existed. And now she breathed the very essence of him. It was a miracle.

She rounded the corner into the kitchen, the smile in her heart shining in her eyes. "Hey you…" The greeting faded.

Lucas Stone turned around, spatula in hand. "Pancakes and bacon okay?"

"Uhh, yeah. Sure. Hi, Lucas."

"Morning, ma'am. How're you feeling today?" He neatly stacked pancakes on a plate beside a pile of crispy bacon and carried it past her to the dining table. She followed him, worried. Where was Brian? Surely he hadn't left her after all! Was he still on the job?

She sat down at the table, staring blankly at her plate as Lucas slid in across from her. She looked up. "Is Brian—" She couldn't finish it.

"He's at the office getting a final…briefing…before your training begins."

Lucas knew she'd agreed to do the mission? Had Brian told him? Or—humiliation squirmed inside her—had he heard her say it over the surveillance equipment last night? Heat flooded her cheeks. Had they *all* heard and seen it? How was she ever going to face any of them?

"Eat up. You're going to need your strength."

She looked up at him in surprise. It was on the tip of her tongue to ask him exactly what he knew, when the street side door blew open on a gust of cool salt air.

Brian. The relief that coursed through her was truly pathetic.

"Hey, pea—" He broke off mid-word as his glance lifted over her head and he spotted Stone. "—Sophie. Hey, Stoner."

"Rip."

She looked over at Brian, surprised. "Rip? Isn't that a rather odd nickname?"

He stepped further into the room, setting down a pair of identical bulky, gray canvas bags. "It's my field handle." At her frown he elaborated. "It's a call sign we use over the radios to identify each other. Everybody has to choose one."

Stone interjected, laughing, "Or if you're unlucky, one is chosen for you. His, for example."

Sophie looked back and forth between the two men. Brian looked a little overheated about the gills, and Stoner was laughing. She replied, "Okay, I'll bite. How'd you get the handle?"

When Brian didn't reply, Stone was happy to jump in. "So there we were, having an important meeting with the big cheeses to convince them to let us in on their super-secret project, and we're all decked out in our best uniforms, spit-polished to the hilt. And Graceful, here, drops his hat. When he bends down to pick it up, his perfectly tailored, snug-for-all-the-girls slacks let loose a resounding *rrrriiiip*. All eyes turn to him and the head honcho says, 'Son, is there a problem?'"

Brian was distinctly red now.

Stone continued, chortling, "And our boy turns around bends over, and flashes his boxers with the words Go Army proudly displayed. Ever since, he's been the Ripper or Rip."

Brian rolled his eyes at her and she quipped, "Hey, at least you aren't Ripper as in 'Jack, the.'"

He shrugged and threw a dire look at his teammate. "You never know. I may still go postal one of these days."

Stoner laughed and stood up to take the dishes out to the kitchen. He made a point of reaching across her and flexing his biceps for her before he picked up the syrup-covered plate, though. She laughed up at him.

He grinned back, unrepentant. "You two have fun today."

"We will."

Brian interrupted. "Speaking of which, if you're ready to go, Sophie, we have an appointment in a few minutes."

"With whom?"

"My boss."

She heard Stoner's sympathetic suck-in of air between his teeth as he disappeared into the kitchen. Her stomach knotted around the heavy meal. "Do I have to?"

"He has some paperwork for you to sign."

She bet. There was the small matter of signing her life away. Literally. Brian gave her no time to fret over it, however. He whisked her out of the house and into a waiting SUV with blacked-out windows. He guided the vehicle down the beach toward the cluster of low buildings that made up the main training facility. He was silent. She got the distinct impression he didn't feel like talking. Unfortunately, when she got nervous, she babbled. She did her best to hold it back, but finally, the prospect of facing a senior officer who knew exactly what they'd done last night—heck, probably *watched* what they'd done last night—was too much for her.

"Is this car bugged?"

"No."

"Any cameras in it?"

"No."

Thank God. She burst out, "Is your boss mad at me?"

Brian looked over at her, surprised. "Of course not. He's royally pissed off at me, but he's not upset with you in the least."

"Then why do I have to see him?"

Brian turned neatly into a parking spot in front of an unmarked building. "Let's go find out, shall we? Don't be afraid. Major Hollister's a good guy." Under his breath he added so low she barely heard, "When you're not at the top of his shit list."

The major turned out to be another crazy-fit looking man in maybe his mid-thirties who came around his desk to shake her hand and offer her a seat. Although his eyes were hard when he looked over at Brian, his gaze softened slightly when he glanced back at her.

"On behalf of the government of the United States, I'd like to officially thank you for agreeing to help us with this operation. I must ask, though, are you absolutely certain you understand what you're getting into and what's being asked of you?"

She nodded. She really hoped he didn't want to dig into the whys and wherefores of her agreeing to do it. "Yes. I understand."

He gave her a long, intense look. "Trust me, ma'am. You don't understand at all. But you will." He looked away, then back at her. "You will."

Sheesh, that sounded ominous. These guys certainly weren't trying to trick her into this mission. First Brian, and now the major had warned her.

Hollister was talking again. "If at any time you choose to withdraw from this mission, there will be no negative consequences to you. You are working with us on a purely voluntary basis. Do you understand that?"

This was taking on the distinct tone of a legal briefing. "I understand," she replied.

"There will come a point in the operation where quitting will become dangerous, not only to you but to the other field operatives working with you. At that point, I can only urge you in the strongest terms to do your best not to abandon my people high and dry. Their lives will be in your hands." She must have gasped, because he added hastily, "But vice versa, your life will rest in their hands, too. And I assure you, there are no finer soldiers on the planet than those you will be working with from here on out. Our unit hand-selects each person from among the best of the best."

"Who exactly are you?" Sophie asked. She was surprised to realize she'd never heard the name of the group Brian worked for.

Hollister sighed. "I can't tell you that. It's classified."

Hmm. She had a top secret clearance, yet even the name of this bunch was classified higher than that? Whoa.

Hollister was speaking again. "I have some paperwork for you to read and sign, Ms. Giovanni."

The first pile of paper was what she expected; statements of the classified nature of this mission, of the requirement for her not to divulge any of the methods or intelligence she learned here. But then there came a warning that she would be trained to use deadly force and the possible ramifications to her if she should ever misuse that training. That gave her pause, but she signed it. Then Hollister pushed one last document across his desk at her.

She looked down at it. A will. She looked up at the two men, who were watching her closely. "Well. That certainly puts this whole project into perspective, doesn't it?"

Hollister smiled, his eyes as cold as the North Pole. "It's just a formality," he replied smoothly. "Every military member is required to have one. Since you'll be attached to our unit as an adjunct, it's required. You know how those legal folks are about their paperwork."

His attempt at levity fell flat, but she smiled at him for making the attempt. At least, she hoped her grimace passed for a smile.

"As you requested, Captain Riley will oversee your training."

Her face exploded into a fiery blush as Hollister continued to stare steadily at her. "I urge you to regard your training with the utmost seriousness, Ms. Giovanni. Your life will, without a doubt, rest upon how well you pay attention to and absorb what the captain has to teach you. I have prepared a list of objectives and training milestones for him. If you give this your best effort, I'm confident the mission will be successful and you will come out of it just fine."

Give the man an A-plus for subtlety. If she wasn't mistaken, she'd just been told in no uncertain terms to keep her hands off the good captain and her mind on her work. She looked the major square in the eye. "I hear you. Loud and clear, sir."

He gave the faintest of nods, then said lightly, "You're a civilian. You don't have to call me sir."

Her mouth twitched. He was a 'sir' kind of guy, uniform or not. He wore authority like a second skin. Kind of like a few old battle-ax judges back home. You called them sir and didn't talk back if you wanted to keep your happy butt out of the slammer.

Brian spoke up. "If you'll excuse us, sir. Ms. Giovanni has a doctor's appointment in ten minutes."

The major stood and held out his hand to her. After a brief, almost painfully firm handshake he nodded once. "Good luck, Ms. Giovanni."

She took a deep breath. *Here goes nothing.*

Chapter 7

Sophie stared down at the ugly black brace encasing her left knee. It clasped her calf and thigh tightly, but the hinged shafts running down either side of her knee were surprisingly light. The doctor said they were titanium.

"And you're sure I can do anything I want with my knee and it'll be okay?"

The doc glanced up at her. "Yup. This brace is purely a precaution. I guarantee it'll prevent you from reinjuring the ligaments you tore before." He glanced over at the X-rays of her knee—one set from the original surgery fifteen years ago and another set less than an hour old. How these guys had gotten a hold of her original medical records so fast, she had no idea. She wasn't sure she wanted to know.

Brian asked, "So we're cleared to launch a full schedule of fitness and operational training for her?"

"Go easy on her, eh?"

Sophie frowned. She wasn't a complete slob. She jogged several miles at a time at altitude on a sort-of-regular basis.

The doctor added, "She's not in the kind of shape of the women you're used to working with."

Women? What women did Brian work with? She might not know much about the military, but she was under the definite impression women didn't do this fancy Special Forces stuff. Maybe the doc meant that team Brian had mentioned yesterday? The Medicis? Medusas? Something like that. A surveillance team of some kind.

Brian replied soberly, "We've only got a couple months at best to whip her into shape."

The doctor opened a cabinet and fished around. "She'll need these then. One at a time. Two if she's completely immobilized."

Brian glanced at the bottle label. His eyebrows popped up in surprise. The doc must have forked over the good drugs. Painkillers, hopefully.

Brian pocketed the brown plastic bottle. "Got it. The usual nutritional supplements?"

"Yup. Plus hot whirlpools and light tissue massage. And keep her moving."

"Roger."

Okay, these two could stop talking over her head any time now.

"Let's go, Sophie," Brian announced. "We've got a lot on our agenda for today."

She followed him out of the office, the brace feeling odd on her knee. It didn't interfere with her walking movement, but as soon as she put the slightest sideways torque on her knee, she ran smack into the rigid brace. That doctor wasn't kidding. Her knee wasn't going anywhere in this contraption. It was strange not to have to baby it, to be able to move without subliminal awareness of not doing anything to hurt her knee. There was freedom in it—and fear. Of the unknown. If her knee wasn't there to hold her back, what was there to keep her from doing new things? Dangerous things?

Good grief. And she'd just agreed to do a secret mission to help capture a terrorist? Who was she trying to kid?

"I know that look," Brian announced grimly as he held open the SUV's passenger door for her.

She climbed inside and he went around and slid behind the wheel. "What look?" she demanded.

"Buyer's remorse. Don't tell me you're already regretting your decision. I haven't even begun to torture you, yet."

She laughed reluctantly. "No. I was just reflecting on what a chicken I am."

He shrugged casually. "Oh. That. No prob. We'll do all kinds of work in fear management."

"You say that like it's easy."

He glanced over at her as he pulled out into traffic. "It is. It's only a matter of knowing what to do and practicing until you get good at it."

Sure. Just flip a switch, and poof, no more clammy palms. No more cold sweats. No more imagined disasters. It was hard to fathom.

Brian parked the car in a lot right next to the beach. What was on their training agenda here? A nice picnic and a bottle of wine, perhaps?

He opened the back door and thrust a pair of tennis shoes at her—her barely used running shoes from home. "How'd you get those?" she exclaimed. "Oh, wait. I forgot. You broke into my apartment."

He grimaced. "Put those on."

"What are we doing?"

"We're going for a little run. To see how fit you are."

Oh, Lord. The sexy stud muffin got to see just what a couch potato she was? Embarrassment crawled up her spine and they hadn't even taken a step yet. Reluctantly, she bent down to tie on the shoes. Her breathing was already tightening up.

"C'mon," he said.

She followed him with lagging steps out onto the beach. Great. They got to run in *sand?* She wouldn't make it a quarter mile.

He directed briskly, "Stretch out some, eh? We don't need any pulled muscles this early in the program."

She dutifully bent down and planted her nose on one of her knees. Her hamstring protested rustily. Her rear end must look the size of Montana in this position. She pivoted so her backside wasn't facing him and moved her nose to her other knee. Lovely. Equal-opportunity pain in the other hamstring.

She made a random creaky pretzel out of herself for a couple more minutes and then he asked, "Ready?"

She straightened up, glaring at him. "Heck, no, I'm not ready. You're some fancy commando, and I'm a legal secretary from Utah who'd rather knit than get out of my chair and vacuum."

He laughed, a friendly, warm sound. "I have no expectations whatsoever of you. Anything you can do over zero is better than I'd hoped for."

"Does that mean I can just declare myself tired now and we can skip this whole slogging through sand and sweating thing?" she asked hopefully.

He grinned. "Nope. It means anything you do today will be a new personal best. We'll build from there."

She sighed. "All right. Just hang on to that zero expectation, okay?"

He led the way out to the water's edge and took off in a

slow jog. Well, for him it was probably a slow jog. For her it was too brisk for comfort. In no time a stitch stabbed her under the ribs and her thighs were starting to burn. The sand turned out to be firmer than she expected. It gave way enough under her feet to cushion her knee, but was hard enough that she didn't flounder with every step.

"How're you doing?" he asked a few minutes into the exercise in torture.

Darned if he didn't sound *perky!* Not the slightest bit out of breath. If she spoke aloud right now, she was going to gasp like an asthmatic fish on a dock.

"Can we…slow down…a bit?" She panted.

"Sure. You set the pace."

"Stop sounding so…damned cheerful." She huffed.

He laughed. "Right. How's the knee holding up?"

She took stock. Surprisingly, it felt just fine. And there was peace of mind in knowing the bionic brace was protecting it.

"If I told you to breathe in through your nose and out through your mouth, would you slug me?"

She glanced up at him. "Oh yeah…Hard."

"Okay. Breathe through your nose and mouth together if you can. It humidifies the air going into your lungs."

Did he mean that fiery stuff burning its way in and out of her chest cavity like molten lava? That air? She scowled in his general direction. Her calves were starting to cramp. And her behind. Then there was her right hip twingeing. And her throat was starting to feel raw.

"Isn't it a beautiful day out here?" Brian declared brightly.

"Stuff it," she snapped.

Laughing, he spurted ahead of her and commenced running backwards in front of her. "You're doing great. We've done nearly a mile. What say we try for two? See that lifeguard tower down the beach? That's two miles from where we started."

She glanced past his shoulder. Could he possibly be referring to that tiny black twig in the distance? Ugh. She staggered onward, with parts of her jiggling she didn't know jiggled. About a week later in her universe, the tower took the shape of a miniature oil derrick and then began to grow in size.

And then finally, blessedly, it loomed over them. She stumbled to a halt, her legs and lungs screaming their protest as she bent down, grabbing the bottom of her shorts and panting like the dying woman she was. Sweat stung like crazy in her eyes, but she was too wiped out to even think about reaching up to brush it away.

"What're you stopping for?" Brian asked.

She straightened slowly, hurting all over. She glared at him. The bastard was barely breathing above normal, let alone perspiring. She asked ominously, "What do you mean?"

"Now we have to run back to the car."

She stared. Blinked. "You're joking, right?"

"No."

"I'm. Not. Running. Back. You can go get the car, drive it down here and pick me up."

"This isn't Daytona. I can't drive on the beach and the road doesn't come this far. We have to run back."

"Ahh. I see. This is the part of my training where I learn to commit murder. And to like it."

He laughed. "Nah, that's next week. C'mon. You've caught your breath. Let's go."

Underneath his cheerful overtone was a distinct undertone of steel. He wasn't giving her any choice in the matter. This was a soldier. An officer. A man used to giving orders… and having them followed without question. Where did the passionate, tender, protective lover of last night disappear to?

"But I can't do it!"

He wheeled around and took a quick, long step that brought him chest-to-chest with her. She was abruptly aware of how big and strong he was.

His voice dropped to a deep, almost threatening timbre. "Let's get one thing straight right now, Sophie. I will never ask you to do something you *can't* do. I don't ever want to hear that word cross your lips again. Is that understood?"

She stared up at him, shocked. "But it's two more miles—"

"You could run ten more miles if you really had to. No can'ts. Got it?"

His voice was hard, but something lurked in the back of his gaze. Compassion. Empathy. Entreaty. *Well, shucks.* "Yeah," she sighed. "I've got it."

She turned and faced back the way they'd come. She couldn't even see the SUV from here. Only two side-by-side sets of footprints winding away in the sand. "Let's go, Rambo."

Brian poured the protein and wheat-greens shake out of the blender and into a pair of glasses. He didn't need the protein hit—he hadn't done anything all day that constituted actual work to his muscles. But Sophie definitely needed it, and he'd promised to do everything she did in the course of her training.

He stepped into the main room where she sprawled on the sofa, red in the face, eyes closed. The poor kid was wrung out. The run had taken the edge off her, but the weight room had done her in. He'd needed to know if she could do a pull-up or push-up. Fundamental to Special Forces maneuvers was the ability to move one's own body weight around. She couldn't do a chin-up but had managed two or three half-credible push-ups. They'd have to start out on light weights and work up to her body weight.

But not today. She looked ready to pass out and it wasn't even dinnertime.

"Here. Take this." He held out the sludge-colored shake.

"What is it? Something I spread on my muscles to ease the pain?"

"No. You drink it. It's a protein shake"

Her gaze snapped to the dark green liquid in dismay. "What protein comes in that color? Ground up caterpillars?"

"Very funny. The soy powder is pale yellow. It's the kamut grass and blue-green algae that give it color."

"Algae? As in pond slime? No way. Give me a steak, juicy and medium-rare, if you want me to eat some protein."

He sighed. "In an operational situation, questioning my orders like this can get you killed. If I tell you to do something, you need to just do it. You can ask questions later."

One brown eye slitted open, glaring malevolently at him.

He grinned down at her. "Despite the color, it's chocolate-flavored. Don't all women love chocolate?"

She purred, "We also love that squeaky sound men make when we yank out their chest hairs. Come here and I'll show you what I mean."

He glanced up at the palm tree in the corner in alarm.

She glanced over her shoulder. "Oh, relax, Brian. I'm so tired I couldn't lift a finger right now, let alone get you in any trouble."

"Could you move if I told you there's a hot tub cranked up all steamy and bubbly on the deck outside?"

She sat bolt upright, then froze, groaning. "You're a cruel, cruel man."

"Let me help you up." He held a hand down to her. Surely hoisting her aching bones off the couch didn't constitute laying a hand on her in Major Hollister's world.

Her hand felt so fragile in his. Slender and weak. What the

hell was he doing, preparing her to march into a nest of terrorists? He opened the sliding glass door and ushered her to the far end of the deck, where a hot tub was, indeed, bubbling merrily. He'd cranked the heat all the way up before they left for the gym. It should cook her about as red as a lobster.

"I don't have my bathing suit on," she protested.

"I'll go inside. You can just strip down and climb in." At her wide-eyed shock, he added hastily, "Or you can climb in wearing your shorts and T-shirt. Go on. I'll get you a towel."

He stepped inside, but not before her groan of pleasure and pain drifted to him. The sound rolled through him, ripping away all his careful control. She'd made sounds like that last night. For him. With him. A fresh wave of lust, at least the twentieth so far today, pounded through him.

He bolted for the kitchen. Must stay away from her. Far, far away.

The phone rang, and he picked it up, abjectly grateful for the distraction.

"Report, Riley."

Hollister. "She held up pretty well, today. Doc says her knee's right as rain. He told me privately the worst of it will be convincing her of that, though. We baby-jogged four miles and hit the weight room. Not much upper body strength. But we'll work on it."

"Where is she now?"

"In the hot tub soaking away her pains and avoiding a protein shake."

"A Bhoukari language instructor is coming over to the house tonight. He'll be there in an hour. Get her fed and loosened up by then."

Riley retorted dryly, before he stopped to consider the quip, "You'll have to send over some booze for that, boss."

Hollister snapped, "Don't even think about it."

Riley winced. "I got the message loud and clear this morning, sir. No worries on that front. I'm not throwing away my career." Not even for Sophie Giovanni. Not even if it was killing him not knowing if she had any clothes on right now—or not.

Chapter 8

Sophie was shocked at how much Bhoukari she remembered. She hadn't spoken or heard it since she was a kid. Yet, in under two hours, a salt-and-pepper-haired Bhoukari gentleman named Samir had her answering simple questions and participating in rudimentary conversation. Best of all, the lesson distracted her from the ominous soreness beginning to set in over her entire body. Where were Brian and those magic pills? He'd disappeared shortly after Samir showed up.

The language teacher had just left and Sophie was pondering the unpleasant prospect of dragging herself up the stairs to bed when the sliding doors burst open on a gust of wind and salt spray. A tall, black apparition loomed there, startling her right up off the couch. She let out a cry of pain and fear.

The intruder pushed back a tight-fitting black neoprene hood and...Brian.

"You scared me half to death!" she accused. "What are you doing?"

"I went for a swim."

"In the ocean? But it's freezing."

"Hence the wet suit."

They stared at each other for several seconds. She couldn't help but notice how the tight rubber clung to him like a second—and highly informative—skin. The guy had an absolutely beautiful body. At a glance he might be labeled lean. But on second appraisal, he was the very pinnacle of fitness, one muscle blending into the next, not an ounce of fat on him anywhere. He might not carry the thick bulk of a five-times-a-week-at-the-gym bodybuilder, but he radiated the quiet strength of an extraordinarily powerful man.

Memory assailed her of that body under her hands, of it lying over her, pressing impossibly deep inside her…she looked up, startled.

His gaze was black. Intense. On fire.

Desire zinged between them like a Vandergraff generator, streaks of blue lightning crackling and snapping all around them. She took a step forward. She wanted to peel the neoprene off him, to kiss everything in its wake, to rouse him to the same fever pitch of last night, to rocket into deep space with him….

Their gazes locked. Every bit of the flames that were consuming her burned in his eyes. He took a step forward. Jerked to a halt. Growled, "Leave. Now. Go to bed. And lock your door."

She fled. Coward that she was, she didn't even remember to ask for one of the little wonder pills. She just ran. And barely felt her sore muscles protest as she hurried to the safety, or prison as the case might be, of her bedroom.

As exhausted as she was, sleep proved elusive. She listened pensively to Brian pacing downstairs—if the repetitive squeaking of the floor was any indication. Then he burst out with a single, vicious curse, and the sliding doors whooshed open once more. He must be going for another swim in the cold ocean.

She knew the feeling. Her body was on fire, and not all of it was the result of the day's exercise. In fact, barely any of it was that innocent.

When she finally slept, her dreams were dark and confused, leaving behind images of tangled limbs and heavy breathing and a tingling, restless need in her core.

"Okay, Sophie. In this session, we'll start learning about unarmed combat."

Brian eyed her many reflections in the mirrored martial-arts studio's walls. He stalked across the deeply padded floor toward her. Her eyes were big and apprehensive and made him want to pull her close and draw her into himself. Into the cocoon of perfect safety he fought a compulsion to wrap her in.

Ripping out his own fingernails would be a hell of a lot easier than trying to get through this session without crossing over the line with her. In spite of Hollister's orders, he was going to have to lay his hands on her today—a lot. And that knowledge sent his thoughts spinning and his pulse and respiration soaring to at least double normal.

Surely the major understood the necessity for touching Sophie while teaching her how to defend herself. Hell, the boss was the one who'd put it in her training syllabus. Hollister might forgive him for touching her professionally in the name of training, but would emphatically not forgive any funny business with Sophie.

"Face the mirror," he directed her.

She turned obediently to face away from him. Her derriere looked invitingly lush in those gray sweatpants and his hands ached to take that rounded flesh into his palms and pull her tight against him—*Stop that!* Since when were sweatpants sexy anyway? Apparently since she'd put some on.

He cleared his throat. "I'm going to put my arm around your neck. I won't hurt you, but I want you to try to break out of my grasp. Okay?"

She nodded and assumed a slightly spread-legged stance. Oh, God. To run his hand down her body, over her smooth belly, plunge into those sexy sweatpants, to cup her hot center, to feel her respond to him, to feel her throb around his finger—Stop. That.

Gulping, he stepped forward and was assailed by the peaches-and-cream scent of her hair. When they got back to the house, he was throwing out her shampoo! He put his arm around her slender neck. Her skin was velvety smooth under his arm and he winced at the thought of the red marks he was about to put on its ivory softness.

He looked into the mirror and she was staring back, her eyes black with intense awareness of him.

"Are there any cameras in here?" she murmured, her voice husky with desire.

He jerked, abruptly aware of her backside pressing resiliently against him. He squeezed his eyes shut for a moment. Control. Focus.

"No," he answered firmly. "No microphones, either. But we're still going to behave. This training is important."

She swallowed hard under his arm and nodded. Both her hands came up to grasp his forearm lightly.

"Ready?" Lord knew, he was more than ready for her.

She nodded, her hair tickling his nose. Ahh, to bury his face in it and breathe in the scent of her—

She ducked fast, yanking him half-over her, then she surged upright at the same time something hooked behind the back of his right ankle. A hard jerk on it and he was sitting on his behind, staring up at her, dumbfounded.

Her eyes sparkled. "Hey, I did it! I dropped the big, bad commando."

Son of a gun. His bruised pride gave way before her musical laughter and he grinned reluctantly. "I gather you've had some self-defense training?" he asked wryly.

"A little bit. My next door neighbor is a Tai Kwan Do instructor and thinks all women should know a few moves to protect themselves."

"He's right." Brian made to climb to his feet, and a hand appeared before his eyes.

"Need a hand?"

He took it, and she leaned back, tugging hard. He shouldn't touch her. But he couldn't resist. His palm tingled, sending jolts of lust pounding through him. Their eyes met again, and damned if she didn't look as hot and bothered as he felt.

"All right, Bruce Lee," he laughed. "Now that we know you can handle yourself, I'm not going to take it so easy on you. Let's try that again, slowly. I'm going to counter your move and show you how to counter back."

For the next half hour, they walked through various self-defense techniques. To the credit of her next door neighbor, Sophie wasn't half bad at slipping holds and knocking an opponent off balance.

But then she was supposed to twist and pull her hand away from his, and instead of resisting her, he went with the move and let her pull him over on top of her. Were he a bad guy, he'd have let his body weight crash down on top of her, effectively knocking the breath out of her and immobilizing her.

But this was Sophie. As they tumbled to the floor together, he threw out his hands and caught himself in a partial push-up so he didn't crush her.

Her gaze reflected shock as his thigh came to rest between hers, and his chest flattened her generous breasts. Memory of those tempting mounds naked and in his mouth washed over him. Of her body clenching around him, hot and tight. Her long legs wrapping around him to pull him closer and deeper. Her nails scoring his back heedlessly in her extreme pleasure. The way her neck arched when she threw her head back at the moment of release.

He groaned involuntarily.

Her gaze snapped away from his mouth and up to his eyes.

So much for keeping this session innocent.

"Kiss me," she whispered.

He closed his eyes, experiencing actual physical pain. "I'm trying, here, Sophie."

"Please."

"You're killing me," he mumbled.

"But you'll kill *me* if you don't. I...I don't usually feel like this."

"How do you feel?" He shouldn't have said the words. He had to keep the fence up between them. But damned if he could stop the question from coming.

"I feel like sunshine flickering through aspen leaves."

He flinched as desire roared through him. He must not give in.

"I feel reborn. Like I walked through fire and didn't get burned."

"Stop!" He rolled away from her violently and lay on his back, an arm flung over his eyes. "I can't have you, Sophie. We can't have each other!"

"Why not?"

"My boss said he'd court martial me if I stepped out of line again."

The crackling energy pouring off her ceased abruptly. "Oh." A pause.

"Can he do that?"

"Oh, yeah."

"Gee. That sucks."

He smiled in spite of the agony of trying to restrain his need for her. "That's one way of putting it."

"But I'm a civilian. Aren't you allowed to see women when you're off duty?"

He lifted his arm to glare over at her. "Off duty being the operative phrase. You're my job, Sophie. I'm supposed to train you. To prepare you for your mission."

She propped herself up on an elbow beside him. "Then you're fired. Now kiss me."

Laughing helplessly, he let his arm fall to the mat. "This is an important mission. You need to take your training seriously. I can't, in good conscience, distract you from it. We've got to stay away from each other."

"Brian, the way you make me feel when you simply walk into a room distracts me. The fact that you're breathing and on the same planet as me distracts me."

Oh, how he knew the feeling. "We've got to stop this. Before it goes any further."

He felt her raise herself up on an elbow beside him and didn't dare peek out from under his forearm at her.

"It has already gone too far," she murmured. "We're past the point of no return, don't you think?" Her inner thigh touched his leg, sliding up his thigh toward parts of him that leaped to attention. Her hand stole across his chest, and his heart galloped wildly.

He jerked away from her, rolled and leaped to his feet, a

violent movement born of desperation. "No! I can't! We can't. We mustn't."

He strode over to the door and grabbed a towel off the shelf there. "Get your things. We're going for a run."

The man started as his cell phone rang. The special one. Prepaid. Untraceable. Wincing, he opened it and said reluctantly, "Hello?"

"What's the news?"

Fouad.

"Someone saw her get on an airplane."

"In custody of whom?" Fouad blurted in surprise.

In his experience, it was never a good thing to surprise the Leader. But then, that was preferable to angering the Leader. And his next words would accomplish that. "Someone from Homeland Security. A man took her to Luke Air Force Base and put her on a business jet."

"Where did the plane go?"

"I'm working on it. We have no contacts who could immediately answer that question. But I've met a girl. She works in the base operations center and can get access to the flight logs."

"How soon? Things are nearly ready to go at this end." Fouad added in a terse bark, "But I want this problem eliminated before we move. Do you understand me?"

"Yes, sir. I will move with all possible haste."

"Sleep with your girlfriend, torture her, kill her, I care not. But find out where the Giovanni woman went and get rid of her!" Fouad was all but screaming by the end of the order.

The man practically whimpered in his terror, "It shall be as you wish."

Fouad disconnected, still muttering as he did so. The man at the other end closed his phone with shaking hands.

Oh, no. It didn't do to anger the Leader. If he didn't find and kill the woman soon, Fouad's scant patience would fail. And then he was a dead man.

Sophie grimaced as yet another stitch stabbed her side like a dagger. It had been three weeks since the exchange in the martial-arts studio. Three interminable, miserable, unbearable weeks. A lifetime, really. Brian crammed so much exercise and training—from unarmed combat to firing guns to surveillance techniques—into every day that each one seemed to take twice the normal time to pass. The world he'd led her into was so radically different from her former life, she hardly felt like the same person. Her apartment, her job, her old friends were a vague and distant memory.

Her reality now was defined mostly by pain, her constant and only companion. Brian had held himself completely aloof from her—grouchy and barely speaking to her except to growl instructions—ever since that fateful self-defense lesson. Other members of his team floated through now and then to resupply the kitchen with food or to provide some special expertise in her training, but mostly the two of them were left completely alone.

Except for the cameras, of course. After her first lesson in electronic surveillance, she'd searched the house and located the extensive network of microphones and cameras throughout it. Whoever'd wired the place had been darned thorough. It made for an uncomfortable threesome—her, Brian and Big Brother.

She took comfort in the fact that Brian was starting to look as haggard as she felt. Which was odd, given that her training barely made him break a sweat most of time. In the evenings when she had her language lessons, he usually went out for a couple hours to get what he called a "real work out." Nonetheless, the strain on both of them was starting to show.

Despite everything, she *knew* he still wanted her. The

harder he pushed her, the more certain she was of it. Her knee was holding up surprisingly well, but the rest of her was a complete wreck. She ached in places she didn't know she had muscles. She went to bed sore and woke up even more sore. Were it not for the hot tub and the doctor's little magic pain pills, there was no way she'd still be going.

This morning's run, she hadn't been quite as miserable as usual so far. Maybe this was the corner the doctor had told her she would turn if she was patient and hung in for the first several weeks of the program. And maybe she was just so exhausted that numbness was setting in.

She stumbled in the sand and fell, catching herself on her hands and knees. Panting painfully, she sat back on her heels to catch her breath

Brian was there instantly, on his knees in front of her. "Are you hurt?" he asked urgently.

Wow. The first sign of humanity out of him in days. "I tripped. I'm fine. Just need…to catch…my breath."

She huffed and puffed for maybe a minute, and then made to stand up. She stepped on her left leg funny and the brace caught, throwing her off balance. She staggered and Brian's arms went around her, catching her and gathering her against him in one quick movement.

"Sit back down." He eased her to the sand, his hands skimming over her knee in concern.

"I'm fine. The brace got some sand in it or something and it hitched for a second."

"Does this hurt?"

He took her foot in his hands and flexed the toe.

"No. I'm—"

He cut her off. "How about this?" He rotated her foot gently in both directions, then bent her knee and straightened it a couple times.

"I told you. I'm fine."

"You're not fine," he snapped. "I've been pounding the living hell out of you, and your body's close to its limits. I can't afford to injure you, dammit. If you're in serious pain or so fatigued you can't go any further, you've got to let me know."

"But that would involve us talking," she snapped back.

His gaze jumped up to hers. "Sophie, you can talk to me."

"Hah!"

"Dammit, I'm worried about you! I don't want to hurt you." He waved his hand toward her knee.

"My knee and I are fine, thank you."

"Then why are you sitting on your butt in the sand?" he shot back.

"Because I tripped and fell, and you overreacted."

"I did not overreact. You're important to—" he hesitated "—You're a valuable asset to Uncle Sam."

That was not what he'd originally intended to say. Who was she important to? Him? Could it be? She sighed. "Thanks for your concern. But I promise you, my knee is fine. I'm fine."

He squatted on his heels, studying her. "You're not fine," he announced. Then he added abruptly, "Let's get out of here."

Something in his voice made her look up quickly. "What do you mean?"

"Let's take the rest of the day off. You've earned a break. What do you say?"

She laughed. "What? Like I'm going to say no? Does a starving man refuse food?"

He stood up and offered her a hand. Abruptly, the mile-long run back to the beach house seemed to fly by. By mutual, unspoken consent, they didn't speak of their plan to play hooky. No need to tick off Big Brother and risk having their escape ruined.

She and Brian headed for the kitchen and packed themselves a quick picnic. He disguised the meal in a couple of plastic grocery bags and they headed out in no time. As the SUV passed through the gates of the military installation and back into the real world, she breathed an enormous sigh of relief.

"I know exactly the place for our picnic," he announced.

She sat back and enjoyed the drive. They wound along the coast on a narrow road perched high above the ocean. Beachfront estates lined the drive with secluded, gated entrances. She blinked in surprise when he turned in at one.

"Brian, this looks like a private home."

"It is. An old friend owns it. He lets me stop by whenever I want to."

"Is he home?" she asked doubtfully.

Brian shrugged. "I don't know. But I wasn't planning on going up to the house to find out. He likes to garden. I thought I'd show you the grounds."

The driveway was lush, framed in overhanging trees and brilliant bougainvilleas in full bloom. A lovely Asian-inspired house topped a hill, but Brian guided the SUV around the base of the hill behind the home and parked the car.

She climbed out, looking around in wonder at the tropical splendor. Layer upon layer of greenery stretched away from them, a crushed gravel path winding into the trees invitingly. Spots of color broke up the verdant palette, drawing the eye forward into the mysteries of the forest.

"This place is beautiful," she breathed.

Brian smiled over at her. "I thought you might like it." He strolled off down the path, which was wide enough for them to walk on side by side.

Birds and crickets and frogs sang, each vying to be the loudest, a joyous cacophony that soothed her soul. She breathed deeply of the rich, earthy air. "It's good to be alive, isn't it?" she murmured.

He glanced over at her and replied solemnly, "Yes. It is. In my career, I've learned to slow down and appreciate moments like this."

She nodded with new understanding. His world revolved around hard work, intense mental focus and unthinkable danger. To let down his guard for a moment, to simply enjoy a place of beauty and peace was a gift indeed.

They wound through the woodland paradise for fifteen or twenty minutes. And then a small space opened up in the path. It wasn't exactly a clearing because the canopy of trees overhead completely enclosed it. A small structure stood in the middle of the glade. For all the world, it looked like a Japanese cottage.

"This way," Brian murmured. He led her to a covered porch and slid open a low, wood and rice-paper panel that came up to about mid-thigh on him. He dropped to his knees in front of the opening, startling her. "It's a traditional Japanese teahouse."

And with that, he crawled inside. She followed him through the opening, bemused. The inside was breathtaking, elegant and simple. Piles of silk cushions served as the only furniture in front of a low wooden table with curved legs. Woven grass tatami mats covered the floor, a stunning water-color scroll hung on the far wall, and an artistic floral arrangement rested on a small pedestal beside it.

"This is gorgeous," she breathed. "But why isn't there a regular door?"

Brian set the bags on the table and started unpacking lunch. "The walk through the woods to get here is designed to remind you of nature's magnificence. Then you enter the teahouse on your knees to remind you of man's humble place in the universe." He gestured to the pile of cushions beside him.

She sank down, smiling. "I see why you like this place."

"Sometimes I *need* this place. When I'm out on a mission and it's going to hell and I'm tired and frazzled, this is the spot I think of to calm myself down and refocus my mind."

She nodded. "It's as close to perfect as any place I've ever seen."

He glanced over at her, a quiet, grateful smile in his eyes. Like he was relieved that she got what this place meant to him. She'd almost forgotten this Brian existed under the grim, demanding instructor.

She helped him lay out their ham sandwiches, carrot sticks, apples and potato salad. The plain meal ought to have looked out of place in this graceful setting, but its simplicity fit somehow. They ate in companionable silence, serenaded by the woodland creatures outside.

After a few minutes, she set down the remains of an apple. "So tell me. Am I going to need this place?"

"How so?"

"Am I going to need a perfect moment in a perfect setting to focus on, when it's all going to heck around me?"

A frown flickered across his face momentarily. And she knew him too well to miss it. He replied lightly, "I sincerely hope not."

"But you can't say for sure that I won't."

"Nothing's certain in life, Sophie."

"No kidding. Six weeks ago, I was going about my regularly scheduled life, working at the law firm and getting used to the idea of being single forever. Accepting the fact that I've turned thirty and my body's starting to go."

He laughed at that. "I've met guys in their sixties who do

triathlons and give the twenty-five-year olds a run for their money. Fitness is a state of mind. Once you commit to it, no matter what age you get started, you can shape and train your body to be as healthy as you want it to be."

She stuck her tongue out at him. "Some of us need a little bigger push than other people to make that commitment."

He reached over and squeezed her hand. "Have you looked at yourself in a mirror lately? Checked a stopwatch at the end of a run? You're doing fantastic. Don't be so hard on yourself."

"I wouldn't be doing anything at all if it weren't for you bullying me and cheering me on. You know, if you ever get tired of this Special Forces gig, you'd make a heck of a personal trainer."

"No, I wouldn't. I don't have the patience for it or the positive attitude."

"That's not true!"

He shrugged. "It works with you. But I wouldn't want to try it with anybody else. I couldn't duplicate the chemistry."

Oh. Well, then. Her cheeks felt warm all of a sudden. She cleared her throat. "So when am I likely to need this perfect memory?"

A shadow passed across his turquoise gaze, darkening it to the turbulent blue-green of a troubled sea. "Well, for one," he replied thoughtfully, "if you're captured, it's an effective technique for POWs to visualize pleasant places as a means of temporary escape from their current reality."

She propped her elbows on the table, studying his face carefully. "Is there a chance I'll be captured?"

Brian exhaled heavily.

She said soberly, "I'll take that as a yes. What will Freddie do to me if he captures me?"

The troubled blue of his eyes went a dark, muddy shade,

like an ocean lashed by a hurricane. Reluctantly, he mumbled, "Use your imagination. Then double it."

Fear fluttered like a trapped bird within her ribcage. She didn't want to think about it. Such a thing couldn't really happen to her. Could it? No. She definitely didn't want to think about it. Except she had to. She *had* to face the possibilities of this mission. Not only for her sake, but for Brian's, too.

She took a deep breath. "Okay, so I have a pretty good imagination. Are you planning to give me any training in withstanding such things?"

He retorted sharply, "Not me. I've already told Hollister he'll have to get someone else to do your POW training."

"Why?"

"I couldn't hit you. It's hard enough for me to wrestle you in your unarmed combat training. At least then you can fight back."

She laughed. "Not that I succeed in tagging you, oh, ever."

He grinned at her unrepentantly. "Nobody said I was going to make your training easy."

They smiled at each other. The moment elongated itself as they each became aware of the other and of their unwillingness to break the fragile connection they'd reestablished. The smiles faded from their eyes, but their gazes remained locked. Her eyes widened as his pupils expanded, turning his eyes as black as midnight. Her breathing waxed light and fast. Her skin tingled. A slow flush climbed his cheeks, and the sight of it gave her a sudden urge to fan herself.

He pushed aside the table at the same moment she leaned forward, reaching for him. They came together with the desperate passion of Romeo and Juliet, star-crossed lovers stealing a moment out of time. A single moment. Just for themselves. An hour with the nightingales before the lark heralded the dawn and ended their secret tryst.

"I've missed touching you," he murmured as his hands skimmed over her.

She knelt before him, her hands roaming where they willed across his skin, "I've been right here the whole time."

"Which made you all the more untouchable," he grumbled.

"Touch me now." It was a sigh of want, a plea of need, from the deepest well of her being.

"Ahh, sweet Sophie. It was all a lie. I couldn't stay away from you if I tried."

Tendrils of joy unfurled in her heart, pulling her forward to meet him halfway, on their knees in supplication to one another. "Then don't try."

Their hands darted about like impatient hummingbirds, touching and teasing, then flitting away to alight somewhere else. As if by magic, their clothes fell away while Sophie burned, hot and cold all at once.

"We shouldn't—" Brian started.

She pressed her fingertips to his mouth. "Give it a rest. We probably shouldn't, but we're going to anyway. We're making a perfect memory in a perfect place."

He grinned down at her, flashing a lopsided dimple. "Perfect, huh? That's a lot of pressure to put on a guy."

She looked him straight in the eye and said deadpan, "I wouldn't ask it of you if I didn't think you could do it."

He burst out laughing and wrapped his arms around her, carrying her down to the silken pillows. "I'll do my best to live up to your expectations, ma'am."

Their laughter sparkled like crystal, scattering diamond prisms of light all around them. He speared his hands into her hair, drawing her up to him, kissing the laughter off her lips. She sipped the nectar of their unspeakable ecstasy at finally being together like this. The relief between them was a palpable thing, a sigh hanging unspoken.

"Ahh, Sophie. I've been dreaming about you every night. I wake with the taste of you on my lips. I've stood in front of your door and argued with myself more times than I can count."

Surprised, she asked, "What do you argue with yourself over?"

"Whether or not I give a damn about my career in the face of my need for you."

"Which one of you is winning?"

He smiled down at her. "My fear of testing your doorknob and finding it locked against me."

She stared up into his eyes, losing herself in their blue-on-blue depths. "It has never been locked against you. Not even that first night when you told me to lock it."

The smile faded from his eyes as he searched for the truth in her words. "Jeez, Sophie—" Words failed him and his mouth descended, a journey of inches between two worlds apart. And then they became one. He kissed her over and over, and she savored the spicy honey-mustard taste of him.

"Mmm. Better than any ham sandwich I've ever had." She smiled.

"You still taste like peaches. You always smell like them, you know."

"It's my shampoo."

"I've started to throw out the bottle more times than I can tell you…" he paused to bury his nose in her hair, and while he was there, he kissed the side of her neck below her ear, sending shivers shimmering down her torso "…but I always stop. I open the lid for one last sniff, and I can't make myself toss it. It would be like throwing away a part of you."

She buried her face in the crook of his neck, "That's so sweet."

"Honey, I'm a lot of things, but sweet is not one of them."

She pushed, rolling him over onto his back among the brilliant ruby-and-emerald cushions. "You are, too, sweet."

He tried to scowl, but ended up grinning up at her. "I'm tough. And macho. And scary."

She leaned down to kiss him. "You forgot grouchy and unsympathetic and a bully."

He looped an arm around the back of her neck. "Ahh, yes. A bully. That's me, all right. I'm a real SOB."

She sprawled wantonly on top of his delicious body. "But you're my SOB."

He whispered, "I like the sound of that." Quickly, he rolled over, his wonderful weight pressing her deep into the haphazard pile of cushions. He kissed her thoroughly, inhaling her into him, drawing her into the magic spell the teahouse cast around them.

The heavy beams overhead were solid, masculine. The delicate panels of paper between them the complete opposite. Light on dark, strong on fragile. Man on woman. A cool breeze blew, and the birds sang on, and the sun smiled down through the leaves.

Sophie's heart took flight. Skin on skin, heartbeat to heartbeat, they soared. He filled her body to bursting with his eager heat and controlled power, but more than that, he filled the void within her soul. It had gaped, empty and yearning, for the past month, aching for him to fill it once more.

"Brian!" she cried out. She clutched him tight, and he drove her higher. She gasped, and gasped again, layer upon layer of explosion building within her. "I've missed you so much!"

"Baby, I've been going crazy for you." He looked deep into her eyes, his body poised, aware that he held her on a razor's edge of release. Their gazes locked, and he plunged so deep within her she forgot to breathe. Shattering glory started through her, one wave after another, brighter and brighter, stronger and stronger.

In that moment, they were the universe and the universe was within them. She cried aloud, arching up into him, and he kissed her with his entire body, absorbing her and her cries of delight into himself. He joined her in an endless moment of perfect sensation, of perfect union, of perfect spiritual alignment.

They collapsed bonelessly into the silk pillows, their bodies spent, their souls merged into a single awareness. She breathed when he did, he sighed when she did. The thought crossed her mind to seek more comfort, and he rolled onto his side, drawing her against his body.

A cool breeze wafted across her skin, and he reached under the table with his free arm to pull out a light silk throw and toss it over them. It rubbed against her sensitized skin, sending shivers of sexual pleasure racing through her again. A moan of pleasure rippled past his lips involuntarily.

He kissed away her smile, leaving a new one in its place. "I should steal the feather out of that flower arrangement and see what sounds I can draw from you with it."

"I'd die of the pleasure," she murmured against his warm, firm lips.

"Ahh, but what a way to go. Death by orgasm. Sign me up."

She traced lazy curlicues across his chest with her finger. "I think I already died. This has to be a little corner of paradise."

He smiled down at her. Outside a bird began to sing, a haunting melody of love and loss and piercing sweetness. The smile faded from his lips as an echo of the song repeated itself more faintly from further away.

"It's beautiful," she breathed. "What is it?"

"Nightingales. The male is singing, trying to attract the female who answered him back. It's said that a male who cannot find a female will sing himself to death trying to draw a female to him."

"How romantic and sad."

His eyelids flickered. "Such is love. It can drive a man to death and beyond."

Sophie stared up wordlessly into Brian's vivid, intensely blue eyes. What was he saying? That she'd gotten under his skin like that? Was he willing to cast aside all he'd worked for, all he'd achieved in the name of love? "I wonder what it's like to love like that," she murmured.

"I feel like that about my work. It's bigger than me. More important than my life. It's a compulsion. Just like that nightingale singing for a mate—for his life."

She stared at him. To death and beyond? She couldn't imagine anything more important than life itself. Except if that was the case...

Why had she agreed to do the mission? Hadn't she weighed the odds of failure against the importance of the job and come up with a rational decision? Was that what Brian was driving at?

Was he warning her again that he always said good bye to the women in his life? The thought sent a sharp pang through her. The thought of the day arriving when Brian breezed out her life as abruptly as he'd breezed into it pained her. No man had ever swept her off her feet so completely. She felt more alive when she was with him than she'd ever felt before.

Fear vibrated within her, low and ominous, that, if he left, she'd never feel this way again. And yet, he'd just told her that his work was his wife, mistress and true love. What kind of a fool did that make her?

She frowned.

He reached up with the pad of his thumb to smooth away the wrinkle between her brows. "I didn't mean to put a frown on your face."

Why *did* she agree to do this mission anyway? Duty, country and honor, right? Except the words rang hollow in her head—every last syllable false. She propped herself up on an elbow and stared down at Brian. Beautiful Brian. Sexy, charming, mesmerizing Brian. Brian, who'd prior to this, managed to completely hold himself away from her in the name of the mission. Why now? Why this? Why today? Why that comment about his job being more important than his life? And then it all clicked.

"You know, don't you?" she demanded.

With that same uncanny simpatico they shared while making love, he plucked the unspoken thought out of her head. "Why you took the mission? Yeah. I know."

"And you want me to reconsider, don't you? Is that was this seduction was all about today? Giving me exactly what I wanted so I wouldn't go through with the mission just to make love with you again?"

He sat up, staring at her incredulously. *"What?"*

"You planned this whole tryst, didn't you? You gave me my *perfect moment* in hopes that once I had it, I'd get out of your hair and go back to my knitting and my desk job. What? Don't you think I'm good enough? Do you think I'm going to screw it up? Is that why you're trying to drive me off?"

"Sophie, I don't know what in the hell you're talking about, but I can tell you, you're talking crazy."

"That would serve your purposes just wonderfully if I were crazy, wouldn't it? Well, I'm not crazy. Yes, I agreed to this whole insane project because of you. Yes, I wanted to make love with you again. Yes, I wanted to spend every moment, day and night with you. And no, I'm bloody well not planning to quit just because now we've had mind-blowing, amazing, incredible, *perfect* sex!"

"What the hell are you talking about?"

"I'm not going to be the one to say good bye and walk away. You're going to have to be the one to do it."

Chapter 9

Brian surged to his feet, oblivious to his nudity. He paced the confines of the paper walls, the woven grass tatami mats rough against the soles of his feet. Sophie huddled on the pillows, awash in the misery that he'd somehow caused her. How could the glory of their lovemaking have crashed so fast into this mess?

The delicacy of the room around her only accented her intense femininity. Something close to obsessive need ripped through him. In spite of his fury, his palms itched to reach out for her, to explore her body, to change her anger and betrayal to mindless passion, to lose himself in her once more.

He burst out, "I cannot believe you think that's what this was about!"

She pulled the silk throw close around her shoulders. "You do everything for the sake of your job. You just said so yourself. So you tell me. What purpose did this little seduction serve this afternoon?"

He ate up another circuit of the room with angry strides, then whirled, glaring. "It accomplished absolutely nothing except jeopardizing the hell out of my career."

"Far be it from me to spill the beans on you. After all, I'd hate to take away the one thing from you that's more important than life itself."

Ahh. Understanding slammed into him like a bolt of lightning. He was too used to dealing with men. Of not stopping to consider how his colleagues might *feel*. He stopped midstride. Turned to face her. Moved swiftly to her side and dropped to his knees on the pillows in front of her. "Is that what this is about?" he asked softly.

"What do you mean?" she asked.

"That my job's more important to me than you are? Oh, God, honey. I've been tearing myself up inside, worrying over you. It's my job to get you ready for this op and send you out, but I'd do anything—up to and including throwing away my career— to talk you out of it and keep you safe if I thought I could do it!"

She stared at him, looking stunned, then declared, "I don't buy it. You're driving me off the only way you can, yet not look like you failed in your job."

What in the hell had gotten into her? Where was this attack coming from? Clamping down on his reaction with the force of a bear trap, he replied evenly, "I beg your pardon?"

"It's too pat an explanation. You taught me how to lie convincingly yourself. You said that when the logic doesn't match up, it's a lie, no matter how honestly the line's delivered."

He stared, truly shocked—an emotion he hadn't experienced in a very long time. Did she honestly believe he'd casually seduce her and try to drive her away, heartbroken, because he didn't think she could hack it?

"I swear, Sophie. My only motive in bringing you here today was to give you a little break from your training. It's killing me to push you like I am. To stand by and watch you suffer day after day. I wanted to give you a moment of joy. Something pleasurable in the midst of the misery I've made out of your life."

"Oh, Brian. I'm not miserable. If you'd have paid the slightest bit of attention over the past few weeks, you'd have seen that."

Dammit, she was starting to cry. He fell completely apart at the sight of those big brown eyes swimming in tears. "Huh. Now who's lying?"

"You've been so wrapped up in your own issues you haven't looked at me. Really seen me." A sob wracked her.

His control as thin as the paper walls, he asked, "Then why are you crying?"

She dashed the wetness from her cheeks. "It's a girl thing. I cry whenever I get emotional. This training has been the hardest thing I've ever done. But, Brian. I've done it! Don't you understand what an accomplishment this is for me? How amazing it makes me feel to know I've done everything you've asked of me and I've given this training my absolute best shot?"

He studied her skeptically. It would be just like her to say something like that to make him feel better. No matter whether or not it was true. She was the kind of woman who worried more about how the people around her felt than about herself.

She continued, "I'm stronger than I've ever been, physically and mentally. I'm more confident. More...alive. You've given me an incredible gift. It's frosting on the cake that you also make me feel pretty. A little desirable, even."

He laughed painfully. "You've been the talk of the entire

base ever since you started running up and down the beach. Entire barracks full of men from here to downtown San Diego are having dirty dreams about you at night."

She gaped, appalled.

He laughed and reached out with a finger to gently close her sagging jaw. "Look in the mirror when we get back to the house. You're a knockout, sweetheart."

"You're blind."

He retorted, "And you're beautiful. Get over it."

She blinked rapidly and looked startled. Hard to believe a woman like her really had no idea of her appeal.

She picked up the thread of her previous logic. "That's why it hurts so bad that you're trying to get me to quit now."

He drew breath to tell her she was talking nonsense, but she interrupted, rushing on. "If you want to end our personal relationship, that's okay. I never expected forever from you. I'm capable of separating the mission from us. I can go on with the training even if you want to break it off with me."

He stalked across the room then whirled, glaring her down. "For the last time, I am not trying to make you quit. And I most certainly am not trying to end our relationship! Trust me, if I wanted to drive you away from me or the job, I'd have succeeded long ago. I'm the guy who's so damned good at what he does, remember?"

Doubt gleamed in her pensive gaze. He swore under his breath. "Please believe me. I'm not trying to get you to quit."

She sighed. "Okay. I'm sorry."

"No need to apologize." He didn't know about her, but his memory of this perfect place had been permanently modified. Henceforth, whenever he reached for the teahouse's calm, the picture would include Sophie's sleek body wrapped around him, her big brown eyes wide in wonder, watching her pleasure as she came apart in his arms. Now he had a perfect memory.

As much as he'd have loved for this afternoon to go on forever, time was inevitably racing on. And theirs here had expired. Like it or not, it was time to say good bye to this place and this moment. Reluctantly, he bent down to gather up their clothes. "It's getting dark out. If we don't get back to the base pretty soon, Major Hollister's going to send out the troops looking for us."

They dressed, packed the remains of their lunch and tidied the teahouse. Sophie paused on her hands and knees in the doorway and looked back one last time in the fading dusk. He prayed she was cementing in her memory for all time the sights and sounds and smells of this little piece of paradise.

If only he didn't have to let her go. But the time was fast approaching when his job would demand exactly that of him. And he dreaded it more than anything he'd ever faced in his entire life. And judging from Sophie's earlier outburst, she was dreading it, too.

"Incoming," Isabella murmured, rousing Vanessa from a quick power nap.

Vanessa Blake, commander of the first all-female Special Forces team in the U.S. military, sat up abruptly, on full battle alert. They'd been out here for nearly three months now, and her whole team was edgy. Looking for a fight.

Isabella reported, "I've got movement in the compound— eight to ten robed and armed men approaching the front gate. And, I've got vehicles approaching from the north."

The entire team notched up their alertness to another level. It wasn't anything they did or said. It was an electricity that came over them; controlled energy waiting for release. The Medusas were ready to move in for the kill. If they were lucky, maybe one of those men in the compound was their target, Freddie Sollem. She'd clearly love for Katrina, her sniper, to get a bead on the guy and take him out once and for all. Then she and her team could go home, the woman Brian Riley was training in California to come help them could get on with her life, and the world would be a safer place. But after months of unsuccessful waiting for Sollem to show a crack in his armor, she wasn't hopeful. At least the guy hadn't shown any indication that he was on the verge of launching a major terrorist attack…not until this incoming convoy, at any rate.

Vanessa trained her binoculars on the puff of dust approaching fast from the east. Several black blobs resolved themselves into military-style trucks, high flatbeds with canvas roofs stretched over arched metal ribs. The trucks' suspensions were compressed and the vehicles swayed sluggishly where the road curved a bit. Whatever load those trucks were carrying was heavy. Really heavy.

"Get a visual on the cargo if you can, Sidewinder," Vanessa directed Misty—the team's Air Force pilot and resident unmanned drone flyer—who was at the controls of an aerial-surveillance drone.

"Gimme a sec," Misty murmured, manipulating what looked like the controls of a video game mounted on a laptop-sized box. "I've got to bring the drone around behind the trucks to peek in the backs."

"Hurry," Isabella piped up. "Those trucks are moving fast. They won't be out in the open much longer."

"Almost there," Misty replied. "Get eyeballs on the monitor. This'll have to be a fast pass so they don't spot the bird."

Vanessa and the others crowded around the monitor playing the video feed from the drone. A strip of asphalt came into view. The drone banked and followed the gray strip. Misty was going to fly her bird right up the trucks' backsides.

"The targets should come into view any second," Misty murmured.

Sure enough, the blurry shape of a truck entered the top of the screen. Isabella quickly tweaked the camera controls to bring the picture into focus. They'd only get one pass on the trucks. Maybe two or three seconds per vehicle. Fortunately, Isabella was the best real-time photo-intelligence analyst Vanessa had ever seen. Two seconds was all Adder needed to identify the trucks' cargo.

Vanessa held her breath as the drone closed in on the trucks. Her gut said this was no caravan of food and toilet paper for the Sollem compound. Maybe they'd finally get a definitive idea of what Freddie was planning.

The rear opening of the first canvas truck cover came into clear view. Vanessa stared hard. A single box, oblong in shape. Bulky.

And then the drone was past.

Isabella gasped.

What had she picked out that Vanessa had missed?

The next truck rushed into view.

"Slow down," Isabella hissed at Misty.

"Can't," Misty retorted.

Vanessa leaned forward. Another box in this truck, looking rather lonely in the middle of the truck bed. Same cargo in the remaining trucks. Six steamer trunk-sized boxes in all. Holding something dense. Metal, most likely. Big. *Like weapons.*

The video picture tilted crazily as Misty peeled the drone off and flew it back out into the desert at a safer distance from the Sollem compound. Isabella sat back on her heels, staring intently at the now-blank screen.

"You need a replay?" Vanessa asked quietly.

"Yeah. I want to verify this one before I make the call."

That was unusual. Isabella was unerring in knowing exactly what she'd seen the first time around.

Aleesha—the team's Jamaican-born doctor and computer guru—typed quickly into the laptop attached to the monitor, and the video sequence they'd just seen played again.

"Slow it down," Isabella murmured, never taking her eyes from the screen.

Vanessa leaned forward, studying the half-time images again. Still boxes. She made out yellow-painted Arabic-style script on the side of one. Vanessa spoke Arabic, but she couldn't read this.

"What does that writing say?" Vanessa asked.

Isabella looked up, her gaze wide with dismay. "It's Urdu."

Vanessa frowned. Urdu was the official language of Pakistan.

Isabella continued. "I think it says 'fissionable material.'"

Vanessa gasped like Isabella had just buried a fist in her gut. "As in nuclear weapons?"

Isabella's gaze was already back on the screen. She leaned in close as the second truck came into view. As the pair of trunks came into view, she paused the image on screen. Stabbed a finger at the top of the rearmost box. "Mamba, enlarge this image here."

A smudge of yellow came into view on top of the box, too blurry to read.

"Digitally enhance it," Vanessa murmured.

"Already on it, girlie." Aleesha engaged the high-tech software that analyzed pictures and forecasted what color missing pixels would be based on the existing pixels around them. The program made several passes through the image, each one clearer than the one before. Finally, the swirling Urdu came into reasonable focus. Vanessa pulled out a small pad of paper and copied down the writing to the best of her ability.

While Isabella continued to study the rest of the video footage, Vanessa reached over and powered up the satellite phone. She dialed General Wittenauer's direct line. It was mid-afternoon in Washington.

"General Wittenauer's office," a familiar female voice answered.

His secretary. Which meant the general was not at his desk. "Hi Mary, it's Viper. I need to speak to the boss. Now."

"He's in a national-security briefing at the White House and can't be disturbed."

Vanessa replied briskly, "Perfect. Patch me through to his cell phone."

There was a brief pause. Then Mary said, "He's in the situation room. A signal won't get through."

"Have the White House operator patch me through to the phone in front of him, then. Don't take no for an answer. I have to talk to him *right now*."

"Is this a matter of national security?"

"Oh yeah."

"One moment, dear."

As grandmotherly as Mary Norton might sound, the woman had worked for JSOC for nigh unto thirty years and was sharp as a tack. She'd get Vanessa's call through.

In less than thirty seconds, a ringing phone sounded in Vanessa's ear. Wow. Mary was good.

Wittenauer muttered low and irritated, "Go."

"Sir, it's Viper. Sorry to disturb you. I thought you might like to know we just got visual on what we believe to be three complete nuclear devices being transported into the Sollem compound."

"What?"

She'd bet that squawk had just brought whatever briefing was in progress in the sit room to a screeching halt.

"Just a second, Viper. I'm going to put you on speaker and I want you to repeat what you just said."

She gulped. Nothing like having to drop a bomb on the president of the United States and his entire cabinet. She repeated her statement. Stony silence reigned for about three seconds, and then every voice in the room spoke at once. The momentary chaos subsided.

Vanessa said, "If you'll have one of your signals technicians come on the line, we'll transmit the images we just collected. You can have your own photo-intel folks confirm our analysis." Not that she doubted Isabella's call for a second.

Wittenauer's voice came back on the line after she'd finished talking to the signals guys and relaying the video data to them. "You sure as hell know how to liven up a security briefing, girl."

Vanessa replied grimly, "Just doing my job, sir."

"Keep up the good work. It goes without saying that you may have any resources whatsoever that you need to continue this mission while we verify your findings at this end and figure out what to do next."

"Roger, sir. Tell Brian Riley he's out of time. I need the Giovanni woman out here ASAP."

"I'll make the call now, Viper."

Out of general principles, Sophie glared at Brian's back five yards or so in front of her. He was pacing her for this run down the beach. The object was to maintain an eight-minute mile for four miles. So far she didn't feel too bad, but they were only a little over a mile into this exercise in torture. It helped her to get mad, and Brian was the logical target. He didn't seem to mind her glares and snarky comments as long as she did whatever he asked of her. And she had to admit, under his tutelage, she was doing things now that she would never have imagined possible six weeks ago.

Abruptly a spray of sand shot up between her and Brian, peppering her in stinging grains. What was that? She slowed down, surprised.

Brian, ahead of the burst, kept going and pulled away quickly. Drat. She sped up to keep the gap from becoming too big.

Another burst of sand exploded on her right. Startled, she swerved left, almost into the surf. What in the world was that? Some sort of training charge placed in the sand for the SEAL trainees? Maybe they shouldn't be running through this stretch of the beach. She stopped, frowning.

"Brian!"

He turned around, running backwards, but then ran toward her when he saw her stopped. "What?" he asked shortly. "You're not wimping out already, are you?"

"Not even," she retorted. "What are those little explosions in the sand?"

He scowled. "What explosions?"

"There were two of them. Like firecrackers. They made a little pop and blew up a bunch of sand."

"I don't hear anything but the ocean and you trying to avoid running."

"Hey. I was doing fine. I feel good. But if there are land mines or something out here, we shouldn't be running through them."

"There aren't any—"

Another burst of sand exploded right at her feet. This sand was wet and really hurt when it flew up at her.

"See? I told—"

"Dammit." Brian took a running leap and tackled her with all the force of an NFL linebacker. His arms wrapped around her waist, he twisted in mid-air so they both landed on their sides. What little wind she had was knocked clean out of her. She lay there gasping for several seconds, absorbing the pain in her shoulder and hip. Thank God they'd been on sand when he did that.

"Hey!" she protested. "That hurt!" A wave washed up on the beach, getting her hair wet and salt water in her eyes. She sputtered and struggled to sit up, but Brian forcibly held her down flat.

"Someone's shooting at you."

She froze beneath him while terror ripped through her. "What? Who?"

"I have no idea," he bit out. "Low-crawl out into the water until it's deep enough to swim. Then head north along the beach. I'll be beside you. Stay on the ocean side of me and use me for cover."

And then it hit her. This was a training exercise. That's why the "sniper" hadn't struck her. She had to give Brian credit. He'd had her going there, for a minute. She didn't relish going for a swim in the frigid water, but it was probably slightly less miserable than running for three more miles at a killer pace. It had turned out she was a natural swimmer, and she'd had no trouble meeting all the swim distances and times Brian asked of her.

"Okay, fine. We go for a swim instead. Can I at least take off my shoes?"

"Get your ass out into that water and start swimming."

She jerked, stung. This grim, furious soldier was totally unlike any Brian she'd seen so far. "All right already." She dragged herself down the beach on her elbows. The sand clawed at her, making for miserable, inch-by-inch progress. Then another wave came in, offering her a tiny bit of relief from the sand's friction. She heaved forward another foot. No wonder sea turtles only came ashore to lay eggs. This was the pits!

Another popping noise and a grunt from Brian.

"You okay?" she panted.

"Ricochet hit me. Not serious."

"You crawled over one of those charges?"

"Sophie…someone is shooting at us. With a gun. I was hit by a bullet."

This *had* to be a training scenario. They were on a military base full of Special Forces soldiers. What numbskull would set up shop and starting shooting in this direction randomly? It was a recipe for suicide. Was Brian's getting "hit" part of the scenario, too? They'd spent the past several days doing a fair bit of first-aid training. "Are you hurt, or do you want me to administer CPR to you out here in the water?"

She sensed his irritation without having to see it. Nonetheless, he answered crisply, "The bullet hit the sand first. Most of its velocity was bled off before it bounced up and tagged me. Besides, the shooter's using a sound suppressor, so the round's probably coming in sub-sonic to begin with. I'll get a bruise, but I don't think it broke the skin. I'll let you know when the next wave hits it."

The next wave? Ahh. Salt water. If there was an open wound, it would sting like fire. The next wave rolled in. "No sucked in breath of macho I-can-take-the-pain. You're okay, then?" she asked as the icy water lifted her up onto her knees.

"I'm okay. Let's go. You ought to be able to breast-stroke in this water."

Her knees banged the bottom and every stroke included digging her fingers into the sand at the bottom of the stroke and pushing off. But in a few seconds, she was fully afloat and actually swimming.

"Head out to sea for a hundred yards or so. Beyond the breakers. Then turn right. And stay beside me," Brian called over the roar and hiss of the surf.

Sophie did as he directed. Her feet were heavy and awkward in her running shoes, and her T-shirt stuck to her torso, impeding big arm movements. They swam in grim silence for several minutes.

She caught a glimpse of Brian's face and nearly forgot to hold her breath as she went under water for a stroke. That was fear in his eyes. Pure, unadulterated, terror.

If he was afraid...then that meant... Her brain locked up.

This was the real deal. Someone was trying to *kill* one or both of them. The thought roared through her brain like an avalanche, annihilating every morsel of reality she'd clung to through this whole bizarre adventure. Who could possibly want to see her die? No one even knew she was here. She hadn't been allowed to contact even her mother to let the poor woman know where she was.

Her arms and legs grew weary, and the cold was bitter. Shivering violently, she struggled to keep her limbs moving in some sort of productive way.

Was Brian really okay? It would be just like him to be mortally wounded and fail to mention it to her. He and his buddies took being macho to a whole new level far beyond any male she'd ever been around.

She pushed on through her abject fear, the teeth-chattering cold and the dismal realization she'd actually rather be running that four miles than suffering through this. Her arms had long since passed through fatigue to burning, to numb, to now just being so damned heavy she could hardly move them. Her brain was moving like molasses in a freezer. She held on to a single thought. She must keep going. Must not drown. Brian would be so disappointed in her.

But finally, even that thought failed her as the cold overcame all function.

"How much longer?" she gasped. "I'm done in."

Brian glanced over at her and swore under his breath. "Let's head in. Just relax, honey, and let the tide carry you."

So relieved that she felt warm tears tracking down her frozen cheeks, she did as he directed. They drifted in to shore perhaps a hundred feet down the beach from a group of sand-covered SEAL students grunting through calisthenics in soaking wet fatigues and boots.

"Hey Rip!" someone shouted from that direction. "We're a little busy here. Take your training elsewhere."

Her feet touched sand, and with enormous relief, she stood up in the chest-deep water. She was never lifting her arms again as long as she lived.

Brian shouted back, "I need a six-man personnel security phalanx around my girl now! This is not an exercise. I've got a shooter a half-mile down the beach using a medium caliber, long-range rifle. Get a team down there ASAP and take him alive. I need to know who he's working for. The shooter's a probable amateur. Can't shoot worth a damn."

The response to his words was impressive. Men scattered in every direction, and in a matter of seconds, six black T-shirted BUDs instructors—all Navy SEALs—were in the water around her and Brian. The BUDs trainees raced down the beach, presumably to cut off the shooter from escaping by sea. Radios and cell phones were at every ear, and three black SUVs peeled away from the SEAL administration building.

One of the SEALs shouted in her ear over the pounding surf, "We're going to bring you ashore now. We may move you around a little roughly, but just relax and let us do our job."

She nodded and shouted back, "Got it."

A little rough didn't quite describe it. The SEALs all but picked her up by the elbows and horsed her up the beach, hustling her across the sand at a dead run into the nearest structure, the students' temporary sleeping quarters. It was crowded with canvas cots and smelled of dirty socks and sweat and salt water. Flinging aside beds and storage trunks, the team raced through the tent. A short pause at the back while a couple men took a look around outside, and then they were on the run again, racing her over to the administration building. At least it had solid walls.

Once inside, they took her directly to an interior office. A naval officer stood up from his desk when she came in. "Miss Giovanni. Have a seat. You're safe now." The guy turned to Brian. "Talk," he ordered. "You've made quite a fuss."

Brian repeated what he'd shouted to the SEALs, albeit in a little more detail, describing when and where the shots were fired and what direction they appeared to have come from.

Sophie was startled when Brian commented, "The weapon might be a bolt-action rifle. The shooter was taking single shots at thirty-second or more intervals. And all three shots were low of the kill zone."

The commander snorted. "No wonder you said the guy was an amateur. Thirty seconds? And all three shots missed?"

Even Sophie knew thirty seconds was a long time to load a sniper rifle. She could do it in under fifteen, and that included carefully clearing the chamber and making sure the spent cartridge had been properly ejected. Heck, she even knew how to make a correction after the first shot for wind or sight alignment.

Brian pulled out his cell phone. Three guesses who he was calling and the first two didn't count. Major Hollister was going to have a cow. How had Freddie Sollem found her? For surely nobody else on the planet had cause to kill her. Was the operation to train her compromised? Was Hollister's own team infiltrated with an informant of some kind?

She wouldn't want to be on his staff in about thirty seconds.

Brian had a short, murmured conversation with Hollister. He closed his phone and said wryly, "The boss just got a little busy. He'll call us back in a while with where we go next. Until then, we sit tight here or wherever the SEALs want to put us. Sir, if you need your office back, we can move the subject."

Herself being the subject in question, of course.

"Stay," the commander replied, smiling. "She's a hell of a lot easier on the eye than the folks who usually come in here. Besides, running the schoolhouse is pretty bland after field ops. I'm glad for the break in the routine."

It was strange after their panicked swim and the frantic race up the beach to then just sit. And sit. Brian had warned her that the vast majority of his work involved crashingly boring surveillance or sitting and waiting. He wasn't kidding.

Two of the SEALs who'd brought her and Brian here re-appeared outside the office door with MP-7 submachine guns at the ready. They passed one to Brian.

She said grimly, "Any guesses as to who that was?"

"Nope."

She retorted, "Aww, c'mon. Even I know who that had to be."

"Could be some crazy out to make a statement to the U.S. military. Could be some kid high on speed with his dad's gun."

"Or it could be Freddie."

Brian replied, "Not Freddie directly. He knows better than to risk coming to the United States. And he sure as hell knows not to shoot at a Navy installation crammed to the gills with SEALs. But I wouldn't bet you a nickel it wasn't one of Freddie's flunkies."

"If Freddie knows I'm here with you guys, getting trained, then does that mean the mission's off?"

Brian didn't answer. Didn't look away from his weapon. But the back of his neck and shoulders went tight. He finally murmured, "Not my call. That will have to be reassessed."

Cripes. To have gone through the past six weeks for nothing? What an awful thought—

Brian replied to her unspoken thought. "Even if the mission's scrubbed, you needed this training. Until Sollem's caught, your life is in extreme danger. Now that he knows we've talked to you he *has* to kill you, come hell or high water."

He was kidding, right? Except logic said he wasn't. Freddie had beat her to the punch. She was a marked woman. Great. Just great.

Chapter 10

Brian drove like a man possessed. The armored SUV ate up the miles as he and Sophie put San Diego far, far behind them. They had no guarantees that Sollem's men weren't staking out the airports in and around San Diego, so the decision had been made to drive to San Francisco, board a commercial flight using assumed names and head for their next destination. Since Sophie had likely been tracked to California in the first place on a military flight, Hollister had decided not to use another military jet and risk an information leak.

If only Sophie were done with her training! They had one more vital piece left, and he didn't relish tackling it.

Sophie slept, no doubt exhausted by the excitement of the past few hours. The sniper had gotten away, Stoner and Scottie had hastily packed gear for them and brought it down to the SEAL compound, and Hollister had ordered the two of them to get out of Dodge.

Hollister was up to his eyeballs in alligators, trying to figure out how in the hell Sollem's man had found Sophie and whether or not they had a leak in the unit. Brian would bet his last dime that nobody on or associated with their team had leaked the information. They were good people, one and all.

Sollem's man had to have tracked Sophie from Utah to California somehow. Maybe one of Freddie's people had seen him drag Sophie out of her parking lot. The location had been far from secure. If that was the case—and it seemed the likeliest scenario—the thought of how close a call Sophie'd had with an untimely demise made him sick to his stomach. He'd gotten to Sophie maybe only hours or minutes before Sollem's henchman.

His cell phone vibrated in his shirt pocket. "Ripper here," he said quietly, not to wake Sophie.

"It's Cowboy." *Hollister.* "Where are you?"

"Approaching L.A."

"Will you make it through there before traffic gets bad?"

Brian grunted. "Traffic's always bad in L.A. We're ahead of rush hour, but it'll still be slow."

"I've got seats for you on the 6:00 a.m. flight out of San Francisco to Calgary."

"Canada?" Brian responded, surprised.

"You said you wanted to take her skiing, right? It hasn't snowed much in Colorado this year, and I don't want to take her back to Utah. That's what the bastard will expect."

No need to ask who the bastard was. Sollem.

"Banff has forty-eight inches of base and more snow on the way. And they have a couple brutal downhill-racing runs like you asked for. You've got a room under the names of Roger and Dawn Jackson." He added dryly, "I figure it's not a stretch for the two of you to pose as a married couple."

Brian didn't deign to respond to the comment. Sometimes it just didn't pay to rise to the bait.

Hollister continued, " I'm working on pulling in a team of operatives to help you with bodyguard duties. When I've got them nailed down, I'll let you know. I'm trying to have them in place before you two get to Calgary, but it'll be close."

"I can handle her solo. She knows the score and is cooperative."

"Nevertheless, I want you to have backup."

Brian laughed. "Don't get me wrong. I'm happy for the help. But I've got it covered until you can get someone into place."

"What's *your* status?" Hollister asked.

"I'm good for now. I'll drive until we're close to San Francisco and then stop at a motel and grab a few hours' rest. I've got the cash Stoner brought me, so we're okay on that score for a while." They ought to be on fifteen grand in greenbacks. It allowed them to avoid credit cards and leaving any kind of traceable trail.

"Have you looked at the identity packages Stoner gave you?"

"Not yet. Are they the Roger and Dawn Jackson legends?"

"Yup. I kept them simple. No need to muck up the situation with a complicated cover story. Sophie's not experienced enough for that."

"She's pretty smart, sir."

"Thank God. Speaking of which…" Hollister hesitated.

Foreboding exploded in Brian's gut.

"We need to seriously consider pressing ahead with the mission even if Sophie is compromised."

"What?" Brian squawked. "But that'd be suicide—" He broke off as Sophie stirred in the seat beside him. He continued more quietly. "Are you nuts? We can't ask that of a civilian."

"You tell me what I'm supposed to do, Brian. I've got a global terrorist about to strike multiple targets with nuclear weapons. Even if he doesn't create a radiation disaster, he's going to royally screw up the economy. How many people will die in the economic upheaval and general panic to follow?"

"But you're asking Sophie to—" He couldn't bring himself to say the word.

"Die?" Hollister finished grimly. "That's entirely possible. I need you to ask her the question. Explain the risks to her. Convince her to at least consider it."

"I need more. I want hard intelligence data on Sollem to show to her."

"She doesn't have the knowledge to make a useful risk assessment."

"That's the way it's going to be," Brian replied hotly. "If I'm going to ask this of her, she deserves the facts. All of them."

Hollister replied, "Stay chilly, bro. Keep your head in the game and your emotions out of it."

He was *way* past that point. But he dared not say so to his boss. Doing that would be a one-way ticket off this mission in about two seconds flat. He subsided into stony silence.

"Call me when you stop to rest."

Brian mumbled something and hung up the phone. He slammed his clenched fist down on the top of the steering wheel. It was bad enough that they'd made him talk Sophie into attempting this mission in the first place. But now they wanted him to talk her into dying?

He'd rather cut off his own arm. With no anesthesia and a dull pocketknife.

He drove on grimly, doing his damnedest not to take out his fury on the drivers around him. He didn't have the slightest idea how he was going to ask her to knowingly sacrifice her life. If she'd have been a hardened operative, it would have been difficult enough. But Sophie? She was an innocent. A sweet, warm, funny, vital woman. A civilian, for God's sake! *It wasn't fair.*

Lives were not chess pieces to be played with lightly and sacrificed casually for a greater good. This woman had a family and friends. An aging mother whom she looked after financially. She had dreams and ambitions. Hell, he had dreams and ambitions where Sophie was concerned.

The stripes on the road blurred and ran together as anguish ripped into him.

The two of them could make a run for it. With the fifteen thousand in cash to get them started, they could get a long way away from here. He could empty his bank account first thing in the morning and they could fly to Paraguay. Some of the best identity forgers in the world worked there. He and Sophie could get new names, new passports, new lives. And then they could disappear. Together.

He crept across Los Angeles in an agony of indecision. A sign announced that the LAX Airport exit was three miles ahead. Should he do it? Should he make the break? They were going to kill her.

Damn it all, he wanted Sophie for himself. For a long time. A little voice whispered in the back of his brain, "Forever."

Yeah. What the voice said. Forever.

Or, she could do the mission and be dead in a few weeks. The remainder of her life could potentially be measured in days. He swore violently under his breath.

But he didn't do forever. He'd spent years perfecting the art of living in the moment. He'd worked hard at teaching Sophie to do the same. He always let go of the past without regrets and never thought too far ahead. But if he talked Sophie into continuing the mission and she died…

No way could he walk away from that. He'd live with regrets over that for the rest of his life. Hell. More than regrets. An empty place in his heart. Guilt that would eat him alive from the inside out.

He didn't for a moment question the necessity of the mission going forward. Hollister would never put anyone at risk, not Sophie, not one of his guys, without a damn good reason for doing so.

Maybe there was another way. Maybe Sophie could stand off in the desert with the Medusas and point out Freddie if he showed himself. Except after the debacle of the shooter on the beach, Brian doubted Sollem would come out of his rat hole any time soon. The guy had to know the United States was planning a move on him if Sophie'd been recruited and was undergoing military training.

Sollem was brilliant. No way would the guy fail to put his informants on high alert for her throughout the Middle East. Inserting her anywhere in that part of the world was a recipe for her death. Certainty began to coalesce in Brian's gut. He couldn't do it. He couldn't send Sophie to die.

Hollister would be severely disappointed in him if he ran. And dammit, he respected his boss. Admired him. Hell, loved him like a brother. He'd happily die for any of the guys on the team. He'd be walking away from many good years with them. Or slinking away as the case might be. Fleeing from duty and honor and country. From everything he believed in and who he was.

Regret joined the other daggers stabbing his innards.

But this was Sophie he was talking about. Wasn't it his job to protect innocent American lives from all enemies, foreign and domestic? He couldn't throw her to the wolves. He just couldn't.

The exit for LAX was in two miles.

If he'd ever wondered what it felt like to be torn apart limb from limb, this was it.

He actually felt sick. Hot and on the verge of puking. *He was supposed to convince the woman he loved to die.*

So appalled was he by the idea of sending her to her doom, he barely registered shock over the realization that he was double-dog, big-time, head-over-heels in love with Sophie. He snorted. And Hollister'd told him to keep his emotions out of it. *Too late for that, boss man.*

Sophie stirred and half-turned to face him. He glanced over at her and she smiled up at him sleepily. His heart flip-flopped like a damned puppy in his chest.

"Hey, beautiful. Have a nice nap?"

"Mmm hmm. Where are we?"

"Los Angeles."

"Do you know where we're going yet?" Her voice was soft and fuzzy with sleep and made him shiver with delight. He couldn't get the idea of forever with her out of his head. To hear that voice for the next fifty or sixty years, to gaze into those big, sweet, melting chocolate eyes of hers any time he wanted to, and have her gaze back at him with love and trust.

Trust. Now there was a word.

Hollister trusted him.

So did Sophie.

And he had to betray one of them.

"Is something wrong?" she asked quickly. So perceptive, his Sophie. She had a sixth sense where his thoughts and feelings were concerned. Uncanny, really. Some sort of secret psychic link.

The LAX exit ramp loomed on the right.

Decision time.

Now or never.

Chapter 11

Vanessa looked up, alarmed, as Isabella held the headset of the satellite phone out to her. "Call's for you, boss."

Vanessa pulled on the headset. Was this the orders to start shooting that they'd been waiting for ever since they spotted what had, indeed, been verified as stolen tactical nuclear weapons? The printing on the boxes identified them as having come out of Pakistan. That country's nuclear weapons program was only a few years old, and they were already losing—or selling off—parts. Scary.

"Viper here. Go."

"Wittenauer, here. I've got orders for you."

"'Bout time," Vanessa muttered.

"Probably not the ones you're looking for, however," the general added. "I need you and Python to egress to the nearest extraction point at top speed. I'll have a fast chopper waiting for you."

"What's up?" she asked, shocked.

"I need the two of you stateside as soon as humanly possible. Jack and Anders will meet the two of you when you get to your destination. They're already en route to the rendezvous point."

"Why?" she asked.

"There's been an attempt on Sophie Giovanni's life. We think Sollem has figured out we're working with her."

Vanessa swore under her breath.

Wittenauer remarked dryly, "I echo your sentiments. I'm sending the four of you to collect Ms. Giovanni and insert her into Bhoukar. It's time to nail Sollem once and for all."

"But I'm the mission commander out here. I can't leave in the middle of the op—"

"Put one of the others in charge. I specifically need you and Python to do this."

"Why us?"

"No time for lengthy explanations. Just trust me. This is how it has to be. Jack and Anders will fill you in when you catch up with them."

"Where are they—"

Wittenauer cut her off. "No time to talk. You two need to get humping. You've got a hard hike to the extraction point. Your ride will be there in three hours. Don't keep him waiting." The line went dead. The general had hung up.

Vanessa stared at the phone. Three hours? It was at least a four-hour hike through deep sand.

"C'mon, Python. We get to see just how healed your heart is after Norway." Karen had nearly died of heart failure during a wild mission last winter. She'd been on convalescent leave for most of the summer and this was her first op back out in the field.

Karen looked up, startled. "What's up?"

"Grab some water and minimal gear. You and I are being

sent home to pick up our housewife commando. Mamba, you'll take command of the surveillance op here while we're gone."

Aleesha nodded briskly.

Karen piped up. "I thought Riley was bringing his girl to us."

Vanessa shrugged. "I don't know the details. But Wittenauer was adamant. You and me. Stateside. ASAP. A helicopter will be at Egress Point Alpha in three hours."

Karen stared. "*Three* hours?"

Vanessa grinned ruefully. "Apparently, the boss thinks we're superwomen or something."

All the women jumped into action, preparing small packs with water, a few basic survival supplies, a couple light weapons and ammo. And dust masks. It was windy tonight and a haze of grit swirled in the air. In under five minutes, Vanessa and Karen were ready to go.

"Ta-ta, ladies," Vanessa said breezily. "Have fun and don't do anything I wouldn't do. I'll get back here as soon as I can."

Aleesha squeezed her shoulder affectionately. "Don' worry, chile. I take good care o' your chickies for ya. Dey be jus' fine till mama hen git back."

Vanessa smiled at her number two then turned and followed Karen into the darkness.

Sophie started as Brian swerved off the highway suddenly, making the guy behind him honk his horn. What was going on? He was acting funny.

"You and me. We need to talk," Brian announced quietly.

"All you have to do is ask for your class ring back and I'll get the hint. You don't have to be mature and talk it out with me if you want to break up."

He laughed reluctantly. "Actually, I do need to talk this out with you. It involves you, too."

Concern tickled the edges of her consciousness. Something was wrong. The certainty of it rattled around deep inside her. She was silent while Brian navigated the crammed exit ramps and threaded his way past airport terminals. "Where are we headed? I gather we're flying out of here to someplace secure to finish my training?"

Brian spoke uncharacteristically tersely. "We're supposed to be driving to San Francisco. Major Hollister has arranged a flight out of there for us tomorrow morning."

"Where to?"

"Canada."

She blinked in surprise. She'd expected him to name some super-secret military installation in the Gobi Desert or the like.

He replied to her unspoken question, "We don't think Freddie will think to look for you in the Great White North."

"Then what?" she asked.

He shrugged. "That's what we need to talk about. First order of business is to get somewhere private and safe, though."

Surely, the two of them couldn't go the airport looming in front of them. Sollem might have informants there, hanging out and watching for Sophie to flee. It was what she'd do in the same situation. The thought surprised her. Six weeks ago, such a concept would never have remotely crossed her mind. But Brian had drilled her for countless hours in military strategy and tactics, creative problem solving and thinking like the enemy. Apparently, some of his teaching had stuck.

She pulled down the car's visor and used the makeup mirror to watch behind them, looking for tails. They headed onto surface streets, which weren't much less congested than the highway. She didn't spot anyone behind them. Whether that meant no one was there or she was just incompetent, she didn't know.

Eventually, Brian made a sound of satisfaction and swerved into a parking space. Must have spotted what he was looking for. He angled the SUV expertly into the spot. Although, compliments of Brian, she was now an excellent, if aggressive, parallel parker, too. She'd enjoyed the offensive-driving classes.

"C'mon," he said.

Sophie looked outside cautiously, up and down the sidewalk for possible threats. She even used the passenger-side rearview mirror to clear the area before she hopped out.

Brian murmured, "Good girl."

She glanced wryly over the hood at him. "Hey. I paid attention in class."

He shrugged and stepped close to her, using his body to block view of her from the street. He muttered, "Not everybody translates classroom instruction into practical usage well."

She glanced up at him. "That's what the next phase of my training is about, isn't it? Field practice."

He didn't reply. A black look flickered across his face. What the heck? Her subliminal concern blossomed into conscious alarm. Something was seriously wrong. The last time Brian had gotten this worked up and refused to talk about it was the day they'd met. That day he held out for hours before coming out and asking her if she'd consider going on a mission to help the United States find Freddie Sollem. They'd gotten through that conversation just fine. There was no need for him to get this tense about talking to her about something again. Unless it was worse….

What could be worse than asking her to risk her life to help bring down a terrorist? Frankly, she wasn't sure she wanted to know the answer to that one. Longing for home slammed into her. She wanted to curl up in an armchair with a good book and watch TV for a couple weeks non-stop.

But that would mean leaving Brian. And she wasn't willing to do that just to feel safe for a little while.

He held the door for her to an inconspicuous restaurant. A Japanese place. They stepped inside and an odor of fish assailed her. At least it smelled like fresh fish. More subtle odors manifested themselves. Hot grease. Teriyaki sauce. A strong green odor of seaweed. Brian spoke in quick, fluent Japanese to a hostess wearing a dark blue kimono and white socks under straw flip-flops. The woman nodded and replied back in a whispery, little-girl voice that they had what he requested and would be honored to allow him its use. She left to prepare it.

Sophie murmured, "Okay, show-off. What did you say to her?"

"I requested a private dining room and the chef's specialities. I hope you like weird seafood."

In a few moments, the hostess was back and led them to a small room bounded by floor-to-ceiling shoji panels in black lacquer and white rice paper. Brian noted that the room next to theirs was occupied by a group of Asian businessmen, already well into their sake. The kitchen was on the other side. Perfect. He and Sophie could talk freely and not worry about eavesdroppers.

He kicked off his shoes at the door and Sophie followed suit. They padded into the space in their socks and sat down at a low, black lacquer table. The hostess put a large wooden bowl on the table and Brian held his hands over it. The woman washed his hands and patted them dry, then did the same for Sophie. The hostess murmured that she would be back with food in a few minutes.

Sophie flashed a dimple at him from across the table. "I see a definite trend to our dates. I gather you're a fan of the Japanese culture?"

He shrugged. "I'm a fan of civilized behavior and simple, elegant things."

"Somehow I'm guessing this stop wasn't on Major Hollister's itinerary for us. Care to explain why we're here?"

He sighed. "We've got a problem."

When he didn't continue, she said, "Let me guess. That shooter on the beach."

He nodded. "Do you know of anyone who has a big enough grudge against you to try to intimidate or kill you?"

She was silent for a time, thinking. Another skill she'd learned from Brian. The hostess brought a platter of teriyaki skewers and a pot of green tea. He waved off the sake. When the woman had left, Sophie announced, "I don't have any enemies who would like to kill me. In fact, I don't really have any enemies at all. Certainly none who want to see me dead."

Brian nodded. "That's what I expected. But I had to ask. The shooter's identity, or at least his employer, seem pretty obvious."

"Freddie," she sighed.

"The very same."

She leaned forward. "Okay, Brian, you've got your private, safe place to talk. So talk."

"What would you like for supper? The nice lady in the kimono will keep bringing out plates of stuff to graze on until we tell her to stop. It's how dinner business meetings are usually conducted in Japan. Our only out is to order full-blown entrees."

"Will she bring out tempura at some point?" Sophie asked.

"Yes."

"Then I'm okay. I love that stuff."

Brian smiled. "Note to self—the lady even likes her Asian food fried."

"I like pretty much anything covered in chocolate, too."

"Ever tried a chocolate-covered grasshopper?"

"No, and I don't need to try one to prove how macho I am, either," she replied quickly.

Brian grinned. "I dunno. They have a nice, fresh, green taste. Not bad with a semisweet dark chocolate."

She reached across the table and pressed her fingers to his lips. "Stop speaking such blasphemy before the chocolate gods strike you dead."

"Chocolate gods?"

"Yes. They're female and hormonal. Don't mess with them," Sophie warned.

"Ahh, Sophie, you make my soul smile."

She stared, startled. Brian didn't say things like that. Ever. What was so different about tonight? Her running alarm unfolded into full-blown dread. He had bad news for her and was buttering her up—and buttering her up huge—before he sprang it on her. Was the mission canceled? Had the past weeks all been for naught?

Except even if the mission was nixed now, this time had not been wasted. With Brian's help, she'd found an inner strength she never knew she had. And of course, she'd found Brian. The mere thought of them together sent warm fuzzies curling through her. She hadn't the slightest idea what tomorrow would bring for the two of them, but she was grateful for every moment she got to spend with him, in his arms or otherwise. He was an amazing man. And he made her feel beautiful. Nope. Definitely not for naught.

"Have you ever thought about going to Japan?" Brian asked, interrupting her train of thought.

"I've never thought about it. But I'd like to travel someday."

"Have you ever been out of this country?" he asked.

The hostess brought in a plate of calamari and pickled vegetables. Neither floated Sophie's boat and she pushed the plate toward Brian.

"If you could go anywhere just for fun, where would you go?" he asked.

What was he avoiding talking with her about? "I don't know. I'd like to see New Zealand. And the Great Wall of China. And the Swiss Alps."

"Ah, mountainous places. The skier in you is showing. Tell me about your ski-racing career."

Okay, fine. She'd play along with this small-talk game for now. He'd already confessed that he needed to talk to her about something serious. He could choose the time for his talk.

But with every casual topic he brought up, the more her alarm grew. What could be so scary to him that he was avoiding it this hard?

Vanessa and Karen finally dropped out of a run as the egress point drew near. It was just over the next ridge in a small valley. Panting, Vanessa flashed a hand signal to Karen to approach cautiously and take a look around for hostiles. Karen nodded, her chest rising and falling about as hard as Vanessa's. The Marine had set a blistering pace, and held it, almost as if she were out to prove that she was back in top form.

On their bellies, they slithered to the top of the ridge and peered over the rim. A black, shark-like shape squatted in the valley. Silent. Waiting. The helicopter.

Karen murmured, "Wanna scare the pilots?"

Vanessa grinned over at her teammate. "You want the captain or the co-pilot?"

"You better take the aircraft commander. You've got more rank to stand up to a butt-chewing than I do."

Vanessa nodded, her grin widening. They traded quick hand signals and moved off quickly. Karen, who'd worked in helicopter maintenance before she became a Special Forces officer was familiar with a narrow, radar-blind area to the rear of the birds and had shared that little tidbit with her team-mates.

Squatting beside the bird's belly, Vanessa and Karen made eye contact underneath the 'copter. Then, on a finger count, they sprang up as one and banged on the pilot's windows with their fists. The two men inside jumped with gratifying violence, and it didn't take a rocket scientist to guess what their moving mouths were saying.

The pilot's door opened. "Very funny. Get in. We're in a hurry."

As the rotors started to turn overhead, Vanessa ran around to the other side and climbed in. Karen slid the heavy rear door shut behind them. The bird leaped off the ground before she'd even buckled her seat belt. Vanessa pulled on a headset while Karen dug around in her pack.

"Ah hah! The good doctor didn't fail you," Karen announced. She held out a pair of little white pills to Vanessa.

She took them gratefully and swallowed them dry. She was tremendously prone to airsickness, but Aleesha—a physician—had found these pills for her. They would shut down the digestive track of an elephant.

The Medusas were in Bhoukar with the permission of the emir of that country, so the helicopter was able to pop up to altitude and fly swift and straight to the south—out to sea, Vanessa noticed out the small window. It was less than an hour until they swooped in for a white-knuckle landing on an aircraft carrier. The pilots getting a little revenge for her and Karen's surprise arrival at the egress point, no doubt.

The door slid open and a deck officer shouted a greeting to them. He motioned them to follow. Vanessa grabbed her pack and climbed out into the noisy chaos of the flight deck. Guiding each of them by the upper arm, the officer hustled them across the deck to a pair of waiting F-18's. Vanessa's eyes opened wide in surprise. Wow. Wittenauer really was in a hurry. She climbed the ladder into the back seat of one jet while Karen climbed into the other.

A crew chief followed her up the ladder, helping her don a helmet and strapping her seat and shoulder belts for her.

"Welcome aboard, Major," a voice said in her ear.

She replied into the microphone inside her mouthpiece, "Thanks."

"Ever been in an F-18?"

"No. I got some training in an F-15, but that's as close as I got."

The navy pilot scoffed. "Old-fashioned Air Force jet." He broke off to answer some sort of takeoff clearance over the radios. Then to her again, he said, "Here we go. Hang on to your hat."

They taxied briefly and came to a stop. Then the carrier's mighty, steam-driven catapult flung them off the ship and into flight so fast she didn't have time to get airsick. The jet climbed steeply, roaring up into the sunset sky. In a few seconds, lights pulled up beside them. Vanessa looked out at another F-18 sliding into position just off their wing. Karen waved to her from the back seat of the other jet and flashed her a thumbs up. Vanessa returned the gesture.

"Where are we headed, Lieutenant?" Vanessa asked.

"My orders are to make all possible haste for Spain. We've got a couple air refueling points set up along the way. Speaking of which, we're about to level off. If you watch the mach indicator by your right knee, you can see when we go supersonic."

Supersonic didn't quite cover it. The jet passed by Mach 2 before the needle stopped climbing.

"Sit back and enjoy the ride, ma'am. We'll have you there in no time."

"How many miles per hour are we going right now?" she asked.

"We're balls to the wall. Fifteen-hundred miles per hour over the ground."

Holy mackerel. What was so bloody urgent about picking up Sophie Giovanni? Vanessa purely hated having to wait for information like this. Despite Aleesha's magic pills, her stomach gave a warning gurgle. The answer to her question had better be good.

Sophie pushed away the remains of the scrumptious tempura and propped her elbows on the low table. If Brian stayed true to form, he'd drop his bomb on her after supper. Sure enough, he started to squirm under her steady gaze.

"All right, Brian. Out with it."

"So here's the thing. Over the course of working with you these past few weeks, I've developed a more than academic interest in you."

She laughed aloud. "More than academic? Gee whiz, that's some compliment, big guy. I feel more than academic toward you, too."

He rolled his eyes, a suspicious redness creeping across his face. "You know what I mean."

She reached across the table and patted his hand. "Time to let me teach you a thing or two. When you're going to tell a girl you like her, you definitely want to take her someplace romantic and private. You got that part just right. And you ply her with fine food and drink. You get an A on that score, too. But then you have to follow up with a romantic declaration of your feelings."

Brian half-scowled through the reluctant grin tugging at his mouth.

"'Feeling more than academic' doesn't cut it. You have to

say something classy like, 'Hey baby. I wanna jump your bones.'"

A chuckle escaped him.

"Or, you could take the sappy route and say something like, 'I can't live without you. I want to carry you off on my white horse to my enchanted castle and wait on you hand and foot for the rest of your life. Oh, and you can have all my credit cards.'"

"All my credit cards?" he exclaimed. "Never!"

She tsked reprovingly. "If you're not prepared to fork over cash to the girl, you can pretty much forget true love and happily-ever-after."

He shook his head. "I've got to go overseas and get me some communist girl with no capitalist ambitions whatsoever."

"Honey, all girls are capitalists. Love of shopping is genetic. It's attached to the Y chromosome."

They grinned at each other for a moment, and then the smile faded from his eyes. He said quietly, "A romantic declaration, huh? How's this? I have come to realize that I have deep feelings for you and I want to get to know you much better."

Waves of hot and cold rushed over her, setting her atingle from head to foot. "Well, okay then," she stammered, "That's not bad as declarations go."

"I may be an ignorant slob, but I think this is the part where the girl makes a romantic declaration back to the guy."

Oh, my. She picked up the dessert menu and fanned herself with it. "No, no. I'm supposed to play coy first. So what brings on this sudden declaration?"

Every vestige of playfulness abruptly evaporated, leaving Brian as grim and serious as she'd ever seen him. "And that brings us to the heart of the matter," he muttered.

Huh? She frowned, alarm screaming through her like fire engines with sirens blaring.

"Major Hollister has ordered me to ask you a question. This isn't my idea and I don't like it one bit. But, here goes. Will you consider continuing with the mission, even in light of this afternoon's incident?"

Continuing…after the shooting…but Sollem knew she was working for her government…he'd kill her on sight…and Hollister still wanted her to approach Sollem and stick a marker on his clothes…but…

But…

Oh my God. Hollister was asking her to die.

Chapter 12

"Phone for you, Major Hollister."

He was way too damned busy for interruptions, but something in the way Scottie announced the call made him look up. "Who is it?"

"National Security Agency."

He frowned. What did they want with him? He picked up the receiver. "Major Hollister, here. What can I do for you?"

"We have a status change on the vehicle you asked us to track this afternoon."

Brian and Sophie. A GPS tracking device was installed inside their vehicle's rear bumper, and their progress north toward San Francisco was being tracked. It was a routine procedure. "What's the status change?"

"Since our last satellite pass eighty-two minutes ago, the vehicle has not moved. It is stationary."

"Are they caught in a traffic jam?"

"No sir. The last telemetry we have shows the vehicle exiting the Highway 405 onto Highway 105 westbound at 5:22 p.m."

"And where does Highway 105 go?"

"Most notably, LAX Airport, sir. Although it also leads toward El Segundo and Playa del Ray."

LAX? Hollister swore under his breath. He asked tersely, "Did the vehicle enter the airport?"

"No sir. It made its way north, toward the Loyola Marymount campus. It parked on a surface street at 5:58 p.m. and remains parked in that location."

"Are the occupants inside the vehicle?"

"Infrared imagery indicates they are not."

"What's the address?" Hollister asked. He copied down the street address the NSA agent gave him. "Are there any businesses nearby?"

"A number of them. It's a commercial area with plentiful shops and restaurants."

"Thanks. Call me if the vehicle moves."

"Will do, sir."

Hollister hung up the phone and shouted to the outer office, "Scottie, get me the L.A. FBI field office!"

"Already dialing, sir."

Sophie stared at Brian in shock. Dismay. Dawning horror. Did he want her to continue with the mission? To die? How Brian got around the table and swept her into his arms, she wasn't sure. But she burrowed into his comforting strength like a terrified child. This was a real nightmare though, not something that could be comforted away by a hug and a glass of water.

"What do you think I should do, Brian?"

He drew back a little to gaze down at her. His voice rough, he asked, "Do you understand what Hollister's asking of you?"

"You did your job far too well. I understand exactly. He's asking me to knowingly go on a suicide mission in the name of killing Freddie."

Brian's arms tightened around her. "We can leave," he murmured. "Take off. I have the money Stoner gave me and I have a fair bit put back in the bank. We'll go to Paraguay. Get new identities. And then we'll disappear. Go someplace you've always wanted to see and start a new life."

Abject relief flooded her. Brian had already taken care of the situation. Of her. She could count on him to keep her safe from all harm. Wonderful, thoughtful Brian.

"How about the South Pacific? There are gorgeous little islands all over down there with pristine beaches and plenty of privacy," he murmured.

What in the world could induce Hollister to ask this of her? The guy might not be the friendliest soul she'd ever run across, but he was an honorable man. Of that she had no doubt. What did he know that she didn't? Freddie must have done something new and outrageous to drive Hollister to such a decision.

Brian continued, "Maybe we could start up a bed-and-breakfast. Something small. Quiet. Just enough to keep us from getting bored. Do you like to cook? I've always enjoyed fixing stuff up. And I could give scuba lessons and run fishing trips for our guests."

And what about Brian's career? He was proposing to abandon it. To become a fugitive for her. To turn his back on everything he believed in, on everything he was. Being a Special Forces soldier was much more than a job to him. It was his passion. His calling. Such an offer from him was touching. Humbling. But to see him give up everything he'd worked for, to walk away from his job, his friends, his most fundamental values…was it really worth all that to keep her from doing Hollister's mission?

"And kids. We can raise a family. How many do you want? Please say you want a houseful. Let's get started on them right away."

Kids? For a second, a vision of dark-haired children with their daddy's blue-on-blue eyes derailed her thoughts. Ahh, that future was tempting. But could she do it? Could she let Brian do it?

"If we leave first thing in the morning, we'll have a solid head start before anyone comes looking for us. And Paraguay's a bitch to track anyone through. We'll be out of there before the Americans even find a trail to follow."

She half-listened in disbelief. She couldn't let him do it. She cared for him too much—heck, loved him too much—to let him do this to himself. There had to be another way.

Whoa. Rewind. She *loved* him?

The thought was a perfect rosebud unfurling in spring. A sweet-tasting snowflake landing on the tip of her tongue. It made her want to sigh with pleasure. Sing with joy. Curl up on a sofa with her best friend and tell her all about the amazing man who'd burst into her life and swept her off her feet. Her heart expanded until it felt like it might float right out of her chest. She was in love.

"Brian?" she interrupted as he launched into a discussion of where exactly would be out of the way enough for their privacy, but not so isolated as to make them feel like prisoners.

He broke off. "What?"

"Stop talking."

Brian stared down at her. Emotions danced through his beautiful eyes too fast for her to identify. And then his mouth was on hers, his lips moving across hers, his arms drawing her up tight against him. His hand plunged into her hair, cupping the back of her head, and he angled his head just right for her to inhale him while he did the same to her. He bore her down to the floor, cushioning her in his arms, kissing her face, her neck, her shoulder. She arched up toward him, aching for the feel of his hard body against hers, his masculine heat covering her.

"Does the door lock?" Sophie murmured.

"Unfortunately, no." Brian lifted his mouth away from her and stretched out beside her, his head propped up on an elbow as he smiled down at her. "All my credit cards, huh?"

She laughed up at him. "Yup. You have to choose. Bachelorhood or bankruptcy."

"Hmm. Tough choice."

She knocked his elbow out from under his head, and he collapsed on top of her. She grabbed his hair and tugged his head the rest of the way down to her and kissed him with all the boundless joy bursting inside her.

"No fair," he complained against her mouth. "You're trying to distract me from thinking logically about my choice."

Her lips curved against his. "I'll let you know if I ever meet a woman who fights fair. You men are completely outgunned in that department."

He gazed down at her. The blue fire blazing in his eyes melted her from the inside out. "Well, then, I guess there's only one thing to do," he murmured, his voice sliding over her like black velvet. "I surrender."

Delight built low in her belly, curling upward and outward until she was so filled with it, she had no voice left to give it wings. She reached up with both hands, placing her palms on either side of his face. Completely robbed of words, she settled for letting her eyes do the talking, letting every ounce of her love for him shine forth.

"Ahh, sweet Sophie," he sighed. "That hostess had better be on the ball and take notice of our shadows on the walls before she bursts in here, otherwise, she's in for a shock."

A new quality entered their lovemaking tonight, a new tenderness, a sweetness that made it so poignant Sophie cried. Brian kissed away her tears and then loved away all thought at all.

But when it was all said and done and she rested boneless against his chest, listening to the steady thump of his heart, something niggled at the back of her mind. The voice of doubt was so small she barely heard it, but she intuitively felt its presence. Over and over during the past weeks, Brian had stressed the importance of listening to her instincts. In spite of an overwhelming urge to close her eyes and her heart against it, she allowed the niggle to drift forward into conscious thought.

She couldn't do it. She couldn't let Brian throw himself on his sword for her. He might be willing, even eager, to do it now, but what about later? One day, down the road, when the crisis of this moment had faded into the past, he would look back and question his decision. He would repent of abandoning his beliefs and his buddies, and would keenly feel the loss of honor. And in his regret, he would resent her.

She'd die if he came to hate her. If he looked at her with remorse and blame. Or worse, if he soldiered on with her, unhappy but too honorable to leave. There had to be another way to resolve this dilemma. She didn't know what it was, but between them, she and Brian would find it. They *had* to find it. Their future happiness depended on it. She sat up reluctantly. One of these days they'd have to try making love in a bed. Maybe with a whole night stretching before them in which to sleep in each other's arms. But in the meantime, they were in a restaurant, and the hostess could walk in any second.

She wrestled back into her clothes, buttoning her shirt hastily. Brian was flushed and his hair suspiciously tussled when the hostess came in—very carefully—to ask if they'd like dessert. Brian said something in Japanese that made the woman fling a hand in front of her mouth and twitter with laughter. The woman bowed herself out of the room, blushing furiously.

"What did you say to that poor woman?" Sophie demanded.

"I told her I'd already had dessert. Peaches and cream."

Sophie rolled her eyes. "As much as I hate to do this, we need to talk."

"About?"

"About what comes next."

"What is there to talk about? We're in agreement. We'll go away together in the morning and start over."

She sighed. "It's not that simple. We need to consider other alternatives."

His brows slammed together. "Why? We've got a perfectly workable solution."

"For the short term, maybe. But I'm worried about the long term."

"How so?"

She really didn't want to debate the possibilities of the future with him. If he even wanted a future with her. She trusted her gut, and it said Brian would come to hate her if she let him throw away everything for her now.

Ignoring his question, she said, "Freddie has obviously done something to up the stakes. Enough that Major Hollister thinks my death is a worthy trade to stop Freddie's latest plan. Right?"

Brian frowned. "That makes sense, yes."

She continued, "I'm supposed to mark Freddie so the Medusas can kill him. Is there another way I can do that? Can I stand off with high-powered binoculars and point him out to the Medusa's sniper?"

"You couldn't pick him out of a stack of photos. What makes you think you'd recognize him at long distance?

Besides, he won't show himself now that he knows you're working with us."

"Good point."

"What if I go to the Sollem compound when Freddie's not there? I can just visit Grandma Sollem and wheedle a picture of Freddie out of her."

"Pictures of him likely don't exist. He's not dumb enough to leave any photo sitting around, not even with his grandmother."

Sophie frowned. "There's got to be another way."

"Why are you suddenly so determined to go through with this? Are you already having second thoughts about us?" Brian demanded.

"Not at all. That's exactly the point. I want a shot at a future with you. But I don't want it under a cloud. I want us to be together free and clear with no restrictions."

"You can't always have your cake and eat it, too."

"No, but we can try. Help me out, here, Brian. You're the experienced field operative. How can I get close to Freddie and still get away from him alive?"

"Don't you think I've racked my brains over this? There isn't a way. As soon as he sees you, he'll kill you. It's that simple."

Sophie closed her eyes for a moment. Gathered her strength. And then said, "Then I guess I'm just going to have to die."

He huffed in frustration. "What do I have to do to talk you out of this?"

"There's nothing you can do. Don't you see? I'm doing this for you."

"Right. You're going to throw yourself in front of a bullet to prove how much you care for me. Explain how that makes any sense at all," he snapped.

Sophie sighed. "Let's just go to Canada. Continue with

whatever training I have left. If we try hard enough, we can cook up some way for me to do the mission and live."

"And if we can't?"

She shrugged. "Let's cross that bridge when we come to it. How many times have you told me before? Stay in the moment. Let's take this thing one step at a time."

In San Diego, Hollister's phone rang. An unfamiliar male voice said, "Agent Maloney here, sir. FBI, Los Angeles."

Hollister sat up straight in his chair. "What have you got?"

"I acquired your subjects in a sushi house. They're in a private dining room in the back of the joint. They're arguing."

Hollister snorted. "I bet. Do you have a parabolic microphone? What are they arguing about?"

The field agent laughed. "No parabolic. I do, however, have a highly effective, one each, high-tech water glass applied to the wall."

Hollister grinned.

Agent Maloney continued. "The man wants to leave and the woman is insisting on going through with the mission."

Hollister lurched in surprise. "The woman's insisting?"

"Correct."

"Have they discussed their specific plans?"

"If the woman gets her way—and it sounds like she will— she wants to go to Canada and continue her training. The male subject is not happy about it, however."

"Son of a gun."

"What are your instructions for me, sir?"

Hollister thought fast. "Don't reveal yourself to them. Tail them for now. At all costs, don't let them get on an airplane at LAX. They're scheduled to drive to San Francisco, check into a hotel for a few hours' rest, then board a flight for Calgary in the morning. As long as they do that, let them continue. Any deviation, however, and I need you to take them into custody. The woman must not be harmed. She's an emphatically non-expendable asset."

"Understood."

"Pull in whatever resources you need. Sky's the limit. Have anyone with any questions contact me directly. And my office is paying the tab."

The FBI agent chuckled quietly. "I have a blank check out of your checkbook, eh? This could be fun."

"Don't mess this one up, Maloney. It's a matter of national security."

Chapter 13

Brian surveyed the breathtaking view from the top of the mountain, a study in black and white, snow and stone.

"I can't do this," Sophie quavered.

Outstanding. That was exactly the point. If she couldn't conquer her fear in a situation where no one was trying to kill her, she certainly had no business proceeding with the Sollem mission.

He replied briskly, "Fear is no more than a primitive part of your brain triggering chemical and physiological reactions in response to a perceived threat. So, there are two ways to attack fear. One is to control your thoughts and perceptions. To talk yourself out of being afraid of whatever initial impulse leads you to fear. The other way to combat fear is to learn to control your bodily reactions. Fear causes an adrenaline dump that, in turn, causes the heart and breathing to accelerate, preparatory to fleeing or fighting.

You can calm both reactions by using self-relaxation techniques."

Sophie stared uncomprehendingly at him, as if one more glance down the mountain was going to send her screaming into his arms. He'd intentionally picked the steepest, iciest, scariest downhill run this part of Canada had to offer for today's exercise. If he seriously wanted to help her overcome her fear, he'd have started her on a bunny hill and worked her up gradually to a monster like this mountain, desensitizing her along the way. But that wasn't the point. The idea was to scare her away from the mission entirely.

"Do I have to learn to overcome fear this way? Couldn't you make me hold a rattlesnake or something?"

He shrugged. "This is your most powerful phobia. If you can overcome this fear, you can overcome any fear." A pang hit him at how frightened she was. This was a mean stunt. Meaner given how truly afraid he knew she was. It was a downright cruel thing to do to someone he loved. But it was the only way to save her from herself, dammit! He hardened his resolve for the hundredth time. He had to go through with this. He hated to hurt Sophie, but what other choice had she left him?

"Are you ready to go?" he asked.

"No!"

"We can't stand up here all day. Time's a wasting."

She took a deep breath. Squeezed her eyes closed. "You're sure my knee will hold up to this?"

"Your knee is irrelevant. It's encased in titanium. The doctor said the brace would hold up to anything you could throw at it."

"You have a lot of confidence in my brace."

"It's not some off-the-shelf number you'd throw on a casual athlete. That brace was designed to withstand the rigors of life as a Navy SEAL. It's a high-tech marvel."

"You're not going to let me off the hook, are you?"

"Nope. You're going down that hill or you're going home."

She sighed and mumbled more to herself than him, "I've learned to shoot a gun. I can drive a car a hundred miles per hour. I know how to rappel down the side of a building. I'm in the best shape of my life. I can ski down some damned hill."

If he weren't praying so desperately for her to chicken out, he'd be amused at her pep talk. He turned the screw a little more. "The ski-patrol guys said this run is wicked icy in the middle. Watch the big turns when you really build up speed."

She stared doubtfully down what looked like a cliff.

He continued implacably. "They said top speed on this course can reach ninety miles per hour."

She murmured absently, "Velocity is related to body weight. Women lose about ten miles per hour on men because they weigh less and lack the strength to let the skis run flat out."

"Eighty miles per hour is still booking," he commented.

"Yeah, it is," she mumbled, frozen as still as an ice statue.

"Look. We don't have to do this. We can jump back in a gondola and get out of here."

"No," she said slowly. "I want to do this. I've carried this fear around inside me for too long. It's time to kill the beast once and for all."

Damn, damn, damn! He asked casually, "How long has it been since you skied? Fifteen years? Beware of your brain sending remembered commands your body can't deliver on. You haven't necessarily developed any skiing muscles in the course of all the stuff you've been doing the past couple of months."

"Good point."

"I'll follow you. You set the pace."

She nodded. She hadn't bothered to ask if he was a competent skier. He probably ought to be complimented by her assumption that he was professional caliber at this sport. Truth be told, this mountain was intimidating even to him.

He planted a pole in the snow and leaned against it, ostensibly settling in to wait for a while.

Sophie closed her eyes and began swaying back and forth gently, leaning left and right in a rhythm only she could feel. After a solid minute of this strange behavior, she opened her eyes.

"You okay?" Brian asked, concerned. Had he pushed her over the edge up here?

"Yeah. I was chair-skiing the course."

"Chair-skiing?"

"Yes. I was visualizing the course and planning my track, anticipating tricky spots, and skiing down the mountain in my head."

"How do you know this course?"

"I looked at the map in the gondola on the ride up the mountain."

He frowned. He recalled her spending a couple moments looking at the resort map…and she'd memorized the entire course in that short a time?

She nodded resolutely. "Okay. I'm ready."

No! She couldn't go down that mountain! But how could he stop her? If she found the strength to do this, how was he supposed to stop her from going ahead with the Sollem mission? "Don't do it," he blurted.

"I beg your pardon?" She looked up at him sharply.

"If you conquer this, what's to stop you from going to Bhoukar?"

Enlightenment dawned in her dark gaze. "Ahh. That's why you've been so grouchy today."

"I'm not grouchy."

She smiled widely at him. "Sure you are."

"I am not."

She sidestepped until their arms touched through layers of nylon. "Brian, I'm not going anywhere on you. I'm right here."

He burst out angrily, "For how long? Another week? Two? And then you'll head into Sollem's compound and it'll all be over."

Her eyes clouded over. "Thank you for your anger," she said quietly.

"What?"

"It's your way of showing how much you care."

His fury evaporated in an instant. She was right. It was actually fear he felt. Here he was lecturing her, all superior, about controlling fear, when his was galloping away with him, wildly out of control.

"Don't do this, Sophie. You don't have to prove to me how brave you are."

She smiled gently at him. "I'm not doing this for you. This one's for me."

That's what he was afraid of. The decision was out of his hands, and he didn't deal well with not being in control.

"C'mon," she said. "I won't take a racing track. I'll cut back and forth across the mountain face and keep the speed down."

He closed his eyes. He'd lost. She was going to take on the mountain, and then she was going to take on Freddie Sollem. And she hadn't the slightest idea how completely unprepared she was for that challenge. If this mountain was an anthill, Freddie Sollem was Mount Everest.

But he knew what she was up against. All too well.

If only he had more time to teach her. A few more weeks. Hell, a few more years. There was so much information she needed…and they were out of time. Panic tightened in a band of steel across his chest.

Okay, buddy. Apply your own lecture to yourself. He counted his breaths, forcibly slowing down the count while he released the tension in all his major muscles. And all he accomplished was making himself lightheaded and faintly sick to his stomach—and still scared spitless.

And then Sophie plunged off the precipice. One second she was standing beside him, and the next she was a dark streak swooping across the face of the mountain. Swearing, he pushed off and went after her.

The trip down the mountain was nothing short of a nightmare. The downhill run was absurd. No human being was meant to fly down this atrocity. It fell away at a crazy angle, cut back on itself at the most awkward possible moments, and it went on for an eternity. At one point, he was sideways to the hill, which was so steep, he could reach out and touch the slope by his ear. And he started to slide downward, his skis skidding sideways across the ice. He gathered speed, going faster and faster, and there wasn't a damned thing he could do about it. Sophie, experienced skier that she was, had shot across the patch of ice and executed a neat switchback turn in the soft snow to the side of the run. She actually laughed at him as he slid past her helplessly.

But eventually, the torture came to an end. Somewhere in the last half of the course, Sophie began to smile, and by the time they reached the bottom, her exultant laughter was drifting back to him. She even assumed a credible racer's tuck and picked up speed at the end, flying toward the finish area. He followed more leisurely, allowing her the moment before he arrived and rained on her parade.

He skied up to her and she lifted her goggles, revealing a radiant expression. Pride in her accomplishment surged through him. No matter what the consequences, she'd done something very few people ever even tried. She'd faced her fear and won.

"Wanna go again?" she panted.

"Hell no!" he replied fervently.

"Chicken," she teased.

"I like to think of it as enlightened self-preservation."

"Right. You're chicken."

"Damn straight." She laughed up at him, and he couldn't help but smile. "How about we try some other trail not guaranteed to break my neck?"

"Let's go."

He followed her eager form toward the line of skiers waiting to board the gondolas. Stay in the moment. Cram as many memories into today as possible. For tomorrow would come soon enough, and with it a pale rider called Death.

"What do you mean, you missed?"

The man cringed, his skin crawling with terror. He'd have preferred the Leader to scream and yell. But this sibilant hiss was almost more than he could stand.

"You failed me."

"I will not give up, my Leader. I will continue without resting or stopping until I succeed."

"You won't get another shot at her. The U.S. government will wrap her in so much security you'll never even get near her or her family."

"I have contacts. People who owe me favors. I can find her."

"Shut up, you fool."

The man's jaw snapped shut.

"Where are you now?"

Sensing the ship sinking around him, he looked out of the phone booth at the hazy Los Angeles skyline and bailed out on the spot. "I'm back in Utah, my Leader. I thought to return to her home and pick up some sort of lead as to where she is now."

"Stay put. I'll send someone to help you. Time is of the essence."

"As you wish."

No way was he sticking his neck into the noose and kicking the chair out from under his own feet. He would gladly martyr himself for God, but letting the Leader kill him as a failure would condemn him to the vaguest margins of Paradise. No thank you. He knew enough to organize his own attack on the infidel horde. He didn't need the Leader and he was not yet ready to die. Not until he could go out in a blaze of glory.

He hung up the phone and stepped out of the phone booth. He dropped the cell phone into a trash bin and walked away quickly.

Sophie had to give Major Hollister credit. He hadn't skimped on getting a nice room for them. This suite, a condo really, was nearly as large as the beach house back in San Diego. It could easily sleep another half-dozen people, and the view of the mountains was spectacular.

She lounged in the hot tub on their private balcony, letting the steaming water soothe away the day's fatigue. Brian was right about one thing. She'd found muscles today that she hadn't used in fifteen years. But it felt good. Really good.

She'd done it. She'd taken on the biggest, baddest mountain Brian could find for her, and she'd beaten it. Finding her love of skiing again was like discovering a long lost best friend. Would the gifts he gave her never end?

It started to snow, a few gentle, lazy flakes floating down on them as they relaxed in the tub. "Could this be any more perfect?" she murmured.

Brian smiled over at her, but the shadow that had been lurking behind his eyes all day was still there. He was freaked out that now she'd conquered this fear, she'd feel compelled to barge into Sollem's house come heck or high water. She was no dummy, though. Brian had trained her too well for that. She couldn't just walk up and knock on Freddie's front door.

They had yet to find a way to get her in and out without Freddie discovering her, but she had faith they'd figure it out. Brian said over and over that necessity was truly the mother of invention. When faced with a do-or-die situation, they would come up with something. Supposedly these Medusas she was going to join up with were a bunch of smart cookies. Maybe they could come up with something.

She started when a noise sounded behind them. A knock on the door. They hadn't ordered room service. In fact, she'd hung out the Do Not Disturb sign herself.

Brian leaped out of the tub as fast as a snake and was over by the door, a pistol in hand before she could hardly blink. She jumped out of the tub as well, shrugging into a robe and sliding into the shadows outside as Brian called out casually, "Who's there?"

"Rip, it's Scat. I come bearing beer."

Brian stepped in front of the door to peer through the peephole. He visibly relaxed and unlocked the door. Sophie started as not one, but four, figures slipped quickly into the darkened room.

Until Brian called the all clear, she was staying put out here, hidden and only a few feet from a railing she could jump over in a pinch. They were on the third floor, but at least ten feet of drifted snow below would act as plenty of cushion for the fall. And Brian had taught her how to do parachute-landing falls.

"Where is she?"

Sophie started. The voice was female.

Brian called out low, "Sophie, you can come out."

She stepped forward into the room, her light Glock pistol still in hand. All four of their visitors immediately made a point of displaying their hands, well away from their bodies and empty.

"Stand down, honey. These are friends."

She glanced over at Brian and saw sincerity in his eyes. She nodded once and pocketed the Glock, keeping a hand near her pocket, however.

One of the men spoke. The same one who'd called through the door. "You've trained her well, Riley."

Brian shrugged. "I need another year to even come close to having her ready."

The visitor retorted grimly, "We probably don't have another week, let alone a whole year."

Brian swore quietly.

The two men and two women stepped farther into the room, setting down suitcases.

Brian spoke, a subtle undertone of reluctance in his voice. "Sophie, this is Colonel Jack Scatalone. He's the supervisor of the Medusas. This is his wife, Major Vanessa Blake. She's the Medusas' team leader. Captain Karen Turner, Medusa team member, and Oberstløytnant Anders Larsen of the Norwegian Defense Force. He's been training the Medusas for most of the past year."

Sophie took in the group before her. They all carried themselves with the same quiet confidence Brian did. Even the women.

She studied them curiously. The ladies looked normal enough. Both of them were pretty, the major a redhead, the captain a blonde. But their eyes…they looked right through a person. On the move constantly, taking in everything and everyone around them.

So. These were the women she was supposed to work with. The fabled Medusas.

The redhead said softly, "It a pleasure to finally meet you, Ms. Giovanni. We've been getting progress reports on you for the past eight weeks. It's nice to finally put a face to the name."

Sophie blinked. "I've been hearing a lot about you, too."

Vanessa laughed easily. "Only half of it's true. The good half."

Sophie smiled. She liked this self-assured, contained lady. She seemed totally at home in her skin.

Vanessa looked around casually. "I hear there's a hot tub around here somewhere."

Sophie replied, "Out on the deck."

"If you'll give me a minute to fish a swimsuit out of my bag, I'd love to join you out there and hear about your training, Ms. Giovanni."

"Call me Sophie." She flashed Brian a laughing glance. "Ooh, a girls only tell-all. Sounds like fun, Major."

"Call me Vanessa, or Viper if you prefer. C'mon Karen, let's go change. I can't wait to hear the dirt on Pretty Boy Riley."

Sophie's smile faded into a frown as the two women carried suitcases down the hall to a couple of the bedrooms like they were moving in. And then it hit her. They *were* moving in. No doubt Major Hollister had sent them as extra protection for her…and maybe even to prevent her and Brian from taking off.

Brian. He must be furious that these four had shown up like this. He was so determined to talk her into running away with him. She looked over at him and thought she detected a certain tightness around the corners of his mouth and in the hunch of his shoulders. The colonel was deep in quiet conversation with him, too quiet for her to hear. She shrugged. Later, when she and Brian were alone in bed, she'd get it out of him. He couldn't resist her when she straddled him and rocked just so….

Vanessa and Karen emerged, wearing bathing suits. Sophie managed not to stare at their spectacular bodies, but it was a close thing. They weren't nearly as muscular as female body builders, but managed to blend extraordinary fitness and feminine grace surprisingly well.

She showed the other women out to the hot tub. As the winter's cold bit her all over with sharp teeth, she eased into the almost unbearably hot water, shivering in delight at the contrast.

The two Medusas slid in beside her.

Karen commented, "This is a far cry from twenty-four hours ago, isn't it?"

Vanessa laughed quietly. "No kidding. It's my first bath involving water in over a month."

Sophie stared. "A month?"

"We've been on a hide in the desert. We don't have enough spare water for wet bathing. We've been using dry shampoo. It's not bad. Kills bacteria on your skin and gets off the worst of the sweat and grime, but doesn't offer much by way of comfort."

"Brian didn't tell me about that."

Karen laughed. "I bet there's a lot he didn't tell you. He didn't want to scare you off."

Oh, how wrong the tall blonde was. He'd done everything in his power to scare her off, the sweetie.

"So tell me about your training, Sophie...."

Inside, Brian watched Scatalone settle onto one of the deep, leather couches and say, "I've been reading your reports on your girl. So tell me about it. Fill in the holes for me. Where is she in her skills?"

Brian restrained an urge to throw up. Hollister knew him too well, damn him to hell for all eternity. His boss had sent in this team of operatives to make darn good and sure he didn't grab Sophie and make a break for it. The net had closed around Sophie and him and they were well and truly caught now.

He had completely, utterly failed her.

She was doomed.

Chapter 14

Sophie adjusted the gauze scarf across her face and squinted against the blinding glare of the sun, grateful for every step Brian had made her run in the sand in San Diego. The sand here in Bhoukar was softer and deeper, but her muscles were used to its frustrating give with every step. Jack Scatalone led the way at the moment, followed by Vanessa and Karen. She was next, with Brian behind her and Anders bringing up the rear. The others regularly shifted the order they hiked in, but she was always kept in the middle of the pack.

The others also carried backpacks of gear, but she was spared the additional weight. It didn't even begin to equalize her ability with the others' but every little bit helped. They let her set the pace and assured her it was okay to go slow, but it was a matter of pride to push herself as hard as she could.

Thankfully, Jack stuck a closed fist up in the air just then, signaling a stop. Without any ceremony, Sophie sank down to the ground, panting. Would they never get where they were going? They'd been walking for nearly five hours. And to think, Vanessa had called it a short hike. Ugh.

"How're you doing?" Brian murmured as he squatted beside her.

"Honestly? Ready to stop. But I can keep going."

He smiled warmly at her, but that constant shadow at the back of his eyes was still there. It had been there ever since Canada, gradually growing darker and more melancholy.

"That's my girl. You're doing great."

Sophie grimaced at him. "You're just saying that."

"No, I mean it."

Karen came over and held down a water skin to Sophie. "He's right. Vanessa and I were just talking about how impressed we are that you're doing this well. We figured the hike in would take seven or eight hours with you along, but we're only about fifteen minutes away from our surveillance post."

Sophie smiled up gratefully. "You know darn good and well I'm dead weight around your necks, but it's nice of you not to say so."

Karen laughed and sank down easily beside Sophie, stretching out her long legs. "When the Medusas started their training, we weren't in much better shape than you're in now. Brian's done a good job bringing you up to a very high level of fitness. But we've had two years of constant physical challenges to harden us."

Vanessa plopped down nearby. "Yeah, and most of those challenges were named Jack."

Scatalone sat down, looping a casual arm around his wife's shoulders. "Do I hear my name being taken in vain?"

Karen laughed over at him. "Absolutely, you miserable old tyrant." To Sophie, she said, "Jack nigh unto killed the six of us in our initial training. Hopefully, Brian was a little more compassionate with you."

Brian piped up. "I was the soul of compassion."

Sophie snorted, enjoying the easy camaraderie of this team. The mutual respect among them was a tangible thing. No way could she rip Brian away from this closeness and these people. They were his family.

"Everyone rested up?" Vanessa asked, looking straight at Sophie. "It'll get dark soon."

Sophie laughed. "By everyone, I assume you mean me? Yes, I'm ready to go. And no, I'm not afraid of the dark. Certainly not with all of you nearby."

The group rose as one. The marching order shuffled again, and this time Anders' broad shoulders were directly in front of her. He was some sort of champion cross-country skier, and he'd commented earlier that walking through sand was a great deal like skiing. He certainly made the going look effortless. Sophie gathered he and Karen had some sort of thing for each other, the way they looked at each other in quiet moments.

They didn't walk too much farther before Vanessa, who was in the lead now, held up her fist for a stop and gave a signal for silence. Vanessa flashed a flat hand, palm down, pushing it toward the ground. Obediently, Sophie sank to the sand. What was going on? Was someone out there?

Brian crawled up beside Sophie and breathed, "We've arrived at the hide. It's at the top of that ridge ahead of us. Sollem's compound is on the other side of the rocks."

Adrenaline screamed through Sophie. This was it. All those weeks of training, all the preparation, all the angst. Could she do it? It was awfully late in the game to consider backing out now. Especially after all the effort these people had expended to get her here. But then, maybe that was the point. Major Hollister was no fool.

She sighed. The thing was, his tactic had worked. After meeting and getting to know these remarkable people, she felt obligated to go through with the mission, no matter what the risk to herself.

As they neared the top of the east-west running ridge, the team went down onto its hands and knees, and for the last few yards, all the way down onto their bellies. Something pressed against the bottoms of her feet, and she looked back to see Brian reaching forward with his hands to give her something to push off against. It made the going immeasurably easier. In a few moments she lay near the top of the ridge, catching her breath. Brian slithered up beside her.

"Wanna get your first look at Sollem's compound?" he asked under his breath.

She nodded.

"C'mon."

She and Brian moved past the rest of the team who were conferring in hand signals. It was only a body length until her nose was right up against the summit of the rocks concealing them.

She'd seen dozens of surveillance photographs of the compound over the two days and knew the layout of the place inside and out, but anticipation buzzed in her gut to see the real thing. Brian rolled over on his side, pulled a field telescope out of a pocket on his utility vest and passed it to her.

Slowly and carefully, like he'd taught her, she lifted her head just enough to peer over the rocky spine. A long wall came into focus with a half-dozen roofs sticking up above. Something moved at the top of the wall and she zoomed in on it. A figure of a man with the distinctive outline of a machine gun in his hands. A chill flowed over her. That man, and dozens more just like him, would kill her without a second's thought.

Fear started low in her belly and expanded, consuming

her entirely in a few seconds. She fought a visceral need to flee this place and keep running until she was far, far away from it.

"You okay?" Brian murmured.

"No. I'm scared to death."

He closed his eyes for a pained moment, and when he opened them, the ever-present shadow lurking in them had almost overtaken his blue gaze. "Let's back down the ridge. We need to slide a little to our east to get to the Medusas' camp."

The entire group moved perhaps thirty yards to the east and approached the top of the ridge again. This time a cluster of beige camouflage nets stretched over a miniature campsite. Vanessa quickly introduced her to the other Medusas—Jamaican Aleesha with a warm, infectious smile; Katrina, a reserved and delicate-looking Korean woman; Misty, blonde, tanned, and gorgeous; and Isabella, dark-haired and striking—and listening intently to a headset.

Yet again, Sophie was struck by how normal these women seemed. If she met one of them on the street, she would never in a million years guess they were trained killers. Of course she knew now, compliments of Brian, that Special Forces soldiers were a whole lot more than that. Still, it was daunting to be in the midst of so many incredibly dangerous people. Even odder was the sense of acceptance as one of them they seemed willing to afford her. It made her desperately want to live up to their expectations.

The next couple of hours were spent choking down a pouch of freeze-dried casserole and taking a nap. And then Brian's hand lightly over her mouth woke her up. "There's movement. We need you to man the binoculars and see if you can spot Freddie."

Everyone was hoping she'd be able to pick out her old classmate from here and point him out for Katrina, the team's sniper. Sophie crawled up beside the small woman.

The sniper murmured, "A group of men are exiting the compound. They'll walk out to the edge of the road and greet whoever's incoming in that convoy of Land Rovers."

Sophie looked to her right and barely managed to make out a puff of dust in the blinding sunlight. "How in the world can you tell those are Land Rovers?"

Katrina smiled briefly and pointed to her right, where Isabella crouched in front of a computer screen and Misty appeared to be playing a computer game. "Sidewinder's flying an unmanned surveillance drone with a camera on it, and Adder's looking at the video imagery."

Sophie didn't have all their various snake names sorted out yet, but the women used them interchangeably with their actual names. On the radios, they only used the snake nicknames. She peered through a powerful set of binoculars at the cluster of men walking across the sand. The light was brilliant, almost unearthly in its intensity. One by one, she examined the men, doing her best to recall the kid who she'd played and eaten and fought with.

Reluctantly, she announced, "I'm pretty sure none of those guys is Freddie."

Katrina murmured emotionlessly. "If anyone gets out of the Land Rovers, have a look at them."

"I thought you said Freddie was in the compound."

Katrina replied without taking her eye off her sniper scope. "I have no idea if he's in there or not. We assume so, since all his top advisors and both his wives are in there right now."

"He has two wives?" Sophie exclaimed under her breath.

"Yup, and about ten kids."

"Wow. I guess he got busy early."

Katrina snorted. "Keep two women barefoot and pregnant in the harem, and the kids stack up pretty quick, I guess."

Sophie shook her head. The puff of dust resolved itself into three white vehicles. They pulled to a stop in front of the standing men, and a half-dozen more men got out. Sophie examined each one of them carefully. "Nope," she said regretfully.

Katrina sighed. "Too bad. We were really hoping not to have to send you in there."

Sophie muttered, "You don't know the half of it."

Vanessa, who'd come up beside her with a pair of field glasses, murmured, "How so?"

Sophie sighed. "It's complicated."

Vanessa muttered to Katrina, "Give us a holler if any more guys show themselves." To Sophie she said, "Come with me."

Sophie turned around awkwardly on her stomach and followed the team leader down the slope to one of the low tents.

"Step into my office, Sophie."

Brian, whom they'd passed on the way down the hill, made to follow them. Vanessa flashed him a hand signal to hold his position. He frowned, but complied as Sophie followed the woman into the tent.

"Can I get you something to drink?" Vanessa offered.

"No, I'm fine."

"You've got to drink at least double your normal intake of water out here. The desert sucks the moisture right out of you."

"Brian's been forcing me to slug huge amounts of fluids."

"Good man, Captain Riley."

Sophie nodded. "Yes, he is."

Vanessa studied her intently. "You like him, don't you?"

"Well, yes."

"It's clear he's totally smitten with you. He reminds me of Jack right after he proposed to me. He hovered over me like I was made of glass." A smile drifted across the major's face.

"Brian has hovered over me from day one. He's determined to keep me safe."

Vanessa sighed. "Safe is one thing that doesn't come with this job. If you spend long enough in this business, you begin to believe there's no such thing as safe anywhere."

"Surely back in the United States, on a military base or at home…"

Vanessa shrugged. "I could be hit by a car tomorrow or a meteor could fall on my head. You just never know."

Sophie frowned. "That's a pretty pessimistic view of the world. How do you refrain from slitting your wrists and just being done with it?"

Vanessa laughed, albeit under her breath. "Ahh, but you see, most of us take the exact opposite approach to life's uncertainties. You never know when your number will come up, so live fast and hard every moment. I'd venture to say I enjoy life a great deal more than most people, simply because I realize it's so precious and fragile."

Sophie considered that for a moment. She understood the sentiment, but was perplexed as to why Vanessa had brought it up now. "You strike me as the kind of woman who doesn't sit around in the desert randomly philosophizing about life for fun. Where are you going with this little talk?"

Vanessa's intelligent gaze snapped to hers. "Brian wasn't kidding when he said you're smart, was he?"

Sophie shrugged. "I'd like to think not."

"Do you fully understand the risks of going into that compound in search of Fouad Sollem?"

Sophie looked her square in the eye. "Yes. It's a suicide mission."

Vanessa exhaled hard. Swore quietly. "There may be another way. An assault on the compound. By all of us."

Sophie reared back in the tight confines of the tiny tent. "Why in the world would you even consider that? The way I hear it, hundreds of armed men are roaming around that place.

Why would you throw away the lives of ten people, when you can minimize your casualties and lose only one?"

It was Vanessa's turn to lurch. "That's not how I think about the lives of my troops. Each one of you is non-expendable." A pause. "Are you sure you're up to doing this alone?"

"I won't be alone," Sophie murmured. "Brian will always be with me. In here." She touched her heart. "Right up till the end."

"Cripes, Sophie. You don't need to throw your life away to prove to him that you love him!"

Sophie stared. "What *is* it with you people? Brian's been trying to talk me out of this mission practically since the moment I met him. And now you? Do you want me to mark Freddie for you or not?"

Vanessa sighed. "You have to understand the moral dilemma this puts us all in. To ask a civilian to do something that may very well cost her life because we're not capable of doing our job without her? That's hard for any of us to swallow, and we're not even in love with you as Brian is."

Sophie stared at Vanessa. In that moment, she felt a deep kinship with this woman, who was a lot like her, just trying to do the right thing out here in an impossible situation. "What would you do if you were in my shoes and it was Jack proposing to throw away his career for you?"

Vanessa nodded. "Ahh. So he did offer to take you and run. Hollister thought he might. No wonder we were sent to collect you in such a sudden rush."

Sophie blinked, startled. So. Her speculation had been right. Hollister *had* sent in reinforcements to keep Brian from disappearing with her. The realization that she'd read the situation correctly gave Sophie little satisfaction, however. She said soberly, "Make no mistake. I don't want to die. But what choice do I have?"

Vanessa stared at her for a long time. Then, in a sudden burst of decision, moved to the tent entrance. "Anders, take over for Cobra. Medusas, Jack, Brian, huddle in here. Now."

Sophie blinked, startled at the command lacing Vanessa's voice. As the others moved toward the tent, she muttered, "Wow. Even my grandmother didn't sound like that, and she was the toughest broad I ever knew."

Vanessa grinned sheepishly. "I practiced that tone in my bathroom mirror for about six months before I got it right."

Sophie grinned back. "It rocks."

"Thanks."

In a few seconds, all six Medusas, Jack and Brian and crowded into the tent with her. There was barely any floor left, and Brian pried up a corner of the tent to let air in as the space got stuffy.

Vanessa got right to the point. "We have to figure out a way for Sophie to get into—*and back out of*—that compound. I hate to call in the bunker-buster bombs and tell them to blow everyone in that compound to smithereens given the number of women and children inside, but I'm willing to do that rather than send Sophie on a known suicide mission."

Sophie started. "But what about the possible nukes?" She'd been shocked to learn about this latest development from the Medusas in Canada. "Wouldn't a full-scale assault on the compound blow up the bombs?"

"They wouldn't blow up—they'd just crack open and release some radiation. But nothing like an actual nuclear detonation. As long as we thought you could go in there un-recognized and mark Freddie, we were willing to wait on blowing the whole place up. But when it became clear Freddie was on to you, we were prepared to annihilate the joint. Then we spotted the bombs. They're the only reason why the whole compound isn't a smoking hole right now. They're also why it's more critical than ever for you to mark Freddie for us—so we can do the smallest precision attack possible on him and try to avoid breaching the nukes' casings."

Sophie shuddered. The stakes riding on her success were almost too high to comprehend.

Vanessa continued, "My orders are to stop Freddie Sollem. Period. No discussion of any fallout, political or nuclear."

Sophie protested, "But there are dozens of women and children in there."

Vanessa turned a hard gaze on her. "And Freddie Sollem is responsible for using them as a human shield. The families in there know full well they're harboring a terrorist mastermind and are voluntarily acting as his shields. Yes, it would be a huge political hot potato to blow up the lot of them. But don't lose sight of the fact, Sophie, that they've chosen to place themselves in harm's way. I can only be responsible for protecting innocent lives up to a certain point. After all, aren't you an innocent, too?"

Brian all but collapsed in relief beside her. The shadows in his eyes receded a little.

Vanessa turned to the others. "Let's put on our thinking caps. Sophie, are you familiar with our free-flow brainstorming techniques?"

"Brian taught me how you folks do it, yes."

"Perfect. Ideas, anyone?"

Jack spoke up from beside Vanessa. "The problem is that as soon as Freddie recognizes her, he'll kill her, right?"

"Correct," Vanessa answered.

"And the original plan was for her to use her friendship with Grandma Sollem to gain entrance to the compound. She was to enter the compound as Sophie Giovanni, old neighbor of the Sollem family."

Nods all around.

"What if she goes in posing as someone else?"

Sophie turned the idea over as Jack continued. "If she barely knows what Freddie looks like anymore, I'd expect he'll have trouble recognizing her, too. Sophie, do you still look a lot like you did as a child when Freddie knew you?"

"Good heavens no! I was a gawky kid with twig legs and braces and stringy pigtails the last time he saw me."

Jack smiled. "May I compliment you on having filled out very nicely, then?"

"Hey, buddy, stick to your own woman," Brian growled.

Low chuckles vibrated all around.

"I'm back to speaking Bhoukari close to fluently," Sophie remarked. "Maybe we could use that."

Vanessa piped up. "A cover story. She's a teacher with some humanitarian aid group. Maybe she's canvassing the women and children in the compound to see if they are getting educations and if she can arrange for them to have a teacher come into this area to work with them."

Jack cautioned, "She's never tried to maintain a legend before. It's a hell of tall order for an amateur." He glanced over at her apologetically. "No offense meant."

"None taken," Sophie replied with a smile.

Brian spoke up. "Freddie will be looking for something like this. As soon as a strange woman walks into the compound, he'll be suspicious and check her out. He'll put her in front of a surveillance camera, recognize her and send in one of his goons to kill her. And then we'll be right back where we started."

Sophie asked slowly, "What if I do the exact opposite?"

Everyone looked at her, surprised.

"What do you mean?" Vanessa asked.

"What if I walk right up to the front door and say, Hi, I'm Sophie Giovanni, and I need to talk to Freddie Sollem. I tell him the U.S. government has kidnapped me and tried to get me to roll over on him, but I've escaped and I'm mad as hell. I'm coming to him to warn him and to ask for protection from those Imperialist bastards."

Brian sucked his breath in hard. "It's too risky."

Vanessa checked him with a raised hand. "Let's develop this idea a little bit. What are the risks?"

Karen piped up. "That Freddie doesn't believe her and kills her on the spot."

Sophie winced. There was that.

They hashed out at least a dozen more ideas, but none of them stood up to intense analysis. Over and over, they kept coming back to Sophie's suggestion. It was the one approach that would guarantee to get her close enough to Freddie to mark him, and it was the only approach any of them thought might actually stand a chance of fooling Freddie for any length of time. At a minimum, it would force him to pause and think— hopefully for long enough for Sophie to make her escape.

Darkness had fallen and the sky was thick with stars through the tent opening before Vanessa rubbed a hand across her eyes and said, "I think we've eliminated every other possibility. And only Sophie's plan is left standing."

She turned to Sophie. "I'm prepared to blow the entire compound and everyone in it to kingdom come and let the diplomatic reaction fall where it will. Or, you can try to convince Freddie you've come to warn him. It's your life on the line. Your decision."

Chapter 15

Brian and Sophie were assigned a tent together—if the low, narrow tarp staked out across the sand could even be called a tent. Sophie crawled underneath it and stopped, startled. Brian had dug down into the sand, creating a surprisingly spacious living area for them. She was able to sit up comfortably and there was plenty of room for both of them to store their gear and stretch out side by side.

"Like my shelter-building skills?" he murmured from behind her.

She moved farther into the enclosure. "This is great."

"Empty this." He passed her a water skin holding about two liters of water. She worked on drinking it while he efficiently unrolled their down sleeping bags.

"It was in the nineties today. Do you really think we'll need those?" she asked.

He glanced up from the sleeping bags. "It'll go down

below freezing tonight. The temperature swings like crazy out here."

"What an incredible climate."

He shrugged. "It makes the people who live in it tough, that's for sure."

She shuddered. "Can I take off my boots?"

"Store them upside down so no scorpions crawl into them." He turned around from securing the tent flap in the sudden darkness. She made out the flash of his smile. "Let me help you with those."

"Yeah, right. Like I want you smelling my stinky feet," she laughed.

"I've worked out here for years. I don't even notice human body smells anymore. Except when a beautiful lady smells like peaches."

"Rotten peaches is about the best I'll be able to do tonight."

His arms slipped around her as they knelt face to face. "You'll always smell like peaches hanging heavy and ripe on a tree, warm in the sun and so juicy they make a mess of your chin when you bite into them."

"Stop that. You're making my mouth water. And I've got to eat dehydrated eggs in the morning."

He chuckled, his hands coming up to frame her head, his mouth pausing a fraction of an inch from hers. The moment stretched out as the humor between them faded, leaving in its place electricity so powerful the hairs on her arms stood up. Desire zinged through her, originating deep in her core and radiating outward until every cell of her being tingled.

His mouth closed upon hers, devouring her whole. She kissed him back with all the passion she'd stored up for the past few days, all the fear, all the desperation of the moment exploding out of her. She flung herself against him, knocking him over onto their sleeping bags, following him down as if she were trapped under the ocean and he was her only air supply.

He pulled her fully on top of him, one knee propped up for her to lean against. He growled, "I can't get enough of you. I'll never get enough of you."

His hand on the back of her neck urged her down to him and they strained against each other, seeking complete connection and momentary escape from the events looming over them. Tomorrow might be about dying, but tonight was about being entirely, incredibly, intensely alive.

They tore each other's clothes off, scattering them all about the small space. Their hands roamed restlessly, and skin slid across skin in delicious chaos. They made love frantically the first time, pounding against their mutual frustration, driving back the rest of the world by main force. It was urgent and rough and explosive. And as she surged up beneath him, nearing release, he captured her mouth with his, swallowing her strangled cries of pleasure and giving his to her in return.

Breathing hard, Brian propped his elbows up on either side of her head, his body still buried deep within hers. They panted in unison.

"Do you suppose they heard us?" Sophie whispered.

"Do you suppose I care?" he whispered back.

"I'd die of embarrassment."

"Honey, what do you think they think we're doing in here? I'm about to send you out alone to risk your life on an incredibly dangerous assignment. They don't think we're sitting around reading poetry."

"Oh, good heavens, I'm mortified."

"If it makes you feel better, I bet Jack and Vanessa are doing the same thing right about now, and Karen and Anders, for that matter."

"Great. We're out here having sex Olympics while the rest of the team listens in."

"They didn't hear anything. We're dug mostly underground and sand's a great noise insulator."

She smiled against his mouth. "Even if that's a complete lie, thanks for saying so."

He smiled back, his lips curving sweetly against hers. "You're welcome." And then he proceeded to do exactly as he'd promised, loving away the hours of the night and distracting them both from the day to come.

But come it did. Sophie woke up in the faint glow of predawn creeping through the cracks in the tarp. She lay there nestled in Brian's arms for a while—hard to tell how long, for each minute seemed to race by at light speed. Funny how time always behaved exactly the opposite of how you wanted it to.

It wasn't fair that she'd found Brian so soon before this mission. But then, if not for the mission, she'd have never met him at all. As corny as it sounded, she'd rather have known him for this short time than never have known him at all.

His mouth moved softly against her temple. When she tightened her arms around him to indicate she was awake, he murmured, "Hey there, sunshine."

"I'm feeling more like a thundercloud at the moment," she muttered.

He raised himself up on an elbow to peer down at her in the dim tent. "The waiting is the worst part of any mission. But once the action gets rolling, you'll forget everything but the moment at hand."

She'd never forget him. Not even in the heat of battle. He was with her all the time, a part of her, and she a part of him. It hovered on the tip of her tongue to tell him she loved him. But what if she died today? Would it be fair to put that burden on him? How would he live with having let a woman who loved him go forth to her death? She couldn't do that to him. No. Better not to say anything to further stress the guy out. He was already stretched as tightly as she was.

"How are you doing, really?" he asked seriously.

She gazed candidly into the shadowed depths of his eyes. "I'm scared. What if I mess it all up? What if I wreck your career? What if—"

He pressed a finger over her lips, stilling the words. "Don't think about it. We don't have to get up for a couple more hours. Close your eyes and go back to sleep."

Brian watched dawn seep through the tent flap, willing it away, begging the gods for just a few more hours here with Sophie wrapped in his arms, safe and sound. The gray light turned pink, then brightened to orange, then blazed with the bursting energy of a new day.

Please God, let it not be Sophie's last day on earth. He couldn't go on without her. If something happened to her, he was going to lie down in the sand and die right along with her. She was his heart. His soul. Hell, his life.

He let her sleep as long as he could. But eventually, Jack poked his head through the tent flap and, with a sympathetic look on his face, hand-signaled that it was time to get going.

They—more specifically, Sophie—had places to go and things to do today.

Brian kissed her eyelids gently and they fluttered open as delicately as butterfly wings. "Good morning, sweetheart," he murmured.

"Mmm, good morning." She stretched her arms over her head lazily, smiling in sleepy contentment. And then her arched brows came together, a faint frown etching her formerly smooth brow.

There it was. The real world had just shoved in rudely between them. He'd held it off as valiantly as he could, for as long as he could. But even he was not invincible against the march of time. He dropped a light kiss on her mouth. "It's time for you to quit being a lazybones and get this thing over with."

She smiled gamely, but her eyes were dark and troubled. "Yes, sir."

"It'll be fine."

"Promise?"

"Yeah. I promise." It was a lie. But a compassionate one. Hell, he'd held a man in his arms once with half his body blown away and told the guy he was going to be just fine, too. This felt even worse.

He helped her find her scattered clothes and don them in the tight confines of the shelter. While she went outside to relieve herself, he warmed up water and added it to a dehydrated breakfast packet. He handed it to her when she returned and she looked down at it distastefully.

"I think I'll pass."

"You'll need the energy later," he said quietly.

Without protest, she began to eat. He suspected she wasn't tasting a bite of it anyway.

He ran scenarios with her for the next hour, describing possible surprises and talking her through how to respond to them. The morning warmed up around them and sweat trickled down his brow, though from heat or abject terror, he couldn't tell.

They wouldn't be able to send her in with much gear. Freddie and his men were too well-trained at spotting such things. And for all they knew, she might be searched before she was allowed to approach Freddie.

Vanessa called the team together to go through the timetable.

As Viper started to talk, Sophie took hold of Brian's hand, crushing his fingers heedlessly. He winced and let her hang on. Vanessa went over the whole plan, including which satellite would be watching the compound, which agencies would be waiting to pick up and track the signal of the burr Sophie put on Freddie, who would launch the air strike on Sollem and what possible bomb packages for that strike would be.

"How long after the burr goes live does Sophie have to get away from Sollem?" Brian asked.

"She's got about three hours. That's how long these nano burrs usually last," Vanessa replied. "We'll have a burr on Sophie, too—several burrs, actually—and as soon as she's got sufficient physical separation from Sollem to survive the blast impacts, we'll call in the strikes."

Brian glanced over at Sophie. "Did you understand that?"

She nodded, her eyes big and dark.

He clarified just to be safe. "Once you've marked him, get away from him when you can. No rush, but get separation."

Vanessa continued, "When the fighter planes are in the air, we'll move in to be in position to recover Sophie if necessary and to take out anyone who tries to flee the scene. The Bhoukari army is standing by to surround the area and apprehend anyone who attempts to flee across the desert. But, they prefer not to be directly involved in this hit if they can avoid it. They'd like us to contain the situation right here if at all possible."

Brian was amazed the Bhoukari emir had even allowed this strike, let alone provided any assistance. It was a huge political risk for him in a country where many of his citizens supported Freddie Sollem and men like him.

Vanessa concluded by saying, "This situation is going to be highly fluid. I'll need all of you to be on your toes today. Everyone ready?"

Nods all around.

Isabella put a hand over her ear to listen to an incoming transmission. She announced, "The Teddy Roosevelt is in position and the F-18s are loaded and standing by to launch. They wish you good hunting, Sophie."

Vanessa said briskly, "Let's do it."

Brian stuck to Sophie like glue for the next half hour, checking all her equipment and going over its uses with her one last time. He helped her hide three nano-burrs at various readily accessible places on her person where they were extremely unlikely to be spotted.

"Remember, as soon as you remove them from their paper backing, they'll go live. As long as the mark's burr is on the tip of your finger, it'll be close enough to your burr that we'll know you haven't placed it yet. Once Freddie's burr separates from yours, we'll know you've marked him."

Sophie nodded, her concentration intense, even though they'd been through all this before. He didn't need to say any of it, and she didn't need to hear any of it, but it gave them something to talk about other than finding a way to say good bye, something to think about other than the desperation tearing them both apart.

Isabella finally forcibly took Sophie away from him to give her a quick briefing on a few local customs within Muslim households in this region. He moved farther down the ridge and paced, too restless even to attempt to sit still. Usually, he retreated into Zen-like calm before a mission. Jitters never got the best of him. But then, he'd never sent a woman he felt like this about into Death's jaws before, either.

"Walk with me," Jack Scatalone murmured to Brian as both men watched Sophie retreat into a tent with Isabella.

He didn't feel like talking to anyone, but since it clearly had been more than a request from the colonel, Brian fell in beside him.

They moved down the face of the ridge well out of sight of any Sollem guards. Jack scanned the horizon to the south. Eventually, he commented, "It's tough letting them go, isn't it?"

"I beg you pardon, sir?"

"It sucks rocks sending Sophie into combat, doesn't it?"

Brian huffed. "That's an understatement."

"Did you do your best in training her?" Scatalone challenged.

"Yes."

"And did she learn everything she needed to?"

Brian sighed. "She learned everything we had time for. But there's so much more I wanted to show her before she goes in there."

"It'll never be enough. To this day, I think of things Vanessa doesn't know yet that I want to tell her. But it's like being a parent. At some point you have to trust you've given them enough tools to get by with while they learn the rest. And then you have to let them go."

"Yeah, but Sophie's not a teenager trotting off to college or her first job. She's walking into a den of scorpions with AK-47s."

Jack put a hand on his shoulder. "You have to trust her. Trust the training you've given her. She's smart and resourceful. Sophie strikes me as having a hell of a level head on her shoulders."

"She does."

"I feel your pain, bro. I've been in your shoes. Except it wasn't just Vanessa I had to send out. I had to send out the whole damned lot of them." Jack glanced back over his shoulder at the encampment.

"You really care for those ladies, don't you?" Brian asked.

"Yeah. They're like family to me. But rough on a guy to love."

"Sophie's not even a soldier."

Jack said wisely, "If she survives this mission, it won't

surprise me in the least if she asks to pursue becoming a Medusa. And hell, with the training you've already given her, she's well along the road already."

Brian started. "Mother of God, did you have to mention that now? As if I don't already have enough to worry about!"

Jack laughed. "Welcome to my hell. Anders is in the same boat you and I are. He almost lost Karen last winter. She went into full cardiac arrest in his arms. He has yet to recover fully from it. This is her first mission back on unrestricted operational status and he flatly refused to let her come out here without him."

Brian muttered, "Hell, maybe we guys should start a club. The Frazzled Significant Others of Medusas."

Jack grinned. "I can tell you this, though. It's worth it. To find a woman who understands every last bit of who and what you are and accepts—hell, embraces—it all…there's nothing like it."

Brian sighed. "Yeah, I noticed. I've never met another woman like her, dammit."

Jack laughed. "She's got it bad for you, too. Trust your feelings for each other. She'll be okay. She's got a hell of a reason to live."

"Lord, I hope so. I only pray it's enough."

Chapter 16

Sophie stood still while Isabella expertly draped the abaya around her and pinned a scarf over her head, tucking in her hair. "All set," the Medusa announced quietly. "How are you holding up?"

"I don't know. Shaky. Ready to get this over with. I'm worried about Brian."

Isabella laughed. "I feel your pain. I'm dating a Special Forces operative, too. I'm a complete wreck whenever he goes out on an op, and he's a complete wreck whenever I go out. It comes with the territory." She leaned in close and murmured, "But the homecomings… they make it all worth it."

Sophie felt her cheeks heating up. The good-byes weren't half bad, either.

Isabella continued, "Don't try to be a hero. Go into the Sollem compound as low-key as you can. You're not there to make a fuss. You just want to give a childhood buddy a friendly warning in repayment for all the kindness his family showed you when you were a little girl. You hope to have a cup of tea with Grandma Sollem, give Freddie your message, and be on your way."

Sophie patted Isabella's hand. "Brian's been over all this with me at least a dozen times, but I appreciate your concern."

Isabella smiled lopsidedly. "I'd do anything to be the one going in instead of you."

"Every one of you would rather be the one putting your neck on the line. You Medusas have big hearts. Thanks for your concern." She took a deep breath. "But I'll be fine."

Isabella smiled. "Yes, you will. This is going to be a piece of cake. Even if the whole mission goes to hell in a hand basket, Freddie will have no idea the kind of training you've got under your belt. He'll grossly underestimate you. It's the Medusas' secret weapon and it'll be yours, too."

Sophie just smiled. Her secret weapon was Brian. He was her armor and her strength.

She stepped outside. Brian waited, wearing a field pack and hiking gear. "Ready to blow this popsicle stand?" he murmured.

She nodded, suddenly choked up. She stared, unseeing, at her watch through a time hack to get everyone's watches perfectly in sync, and then it was time. Brian and Sophie hiked south, directly away from the ridge.

"How's her signal?" Brian muttered into the microphone clipped to his collar. He listened for a moment and then flashed her a thumbs-up. Her own burrs were working, then. She had one in the heel of her left shoe, and one in her stomach that Isabella had given her to swallow as a capsule. Both of her burrs had sizable batteries and would operate for several days. Good Lord willing, she wouldn't need them for that long, though.

She and Brian slogged through the sand in silence. The afternoon's heat stacked up around them, layer upon layer of stifling air, whipped by a dry, hot wind full of talc-fine grit. The dust stuck to everything—to her eyelashes and the sweat dotting her brow, even to her teeth.

In about an hour, they arrived at a desolate strip of asphalt that stretched away into nothingness as far as the eye could see in either direction. Whorls of dust skittered past, threatening to bury the paved strip until another gust came along to clear it. The effect was of a shifting, mirage-like image of a ghost road.

And then a large, linear puff of dust appeared in the east. Brian pulled out his field telescope and had a look. "It's your ride," he confirmed.

She looped her arm in his elbow and leaned her head on his shoulder. He turned, wrapping her in a fierce embrace. There was no time for words. Which was just as well, for neither of them had any. Far too much was left unsaid between them to begin to express in the remaining seconds they had left. Sophie fought back a rush of hot tears, her throat clenched around a sob.

Brian's hand slid to the back of her head, pressing it down onto his shoulder. His cheek pressed into her hair. She inhaled the scent of him. Dust and sweat and that indefinable male essence that was uniquely Brian.

"Think of the teahouse," he muttered. "Of our perfect moment."

The sound of a car motor intruded upon the silence of the wind and whispering sand.

Brian's cheek lifted away from her head and she leaned back enough to look up at him. She could swear a little extra moisture glistened in his eyes.

He said simply, "I'll be waiting for you."

She reached up on tiptoe and pressed her lips to his. Their

mouths were dry, their lips cracked from the harsh desert sun, but she didn't care. She let out a wordless moan, low and heartbroken. She tore away from him went to the white Mercedes that pulled up beside them. The driver rolled down the front passenger window and said something in Arabic. Brian nodded and said something back. Sophie recalled Vanessa mentioning a pair of recognition phrases that would be traded with the taxi driver.

Brian opened the rear door for her. He handed her inside, his fingers trailing across the wet tracks on her cheeks. He lifted his fingertips to his mouth and kissed her tears. Without a word, he closed the door and nodded to the driver. He stepped back.

Sophie reached up, pressing her palm to the cool glass. The taxi pulled away, and she turned, watching him stand there alone and tall beside the road until he disappeared, swallowed up by the desert and her tears.

Thankfully, the ride took about a half hour. Enough time for her silent sobs to fade away and for her to collect herself. The driver said nothing. He glanced up at her occasionally in the rearview mirror, but seemed to respect her privacy. She rehearsed what she was going to say in Bhoukari under her breath.

Her thoughts turned to Brian as they looped out of a dusty, unremarkable village and headed back east, toward the Sollem compound. She drew a shaky breath and tears threatened yet again.

Steady, Sophie. Stay in the moment, Brian's voice whispered in her head.

Right. In the moment. She focused on her cover story, blocking out everything else as the long, familiar, white walls came into sight ahead. She'd made her way to Bhoukar from the United States and was out of her element. Scared. Unsettled by the foreignness of this place. But she was determined to see her old friend and pass him a warning. The sun was drawing near the horizon and the first tints of sunset were beginning to paint the compound a soft peach hue.

Peaches...

Focus, darn it!

The driver slowed as they neared the compound, and at least six guards charged from the front gate as the car approached. They looked like angry fire ants swarming forth.

Show time.

Suddenly, one of the guards jumped in front of their vehicle. The taxi driver slammed on the brakes, pitching Sophie forward hard enough that she had to catch herself against the back of the seat. Shouting erupted outside the window. Male voices. It took a moment for the angry cacophony to resolve itself into Bhoukari words. They were ordering her out of the vehicle. Now.

She took a deep, unsteady breath. Too late to second guess herself. *Get in the game, baby. I'm with you.* A sense of calm came over her. This was for him. For them.

She opened the door and stepped out. Two armed men rushed her, grabbing her roughly by the upper arms through her black robe. They dragged her toward the high, carved wooden gate. Fear screamed through her. The enormity of what she was attempting slammed into her, all but drowning her in choking terror. What in the hell was she doing?

Brian tore into camp, his entire body on fire from the long sprint back to camp through the sand. "Did I get here in time? Is she inside yet?"

Isabella nodded infinitesimally toward the compound. "The cab just pulled up."

He flopped to his belly and slithered forward to see over the spine of rocks. He pulled out his field glasses...and hissed with displeasure as the guards manhandled Sophie.

One of them all but yanked her off her feet, and he lurched up involuntarily.

"Down, Tonto," Isabella said sharply. "There's nothing you can do. And Sophie knows what to do."

Brian's gut twisted like a nest of restless snakes, nonetheless. Clenching his teeth until his jaw ached, he watched Sophie shake off the men's hands and say something to them. Both guards backed off.

"Good girl," Isabella muttered.

"What did you tell her to say?" Brian asked, surprised.

"I told her to order them to take their hands off a properly covered woman. And not to say it too nicely."

"Thanks."

Isabella smiled sympathetically at him. "Maybe you ought to go back to camp. You can pace down there in peace. I'm too busy for you to have heart failure on me up here."

His anguished gaze snapped to hers. "I'll be okay. If Sophie can do this, so can I."

"Then help me track her signal against the overlays on my computer. I'm using a satellite photograph on the screen, and on this tab over here, I've got her signal flashed up against our schematic of the compound. You flip back and forth between the images with this button here. Got it?"

He nodded, has gaze fixed on the tiny pinpoint of light that was Sophie. His need to jump through the screen and join her was nearly unbearable. He couldn't do this. He couldn't sit here and watch her live or die, completely helpless to protect her. What the hell had he been thinking to let her talk him into going through with this?

The guards hauled her just inside the front gate, where a man wearing a cobbled-together military uniform of sorts met her and demanded to know her business.

She announced, "I need to speak to Fouad Sollem. I am an old friend and I come with news for him. Please let him know I'm here."

The man stared at her, overlapping layers of dismay, shock and fury painted on his face. "Who are you?"

"Take me to Sollem." Isabella had been extremely specific. Under no circumstances give her name before she got inside the main building. And, once inside, she wasn't to tell anybody her full message short of speaking to Sollem himself.

The sudden dark inside the sprawling, heavy-walled house they took her to was blinding. She blinked, trying to clear the stars from her eyes, but it took several seconds for a wide hallway to resolve itself. Devoid of furniture, the walls and ceiling were built with elaborate Arabic arches and decorated with multi-colored mosaics in complex geometric shapes.

The second door on the right opened and a man in a white robe, much like her black one, stepped out. Definitely not Freddie. This man was too old by a dozen years or more.

"Who are you?" he asked brusquely.

She repeated her story.

"What is your name?"

"Sophie Giovanni. I grew up next door to the Sollem's. Grandma Sollem babysat me for years. Is she still alive? I hope so. I'd love to see her again."

"Stay here." He retreated into his office

Like she was going anywhere, flanked by scowling guards? At least they were keeping their hands off her for the time being. She pulled her head scarf a little farther forward over her forehead as if it could protect her from them. *Patience, sweetheart. Be calm. Relaxed. You're the one doing Freddie a favor. He should be grateful to you.* Brian's remembered voice washed over her frayed nerves, calming them.

Soon, she thought in response. *I'm coming back to you to collect on that future I want with you.*

Several minutes elapsed.

Another man walked down the gallery toward her, his white, floor-length shirt billowing around a lean frame. In heavily accented English he announced, "You will to come with I."

She nodded and followed him down the hall. He led her into a small parlor with a pair of giant sofas. He gestured to one of them. "Please to sit."

In Bhoukari, she said politely, "If you're more comfortable in your own tongue, I'm happy to practice my Bhoukari. Grandma Sollem taught it to me when I was very young. I must apologize, though, for my many mistakes marring your beautiful language." Isabella had said to lay on the politeness thick. It would tend to invoke ingrained rules of hospitality, which were ironclad in this culture.

Indeed, the man seemed taken aback. "Would you like some tea?" he asked stiffly in Bhoukari.

"I'd love some. Hot. With orange slices." That was how the locals drank it.

His eyebrows climbed even higher. He turned and left. She studied the walls. Then the ceiling. Then the Persian rug beneath her feet. Then the walls again. It wasn't hard to act bored for the pair of cameras she spotted, one high in the corner, and the other peeking through a tile mosaic on the opposite wall. She loosened her head scarf, but did not remove it. She waited. And waited.

And still she waited. But finally, the door opened and several men came in. They wore authority with ease. These guys were a definite step up the pecking order around here.

The three men sat down opposite her on the other sofa. "Miss Giovanni, you will understand if we ask to see some identification?"

"Of course." She dug in her purse and handed over her

passport. The three men leaned close to peer at it together. A short, muttered conversation ensued, most of which she couldn't hear.

"What is your message for Mr. Sollem?"

"Thank you so much for your *hospitality*. I know it's most unusual to receive a *guest* in this way, particularly in such an isolated location." She leaned on the buzz words, reminding them of their responsibility to play nice with her. "With all due respect, my message is for Mr. Sollem, and not for any of you. I will give it to him myself."

The men scowled at that. One said, "Mr. Sollem is extremely busy. I am his close and trusted associate and will most faithfully relay your message."

"It's so kind of you to offer!" she exclaimed, all innocent exuberance. "But I'm in no hurry. I'll wait until Freddie has a spare minute. My message for him is really important, but it's between me and him."

"It is not proper for an unmarried woman to speak alone to a married man," one of the men announced.

Isabella had anticipated this one. Sophie replied smoothly, "Of course, I want a chaperone. After all, I have my reputation to protect, as well. I've known Grandma Sollem my whole life. I would be honored to have her act as our chaperone."

The trio subsided again, muttering among themselves, then arose as one and left the room, frowning darkly. Round one to her. How many more layers of flunkies did she have to wade through? The Medusas had no idea. In fact, they were interested to find out, because it would give them insight into the structure of Sollem's organization.

Another wait stretched out. How long had she been sitting here? She peeked at her watch. Nearly two hours. Brian must be back at the encampment by now.

Climbing the walls with impatience if she knew him.

* * *

Heart failure was starting to sound better than sitting here, watching Sophie's signal blinking, minute after excruciating minute in the exact same position. She made it inside the main building easily enough. But now she seemed to be parked someplace. Probably being interviewed by various subordinates of Sollem's while they tried to figure out who the hell she was and what she was doing there.

He was going to have an aneurysm any second. His head was going to explode and it wasn't going to be pretty. All the things he should've said before she left crowded forward, taunting him. He should've told her she'd changed his life. Made him think of kids. Family vacations and long nights and lazy mornings in bed with her. Of forever. He should've had the courage to tell her he loved her, dammit! Now she was out there all alone, risking her life, very possibly about to die, and she didn't know. A slow burn of acid ate at his stomach. How could he have sent her out there without her at least knowing that?

Vanessa reported from further down the ridge, "They've doubled up the patrols on the walls."

Brian smiled grimly. He'd bet Sophie's arrival had thrown a nasty monkey wrench into the works around the compound. Indeed, Misty had ventured a high flyover with a drone not too long ago, and activity in the compound was much higher than usual. Isabella was still doing head and weapon counts on the images to get a more accurate idea of the strength of Sollem's organization. Sending in a long-lost childhood friend, an American woman at that, was a hell of a kick to Sollem's hornet nest.

"When is something going to happen?" Brian groused.

"Patience, Rip," Jack murmured. The colonel was on babysitting duty with him right now.

Brian rolled his eyes at the colonel. She had to be all right. She had to.

He blinked at the screen before him. Had Sophie's signal just moved? It hadn't been far, but he could swear it had. He replayed the video feed for the past few seconds. "Hot damn. We have movement."

Sophie had all but dozed off when the door opened once more, jerking her to alertness. This time a procession of black-robed women entered, a broad, bent figure bringing up the rear. Sophie stared. The Medusas had thought the chances of her seeing Grandma Sollem were slim.

She leaped forward as the old woman sat down heavily, and knelt at the woman's feet. "Grandma Sollem!" she exclaimed in genuine joy. "I so hoped to see you. You look well. How are you?"

"I am old. And you have grown up into a beautiful woman, little Sophie." She took Sophie's hand in hers, examining it critically. "What's this? No husband? Why not? You American women are too independent. You do not understand a woman's place is in the home, raising a family and serving her husband."

Sophie smiled warmly. "I only recently found the right man."

Grandma Sollem nodded her approval. "I would know you anywhere, child. The sweetness in your eyes has not changed at all."

The old woman all but turned and looked into the camera in the corner when she said that. So. Grandma had been sent in here to verify her identity. Now that they knew she was, indeed, exactly who she said she was, what would they do with her?

"What brings you way out here to the end of the earth, child?"

They'd sent Grandma in to pump her for information, too, had they? She looked into the old woman's shrewd eyes.

"First and foremost, I came to thank you and your family for being so kind to me all those years ago. I never forgot you. And see, I still remember your language." She smiled brightly. But then she let the smile fade and leaned forward. "I am worried about Freddie, Grandma. I had a…run-in…with my government over him. While I was in custody, I learned some things which may be valuable for him to know."

There. That should send the folks on the other end of the cameras into a fine tizzy.

Grandma Sollem leaned back, startled, a calculating look in her eyes. Whoever said that women were weak and ignorant in this part of the world had never met Grandma Sollem. "You will stay for supper," Grandma announced.

"Why thank you! I'd love to talk with you some more."

After the meal, a pair of grim-looking men snagged her as she left the dining room. The other women skittered wide around this pair. Finally. Now she was getting somewhere.

One of the men took her firmly by the arm. Her instincts told her not to protest such treatment with these two. They took her through a maze of rooms and down a narrow flight of stairs into another hallway full of closed doors. They stopped in front of one and thrust her inside.

She stumbled as the door closed sharply behind her. She turned around. A woman stood there. Grim. Unsmiling. "You will undress."

Brian huddled over the computer monitor with Isabella again. "She must have gone underground. The schematic shows her having just walked through that wall."

Isabella nodded. "I concur. Let's map her movements. It'll give us some idea of how extensive the bunker is."

He nodded, exultant. Sophie must have gotten past all

their third degrees to be allowed underground like this. Phase One complete. Pride surged through him. Good girl. Now to find Freddie.

"Excuse me?" Sophie exclaimed in dismay.

"You will disrobe in front of me, or you will do it in front of them." The woman jerked her head toward the hallway.

"What's this all about?" *Show just enough outrage to look like an innocent, but don't push it too far,* she heard Brian murmur.

"Security around the Leader is extremely tight. You did not expect to just stroll in off the street and see him, did you?"

Sophie frowned. "This is a heck of a note. Here I am risking my neck and doing him a favor, yet I'm the one who has to strip down."

The woman shrugged, waiting.

Sophie stripped off the cumbersome black robe gladly. Beneath it, she wore western clothes—charcoal slacks and a gray cotton blouse. She kicked off her shoes and socks, took off her pants, and unbuttoned her shirt, handing it all over to the woman for inspection.

As the woman poked her hands down into the shoes, she said without looking up. "Everything."

"Oh, honestly." Sophie cringed mentally and reached behind herself for her bra hooks. *No worries, sweetheart. She sees the same thing every time she takes a shower.* Clinging to that thought, Sophie peeled off her underwear in mild distaste. But when the woman made her bend over and inspected her body cavities rather more thoroughly than the Medusas had anticipated, Sophie'd had enough.

"Look, enough is enough," she declared in genuine outrage. "I came here to give Freddie a warning that could save his life. If he's so damned suspicious of the kid next door, then I'll just skip giving him the warning. I was trying to be a good neighbor, but I don't have to put up with this." She hadn't spotted a camera and prayed there weren't any, but the room was probably bugged. Whatever. She was annoyed, and not about to pretend otherwise. It all went along with her cover story, anyway.

The woman shoved her clothes across the table. "Get dressed."

Sophie dressed quickly. The woman had taken the penknife from Sophie's purse and her cell phone, but neither was any big loss. She had a hard ceramic blade in the heel of her shoe and there wasn't a cell phone tower for a hundred miles in any direction.

"Come with me," the woman said tonelessly.

Sophie followed her out into the hall. The grim men took over again. They led her down a narrow flight of stairs that looked like something out of an ancient pyramid. Both the tunnel and steps were roughly carved directly from the bedrock. It was steep and so tight her shoulders almost brushed the walls. The ceiling was only a few inches taller than her head.

"We have another stairwell," Brian called out. "There's a second level to this bunker system. And from the amount of time it's taking her to move down it, I'd say we're looking at something a couple stories underground."

"Roger," Jack replied. "I'll relay that to the Teddy R. They'll need to send the bunker-buster package and be prepared to make multiple strikes on the same target."

Once she marked Freddie, how was Sophie going to find her way back up to the surface? What was probably the only stairwell into or out of the bunker would be closely guarded, and she couldn't very well sneak up it. Sollem would have to let her go voluntarily, which narrowed her options considerably. His panic bubbled up very close to the surface. She wouldn't know what to do! He had to get in there. Find her. Find a way out! Adrenaline screamed in his gut for action. He had to do something.

He could sneak away from the Medusas. Make his way down to the compound. Go in over the back wall. They knew which building held the stairwell to the bunker. He could infiltrate it. Make his way to Sophie.

He glanced around furtively.

"Don't even think about it," Scatalone rumbled behind him.

Brian whirled, startled.

"I know exactly what's running through your mind, buddy. I'll take you out before I let you blow this op. Sophie's got it under control. If you go in there, you'll only get her killed."

Brian cursed violently under his breath. Scat was right. But that didn't mean he had to like it.

Forty-two steps later, the steep tunnel flattened out before Sophie into a distinctly bunker-like hallway, low and carved out of red sandstone. They stopped in front of a plain wooden door. One of the men knocked. "The American is here, my Leader."

A male voice from within said with sharp authority, "Enter."

Sophie's adrenaline spiked sky high.

The door opened before her.

Chapter 17

She stepped inside a spartan room, furnished like an effi-ciency apartment, with a kitchenette in one corner. One side of the room was taken up by a large table, and the wall beside it was covered with a giant map of the world. All that she noticed in a glance. But it was the man seated at the end of the table who captured her full attention. The moment she laid eyes on him, there wasn't the slightest doubt in her mind she was looking at Freddie Sollem. Not only did she recognize the shape of his face, leaner now and morphed into adulthood. But his eyes...

Oh, yes. It was Freddie.

He wore power like a cloak, surrounding himself in folds of danger. She walked forward, half mesmerized by the charisma of the man before her.

"Sit," he commanded sharply.

Her first impulse was to obey without question, but she

checked herself. Laughed lightly. "I'm not a dog, Freddie. How are you? It has been a long time. You're so grownup."

He said nothing, just stared at her narrow-eyed. She took another step closer. He shifted in his seat, and for the first time, light from the small overhead fixture fell on his face. Sophie suppressed a gasp of dismay.

He knew.

His saber-sharp, aware eyes looked right through her. Without a shadow of a doubt, he knew exactly why she was here and what she was up to. It was creepy in the extreme. They all had terribly underestimated his intelligence. He wasn't a step ahead of them, he was a mile ahead of them. Her thoughts raced in panicked circles. What to do? Step back and punt? Play out the original plan? Improvise? At a minimum, Freddie would have seen her abrupt fear by now. That was a dead giveaway, darn it.

The plan was to face this guy head on with the truth—or at least some of it. And she didn't have time to think up anything else. "Freddie, you're scaring me, glaring like that. What's wrong?"

For the first time, he blinked. "You tell me, Sophie. What is so wrong that you would come all the way to this godforsaken corner of the world to speak to me so urgently?"

Take the offensive and knock him off balance. It has been a long time since he was confronted with a Western woman. He won't expect you to treat him as an equal.

Thank you, Brian. She shifted into English and allowed the faintest hint of scorn to enter her voice. "Godforsaken? But don't you tell your followers that God is firmly on your side?"

His black brows slammed together. He waved an imperious hand, and the two men who'd brought her here left the room. Outstanding. That would make her job a whole lot easier. "How dare you speak to me of God?"

She rolled her eyes and took a step forward. "Oh, puh-lease. It's me. Sophie. The kid who scraped you up off the ground when you fell out of that tree and broke your collarbone. I've seen your mother pull down your pants and tan your bottom. Don't get all huffy on me."

For just a second, she saw a flash of the kid she used to know, the relaxed American with the quick sense of humor. But then the child disappeared, replaced by this menacing stranger. "What are you doing here?" he demanded in English.

She took another step forward and replied, "I had a little visit from Uncle Sam a couple months ago. They arrested me for having grown up beside you. Maybe you can tell me why they did that?"

He shrugged. "I wouldn't presume to know the mind of your government."

"Liar, liar, pants on fire," she quipped wryly. It was a line they'd used frequently on each other as kids. Disbelief at having just said that to one of the deadliest terrorists on the planet drifted through her mind. *Stay in character. You're just here to give him a friendly warning.*

A ghost of a smile passed across his face. "What did your government tell you about me?"

Perfect. Now he was the one fishing for information. She took another step forward and pulled out the chair next to his. Sat down in it. He didn't seem to mind the proximity. The back of her neck started to itch where the first burr was taped under her hair.

"They said some wild things about you. Accused you of terrible crimes. And they questioned the living heck out of me about you. I'm afraid I let it slip that you were crazy for *Star Wars* and wanted to be Luke Skywalker when you grew up."

He let out a startled snort, but the humor left his eyes almost as fast as it appeared. That laser-sharp gaze of his took aim at her once more. "What else did they say?"

She looked at him candidly. "They said you're planning an attack on the United States. A big one."

He leaned back in his chair abruptly, staring at her as if he were dissecting her brain. Either he hadn't expected her to know that or to admit it if she did. "What sort of attack?" he asked smoothly.

"With bombs. Maybe even nuclear. Is it true?"

"Did they send you to ask me that?"

She smiled without humor. "No. I'm not supposed to be outside the United States right now. And I'm quite certain they don't want me talking to you." It was most certainly true that Brian didn't want her here, and she let that truth infuse her words.

"Then why did you come?"

"Your mother practically raised me. You were like a brother to me. I have always thought of you as family. And I was offended at being snatched off the street and detained for questioning by my own government. I'm a legal secretary now, by the way, and what they did to me was not only illegal, but a violation of my Constitutional rights. And that makes me mad."

Freddie was utterly still.

Brian had taught her the interrogation technique. Create an uncomfortable silence and see what the subject babbles in his or her need to fill the gap. She schooled herself to patience and let the silence stretch out. Two could play that game.

He leaned forward in sudden decision. "Why should I believe you? In all these years you've never contacted me. Why now?"

"I knew where to find you and Grandma Sollem after the government questioned me. They told me where you live. Showed me pictures of this compound, in fact."

That made him twitch.

"And I hadn't been arrested and badgered before now."

"Why should I believe you?"

She shrugged. "I have no reason to lie. I don't know if you're planning an attack or not. It's none of my business, beyond the fact that I'm an American and I sincerely hope you're not planning anything so vicious against innocent victims. But I thought it was the least I could do to let you know that Uncle Sam's on to your plan."

"Did they send you here to dissuade me from following through with the attack?"

She laughed. "If they wanted to do that, a bunch of bombs dropped on top of your head would be more their style, don't you think?"

Sardonic amusement lit his eyes.

She was tempted to say more, but Brian's voice whispered not to oversell her case.

Sollem demanded, "What else did you learn about me?"

"That you're brilliant—although I already knew that. You were always the smartest kid in class. I learned that you're supposedly a fanatic. And that my government is afraid of you. They want to kill you."

"Why haven't they if they know where I am?"

She shrugged. "I have no idea. If I were you, I'd seriously consider moving someplace else, though. Soon. And may I just say it's not very nice of you to put your family at risk by surrounding yourself with them like this?"

He stared straight into her eyes and said baldly, "I'm not a very nice person."

"Why do you do it, Freddie? What do you hope to gain by killing so many innocent people?"

"How many of my people has the West killed? They were innocent of anything other than being born in this part of the world. And yet they had their homes ripped away from them, their livelihoods destroyed, their children slaughtered."

He stood up and began to pace while he delivered a diatribe

about the injustices of the West against his people. It was exactly the opportunity she needed. She reached up under her hair to itch the nape of her neck. With her fingernail, she peeled back the edge of the little bandage and scratched what felt like a grain of sand off the paper hidden there. It lodged under her fingernail.

He took a lap around the room then circled around the far end of the table, heading back toward her. As he swept past, ranting about the rape of the Middle East for oil and land, she held out her hand and let his robe brush her finger. She checked carefully under her fingernail. The burr was gone.

Mission accomplished.

"She did it!" Brian pumped his fist. "Sollem's burr just separated from her signal."

"Take a time hack," Vanessa ordered.

Brian glanced down at his watch. 10:17 p.m.

The entire team clustered around the computer terminal to have a look at the twin signals flashing on the screen, Sophie's green and Sollem's red. The red signal was moving, circling around the green one.

"Looks like she's stationary, maybe sitting down, while Sollem paces around her," Isabella commented.

Vanessa nodded. "She's got him thinking, then. The intel reports on Sollem said he doesn't hem and haw over making decisions. If he's pacing, he's trying to figure out what's up with her."

"Hang in there, baby," Brian muttered under his breath. "All you have to do now is walk out of there."

Sophie took a deep breath. Now for the hard part. Talking her way out of here.

Freddie turned to face her. Challenged, "What have you to say for yourself?"

"I'm not the president of the United States or Congress. I'm just one person. I didn't come here to argue politics with you, Freddie. I just came to warn you that the Americans have found you and know what you're up to."

"You realize that I cannot let you go, don't you?"

She blinked, genuinely stunned. "I beg your pardon?"

"Your government is exactly right. In a very short time, I am, indeed, going to launch an attack against your country that will make 9/11 look like child's play. I cannot let you return to America and confirm that to your government."

"They don't need my confirmation, Freddie."

"Stop calling me that!" he flared up. "That boy is dead. I am Fouad Sollem, the Sword of God!"

Maybe it hadn't been such a good idea to provoke him into that sectarian rant. He radiated fury now, and it was frightening.

She said reasonably, "You haven't told me anything my government doesn't already know. And now that you know America has located this place, you'll move anyway. I don't know anything that will harm you or your plans."

"Ahh, but you have seen my face, Sophie."

"A lot of people know what you look like."

"Not who will share that information with your government."

"Look, I'm mad as heck at what the U.S. government did to me, and I came half-way around the world to warn you. Why would I turn around and betray you to them?"

He shrugged. "They will find a way to make you talk. They are infidels with no morals. I cannot risk having you fall into their clutches."

She retorted, "I'm not going to argue with you about who's acting immorally, here. There is one thing I know for sure, though. The United States has technology you haven't even dreamed of. Keeping me here won't protect you from them. You're up against a formidable foe. They won't leave quietly into the night if you go through with this attack. They'll hunt you to the ends of the earth."

"Their record with finding sons of God at the end of the earth is far from perfect."

She looked around scornfully. "This hole in the ground will look as luxurious as Versailles before they're done with you. If you relish living in a cave, eating camel jerky and drinking sour goat milk, be my guest. It's not my idea of a life."

"And that is why you and your kind will lose. You are soft. Spoiled. Married to your material goods. Americans' love affair with toys will be the death of them."

"Some of those toys may be the death of you, too," she said softly.

He whirled and said savagely, "Is that a threat?"

"No," she replied evenly. "It's a statement of fact. You're one man trying to take on the greatest military and intelligence machine the world has ever seen."

He smiled wolfishly. "And I am the virus in that machine. Tiny. Insignificant. My people creep through the forgotten corners of the machine, planting the seeds of destruction. And the machine cannot see its own weakness."

"You and I are going to have to agree to disagree. I came here because I owed you and your family a debt of gratitude. I've passed along my warning, and now we are even. A taxi should be here shortly to pick me up. Have a nice life, Freddie—or Fouad, if you prefer. I wish you peace."

"Peace?" he snorted. "I think not. The path to Heaven lies in violence."

"Your Heaven. Not mine."

"Exactly."

He leaned over the table and pressed a button on the telephone sitting there. In rapid Bhoukari, he told someone to come in.

"Take her to a cell and lock her up."

"Freddie! I can't hurt you. Let me go!"

His eyes were stone cold as he stared down at her. "You may yet be of some use to me as a hostage, or perhaps as a spokesperson. I will not kill you just yet. I don't know why you came here, Sophie Giovanni, but you are lying to me. Make your prayers to your god, for you will not leave here alive."

Shocked, she stared at his back as he swept from the room. She didn't bother to resist as the two men who'd brought her here dragged her to her feet and goose-stepped her almost to the end of the long hall. They tossed her through a doorway into a black space and slammed the door shut behind her.

The darkness was complete except for a slit of light coming under the door. As her eyes adjusted to the dark, she made out a tiny box of a room. A chair sat in one corner, a bucket in another. A light bulb hung from the middle of the ceiling. She made a couple of circuits of the room. If nothing else, it would tell Brian and company that she was inside a small room at this spot.

If she was lucky, she was far enough from Freddie's signal that the air strike was being called in at this very moment. She took a glance at her watch. 10:22 p.m. It would take about twenty minutes after Freddie moved far enough away from her for the jets to launch and fly here. She sat down on the chair to wait.

But when eleven o'clock came and went, panic began to set in. The strike should have happened by now. Freddie must be too close to her. Damn. She had to get out of this room and move away from him before the Medusas had no choice but to call in the attack.

Except she had no idea where to go to get away from the terrorist. *One problem at a time. Get free, then worry about where Freddie is.* Brian's voice in her head soothed her and focused her thoughts. Time to put some of that fancy training he'd poured into her to use.

Brian paced back and forth below the ridgeline, his panic running wild. "We've got to do something. She's obviously imprisoned, and can't get out of there."

"We've still got a little time," Vanessa said calmly enough. But her eyes were dark with worry, too.

"Let me go in. It'll take me a half-hour to hump over to the compound. That'll give me an hour to get inside and find her and a half-hour to get out."

Vanessa replied, "Brian, she's behind so many layers of security you'd never get to her in time, assuming you even managed to get past them all. It would be suicide for you and could trigger an order to kill her."

"I'll take that chance."

Vanessa shook her head. "I'm sorry. I can't allow it."

Frantic, Brian barely managed to refrain from tearing his hair out. "But we've got to do something!"

Vanessa sighed. "Like what?"

"Stage an attack. Draw Sollem up to the compound's walls," he threw out desperately.

"It might have the exact opposite effect and cause him to hunker down even more tightly in that bunker next to her."

"Then we wouldn't be in any worse position than we're in now. If those bunker busters get Freddie, they're going to blast Sophie to smithereens, too."

Vanessa gazed across the sea of sand at the Sollem compound. Glanced over at Jack. "What do you think?"

"We could position some people close to the compound. Then we wait till the last minute. If Sollem doesn't move in the next hour or so, we start firing at the walls."

"We don't have a lot of go-boom to throw at the compound."

Brian dived in hopefully. "It doesn't have to be a lot of fire-power. It only has to be loud. Just enough to make them think they're under attack. Sophie's arrival has to have put them all on edge anyway. Some American waltzing in and announc-ing that Uncle Sam knows where they are has got to make them nervous as hell."

Vanessa nodded. "Isabella, you and I will pack up camp while the rest of you make your way to the compound. Once we start shooting, our cover will be blown and we'll have to bug out. Adder and I will watch the monitors here and I'll make the final call based on whether or not Freddie moves in the next hour."

The group burst into motion. In a matter of minutes, the party was armed to the gills and loaded down with almost all their ammunition. Brian was so thankful to be doing some-thing, he almost felt lightheaded.

As they prepared to head out under Jack's command, Vanessa put a hand on Brian's arm. "I know you're torn up. But promise me you'll follow Jack's orders and not be a cowboy. We all want to get her out of there alive, and we'll have a better chance if we work together."

He exhaled hard. She was right, dammit. "I hear ya," he grumbled.

She smiled. "If there's anything humanly possible to be done to get her out, we'll do it. She'll be fine."

"I sincerely hope you're right."

Sophie took apart the heels of both shoes and retrieved the various hidden supplies, shifting the tools into her purse where they would be readily available. She went to work on the old doorknob-and-lock assembly. She wasn't all that great at picking locks and it took her forever to get it right. But eventually, the knob turned under her hand. She checked her watch. 12:02 p.m. One hour left before the Medusas would have to call in the airstrike. If she didn't get away before then, she'd end up as dead as Freddie. And she'd never get to tell Brian how she felt about him. That she loved him and she wanted to spend the rest of her life with him. Dammit, she *had* to get out of this bunker!

She dragged the chair into the middle of the room and stood on it. Quickly, she unscrewed the light bulb and, using her harder-than-steel ceramic knife, pried at the socket. In a moment sparks flew, stinging her cheeks. She dug some more, hooking and tearing at the wires. The strip of light seeping under the door flickered and went out. *Yes*.

She raced for the door and slipped out into the hall. An emergency generator could kick in any second. Frantically, she felt her way down a wall away from Freddie's quarters, toward the door she recalled at the end of the hall.

Her hands encountered wood. She tried the knob. Locked. Voices shouted in the darkness and flashlights sliced across the tunnel behind her. Pulling her black scarf across her face, she used her shapeless black garb to fade into the shadows.

A breath of cool air moved across her ankles from under this door. A large room then. Maybe with a hiding place or two. She'd never tried to pick a lock in the dark, but there weren't any other options. She couldn't very well stroll back toward the men running around at the far end of the hall. Her absence would be noted soon, and then they'd come looking for her. Panic climbed the back of her throat at the thought. She doubted Freddie would think she was worth the trouble of keeping alive if they found her.

She worked frantically, trying to picture the lock in her mind's eye. A glance over her shoulder revealed a stream of men rushing into what must have been an armory and streaming out with weapons. They were heading for the stairs. Please, God, let them think the power failure was part of an attack from outside the compound.

Breathe, sweetheart. Be quick but don't hurry.

Mentally, she sobbed back, *I love you*. She had to tell him that in person before she died! Why, oh why, had she been such a coward and never said it to him before?

After countless, endless minutes, the knob finally turned. Praise the Lord. She slipped inside the dark space. It felt big. If only she'd been able to smuggle in some sort of flashlight. She only had a half-dozen matches. She took one out, struck it on the rough strip installed on the bottom of one of her shoes and held up the light.

It was a storeroom with crates stacked all around. She moved toward a tall pile of boxes in the middle of the space. Her match guttered. She stopped moving, but it guttered again. A breeze of moving air, then.

She looked for some sort of air vent or fan, but didn't see any in the walls or ceiling. Her fingers began to burn and she dropped the match, sticking her singed fingertips in her mouth. In the dark, she bent down and picked up the spent match. Brian had taught her under no circumstances to leave evidence of her passing.

She walked forward, her hands out in front of her. *Canvas.* She moved around the tarp-covered crates. She tripped over a pile of what felt like packing material— long, wooden shavings and flat, rough planks like the pieces of crates. She kept going. The noises in the hall outside faded.

She hissed in pain as her shin connected painfully with something sharp. She felt for the obstacle. Some sort of electronic switchboard with a smooth, metal surface curving away to the left of it.

Could it be?

She risked another match. And stared in shock at the sight which illuminated before her. *The bombs.* Three of them lined up side by side. She'd found them. Son of a gun. Not in their wildest dreams had Brian or the Medusas expected this windfall. But she wasn't about to look a gift horse in the mouth. The match burned out and she put its remains in her pocket. She thought fast.

If she'd moved far enough away from Freddie, jets would be streaking toward this position. Would she and the bombs be safe, or would these weapons be damaged in the blast? There was no danger of them detonating—nuclear bombs were actually far too stable for that. But, if the containment chambers were breached, they could release a whole lot of radiation. Certainly a fatal amount for anyone standing this close to them.

She needed to get away from the weapons.

But…

She also had an opportunity to sabotage them. To keep Freddie from using them to harm anyone. She weighed her choice. If she and the bombs were inside the blast radius, radiation would be the least of her problems. If they were out of the main blast radius, she'd be okay regardless.

What would Brian do?

No doubt about it. He'd stick around and disable the weapons. He was that kind of guy. And it was why she loved him. How could she do any less herself?

Brian all but fainted in relief when Vanessa's voice crackled across his earpiece. "We've got movement. Sollen has moved—quickly—away from Sophie's position, and she's on the move in the opposite direction."

"Far enough apart?" Brian asked.

"Not yet."

Jack murmured, "Something's going on at the compound. The lights have all gone out. What do you have on satellite imagery, Viper?"

Vanessa answered, "Standby one." A pause, then, "Men are running around like chickens with their heads cut off. They're acting like they know y'all are coming."

Brian frowned. How was that possible? This team was highly trained in stealth techniques, and there'd been no slipups that could've given away their position to Sollem's men.

Jack asked, "What if Sophie has knocked out the power and caused a panic inside? Would she know to do something like that?"

Brian replied without hesitation. "Absolutely."

Jack asked, "Does it look like Freddie has come up out of the bunker?"

"Not yet. He's near where we marked the staircase down to the lower level, but it doesn't look like he's gone up the stairs."

"Cautious bastard," Brian growled.

Jack grinned over at him wolfishly. "What say we add to the chaos a bit and see if we can coax our boy out?"

Brian nodded. Oh, yeah. He was so ready to start killing.

Feeling around the edges of the targeting computer in the dark, Sophie looked for the latches that held it in place. She hadn't been paying much attention the day Brian showed her the schematics of tactical nuclear bombs, in addition to a dozen other high-tech weapons. But she recalled the whole targeting computer, essentially a laptop minus the screen, should lift off.

She found what felt like a latch. Pried at it with her fingers. Broke a nail. Swore under her breath. She pulled out the knife and pried up the latch. It released with a metallic click. She tried to lift the computer. It felt like at least three more locking points held it down. The other locks were easy to find—one opposite the first lock and two more centered on the other sides of the device. She lifted the computer away from the bomb. Quickly, she shrugged off her robe and wrapped the device in the fabric. Setting the whole bundle on the floor, she gave it a hard stomp with her foot. Muffled crunching sounds came from the device. She gave it several more hard stomps. Unwrapping the robe, she inspected the bent and broken results of her efforts by feel. Perfect.

She'd been out of her prison cell for about twenty minutes. If she was far enough from Freddie, the air attack should hit any minute. Until then, she might as well occupy herself with destroying the targeting systems of the bombs. She didn't know enough to attempt to wreck the bombs themselves. Besides, from what she vaguely recalled, nuclear weapons were sealed in metal casings that would take a welding torch even to think about breaking through.

She finished the second bomb and had just moved on to the third when noise erupted in the hallway again. A lot of it. Men shouting back and forth. She froze, crouching behind the bomb, listening to their shouts. Damn. They were conducting some sort of search. Must've discovered she was missing. *C'mon, air strike. Hit already.*

The overhead lights flickered and burst on, blinding her, and she squinted hard into the sudden light. Dang. Power had been restored. She was near the back of a very large room with crates piled all over the room. Labels announced everything from canned fruits to rocket-propelled grenades. The compound's warehouse.

As she got her first good look at the bombs, she was startled by how large they were. Fat and ungainly looking, she frowned at them. How had Freddie's men gotten these things down that teeny little stairway she'd come down? And those crates over there. No way would they fit down the stairs. There had to be another exit. She looked around for it. In the back wall behind her, a large, dark shadow might conceal some sort of tunnel.

"Don't bother," a male voice said coldly behind her.

She whirled, violently startled.

Freddie. Pointing a very large, very lethal-looking pistol at her.

Busted.

She only barely managed to maintain her feet as sick fear rolled over her. She was so nauseous she could barely stand. *She wouldn't get to tell Brian she loved him.*

Somewhere in the back of her head, a little voice started to scream. And kept on screaming.

His eyes glittered snake-like, in cold rage. "You little bitch. The Americans sent you in to sabotage my operation, didn't they? I knew you were lying!" He advanced menacingly.

Frantically, she looked down at the electronic keyboard in front of her. She pressed a bunch of buttons randomly. The screen lit up and several beeping noises emanated from it.

"Stop right there, Freddie. I'll blow this thing up."

He laughed. But he stopped advancing. "You don't know how to detonate that."

She laughed back scornfully. "These things are designed for American Army grunts, remember? They're so simple a monkey could operate them."

A hint of doubt flickered across his face.

She glanced down again. She remembered that the detonation switches on several of the weapons Brian had briefed her on were covered by a red flap of some kind. She spied one of those now. She reached over and flipped up the switch cover.

"You'll die," Freddie bit out.

"So will you."

"You won't kill yourself to stop me. You don't have that kind of moral spine."

Her gaze narrowed. "Don't I? Are you so sure of that? I had enough spine to waltz in here all by myself to find you."

Definite alarm crossed his face at that. But then resolve replaced it. "Blow us both up, then. I'm ready to meet my god."

"I'll bet you are. In hate and fear and violence. You've murdered hundreds of innocents. Their blood is on your hands. It stains your soul, Freddie. Your Heaven is going to be a very hot place, I think."

"I'll take that chance," he snarled. "But you won't." A message scrolled across a black panel on the targeting computer in red letters. *System arming.*

Holy cow.

Freddie snapped, "No American is willing to die for what they believe in."

"Ahh, but there you're wrong. Why do you think American soldiers volunteer to be in our army by the tens of thousands? We don't force a single one of them into putting their life on the line for their country. They do it because they believe in what it means to be an American."

"A few misguided souls may do it for patriotism. But mostly they do it for money. For jobs. I'll grant you they may even do it for education."

She shrugged. "I disagree. But even if you're right, they still put on a uniform, lay their lives on the line, and die for that flag on their arm. It's a chance they're willing to take."

"But you're not a soldier. You're a civilian. Just some woman playing at being God."

She smiled coldly. "Unlike you, I harbor no such delusions."

The computer blinked. *System armed.*

She reached down deliberately and put her finger on the

red button. "So, Freddie, What's it going to be? The bomb is armed and ready to go. You and I seem to have achieved a Mexican standoff. Shall we die together, or do I have your word that I walk out of here, unharmed?"

He made a noise somewhat akin to laughter, except it was hollow and furious. "You think you can defeat me? Me? The Sword of God? You can't do it."

She stared him square in the eye. "I can and I will. Unlike you, I have known a moment of perfect happiness in my life."

And as the words left her mouth, she realized with shock that they were true. With Brian, she'd achieved something so rare and special that very few people were ever so blessed. She *had* to live. To tell him what she'd figured out when faced with her own death. She couldn't let him go on, never knowing what an extraordinary gift he'd given her.

Except, Freddie had the gun and other ideas. There wasn't the slightest doubt in her mind that he would never let her walk out of this room alive. Despair robbed her of breath and the scream at the back of her head rushed frighteningly close to the back of her throat. This couldn't be happening to her. It was her worst nightmare, come horribly true. What to do?

Do what you have to, Brian's voice whispered calmly. Understandingly.

And in that moment she understood Brian's last and greatest gift to her. Courage. To face life head on and do what was necessary and right, no matter what the cost.

"You lie!" Freddie screamed. "You won't do it!"

He leaped forward.

She looked up at him. Met his gaze.

Smiled.

And pushed the button.

Chapter 18

"We've got a problem gentlemen," Vanessa's voice announced in Brian's ear. Crap. Now what? He lifted his finger away from the trigger of his weapon.

"What's up?" he replied shortly.

"Sollem's signal is almost on top of Sophie. I'd estimate they're in the same room."

How did he have any more adrenaline left to dump into his system like this? He felt faintly nauseous as his stress meter pegged out once more. He muttered, "Freddie's probably questioning Sophie about what the hell's going on, wondering if this is a full-blown American assault."

"We're running out of time. You've got to draw Sollem away from her and soon," Vanessa bit out. "You are greenlighted for the attack. Go get 'em, gang."

Brian took aim at the nearest guard on the east wall of the compound. His finger depressed the trigger of his weapon.

The assault rifle kicked hard in his hands, and it felt good to be handling the weapon. The reaction to their barrage was impressive. Dozens of Sollem's men popped up above the walls, firing wildly. What they lacked in accuracy they more than made up for in sheer volume of lead. Hell, there was no need for the American team to fire back. These guys were lighting up the night like an entire infantry division was incoming. If the explosion of noise alone didn't draw Sollem outside, nothing would.

"Take cover!" Jack shouted over the radios.

Sophie looked down at the bomb. Nothing happened. Damn! Wait. Something *had* happened. A timer was counting down on the face, a few seconds below ten minutes.

Freddie laughed where he stood. "Nice try. But there's a delay programmed into the bombs."

No. No, no, no! He'd known all along she wasn't capable of blowing them both up. In sheer frustration, she reversed her knife and brought the butt down violently on the keypad. Pieces of plastic scattered all over the place as she destroyed it.

She looked up grimly. "Yeah, but now you can't disarm it. I broke the off button."

Freddie's eyes opened wide in rage. "You bitch!" he howled.

She dived for the ground, correctly anticipating that he'd raise his pistol and fire it at her. Metal clanged off the bomb casing.

She called out, "Are you sure you ought to be shooting at a live nuke, Freddie?" Her brain kicked into overdrive. Given his horrified reaction, he wasn't planning to die tonight. Which meant he'd try to disarm this thing. Which might give her a window to attempt an escape. There had to be another way out of here. The only possibility was that dark niche in the far back corner. She could see all the other walls and they were solid rock.

He continued to fire wildly, screaming invectives in Bhoukari. She crawled on her belly for some crates beyond the bomb she'd just armed. Once she got behind them, she came up onto her hands and knees and moved away faster. Freddie's weapon stopped firing. If she was incredibly lucky, in his tantrum he'd used up all his bullets and didn't have another clip on hand.

"Come out, Sophie, and I won't kill you."

Yeah, right. She ignored the taunt and ducked into the shadow behind a decent-sized crate. She listened for movement. Feet scuffed on the floor. It sounded as if he was moving toward the ticking bomb.

He started swearing again. Something about how the hell to turn this thing off. It sounded as if he hit the targeting computer several times with something hard. Maybe the butt of his pistol. Running footsteps—away from her, thank God. A door opening. Freddie's voice shouting out into the hallway for someone named Mahmoud.

Now was her chance to move.

She peeked out from behind the crate. Freddie's back was to her. She darted across the last open space between her and that dark corner. The walls were crudely chiseled and rough outcroppings of rock overlapped, creating heavy shadows. Pulling her black garb close around her lest it snag on something, she eased forward.

Somebody shouted something at Freddie. She started. There was gunfire outside the compound. *Brian.* The Medusas must be creating a diversion for her. Bless them. Freddie shouted back, demanding Mahmoud again. She used the men's argument to slide around a large outcropping.

Bingo. A broad tunnel was hidden behind it. The floor had been smoothed, but the walls were in their rough, natural state. She moved forward as quickly as she could without making any noise. Good Lord willing, Freddie would be occupied for the next few minutes trying to disarm the bomb. Small lightbulbs strung at long intervals provided enough light that, as soon as she got a few dozen yards from the storeroom she was able to take off running.

And run she did. Like the wind.

"She's moving," Vanessa announced tersely. "Away from Freddie." Brian all but lost control of his bladder at the announcement.

"Where is she?" he retorted sharply.

"Moving east. She's weaving like she's dodging obstacles. But she's coming fast. She's running."

Jack ordered quickly, "Everyone but Ripper shift position to the west wall. Let's pull them over that way like we're preparing to storm the gate. Rip, you hold position on the east wall. Lay down covering fire for her if necessary when she comes over the wall."

"Roger," Brian acknowledged.

Vanessa announced, "I'm calling in the air strike. I'll make a radio call when the bombs are sixty seconds out for you to take cover. The planes are airborne, loitering just off shore, so in about ten minutes, have a spot picked out."

Brian glanced at his watch, then back at the wall. *C'mon, Sophie. Run to me, baby.*

Thank God for all those miserable runs on the beach Brian had subjected her to. The tunnel wasn't steep, but went steadily uphill. In a few minutes, she was huffing like a winded racehorse. But then she thought about the possibility that Freddie had sent men up this tunnel after her. When that thought gave out at bringing her new energy, she thought of Brian waiting for her at the end of this tunnel.

Of course, she had no idea where this thing came out. For all she knew, she was going to pop up in the middle of Freddie's bedroom. But once she was on the surface, she would at least stand a chance of making her way out of this nightmare. And she wouldn't be buried alive in that damned bunker.

The problem with this tunnel was it was the only way out of that storeroom. Freddie's flunkies would know exactly where to find her. All they had to do was chase her up this tunnel till they caught her. Or worse, send some guys to wherever it emerged and just wait for her at the exit.

Surely, the Medusas had called in the air strike by now. Unless Freddie himself was chasing her up this tunnel, which she seriously doubted, she had to have plenty of separation from him. To distract herself from her heaving breath and the knives stabbing her legs and sides, she considered whether or not the nuke behind her would blow up if the bunker busters hit it. If it did, the F-18 pilots were in for a hell of a surprise in their rearview mirrors when the mushroom cloud went up.

I'm coming, Brian.

As her oxygen stores depleted and her feet grew heavy, she remembered that first run he'd taken her on—the two-mile run that had turned into four miles. He'd said she could run ten more miles if she really had to. She'd made it all the way back down the beach that day. She could keep going now. Yes, she felt like crap, but this was her life. Her and Brian's future. Kids and old age and years of going to sleep and waking up in Brian's arms.

She dug deep. Accepted the pain. And kept on going.

"She's approaching the wall," Vanessa murmured. Brian scanned the deserted expanse of wall eagerly. Any second now, she should pop over it. Jack's tactic had worked. Undisciplined mob that they were, all of Sollem's men had run for the gate when the firing concentrated entirely on the west wall. Sophie ought to have a clear shot at escaping over here.

"Do you see her?" Vanessa asked.

"Negative," he replied, startled.

"She's outside the wall."

He scanned the entire compound again. How in the hell could he have missed her? "No, she's not. I have no visual on her."

Vanessa swore. "Damn. Then she's still underground. She must be using some sort of escape tunnel."

Brian thought fast. "Vector me to her position. I'll follow above ground until she surfaces."

"Ping your position," Vanessa replied.

Brian pressed the position transmitter on his personal GPS locator.

"Gotcha. Her current course will take her approximately thirty yards to your north. She's moving east by northeast."

Brian looked over his shoulder. "There's a big upthrust of rocks over that way. I'll make for it."

"Call me when you get there and I'll update your vector."

He was already moving and merely clicked his radio button twice to acknowledge the comment.

I'm coming, sweetheart. Keep running.

Sophie thought she felt the air growing drier. Colder. The tunnel curved just ahead. Her watch showed maybe two minutes before the nuke behind her was set to blow. That was the other problem with this tunnel. The shock wave from the bomb would travel right up it and make vapor of her. Nonetheless, she slowed down. She tried to control her breathing, to keep it quiet, but that was hopeless.

Panting, she eased forward. Please God, let there not be guards waiting for her.

* * *

"She has stopped. Twenty yards, bearing zero-five-zero from your position."

Brian looked over his shoulder. That might be a cave over that way. Pockets and fissures were plentiful in this outcropping, and he was having to proceed slowly, clearing every one before he passed in front of it. He double clicked his radio.

Stealthily, he glided toward the possible cave entrance. And froze.

Was that movement?

He waited, as still as a rattlesnake about to strike. His night-vision goggles pierced the darkness of the opening, made a gray-green blob out of it. There it was again. Yup. A human shape. Somebody was standing inside that opening. Was it Sophie?

His first impulse was to dash forward and pull her into his arms. But the soldier in him held him back. He took a slow step forward, trusting his camouflage gear to hide him. Another step.

Another shape came into view. Two men. Both armed. Both peering into the cave. This must be the tunnel exit. And the bastards were waiting to ambush Sophie. Thank God he hadn't run up and hugged the first one.

Fury roared through him. He swung his rifle up and aimed in one quick, smooth movement. Tap, tap. Tap, tap on the trigger. Two quick shots to the back of each man's head and they both dropped to the ground. He waited for more men to emerge. Nada.

That didn't mean there weren't more men hiding in the cave, though. Crouching low, he crept forward.

"Sixty seconds till bomb release," Vanessa announced.

Crap. He *had* to find Sophie! He started a countdown in his head. *Fifty-nine. Fifty-eight.*

"You're maybe ten yards from her position, Rip. She's due west of you."

He didn't acknowledge the call at all, which would signal Vanessa that he was in full stealth mode.

He rounded the opening of what turned out to be a good-sized cave. No other heat signatures appeared inside. Just the two rapidly cooling blobs on the floor. *Forty-seven. Forty-six.*

There was no time, dammit! He had to find Sophie and get both of them under cover! This cave might very well collapse when the bombs and debris started raining down.

He took a chance. Called out low, "Sophie. It's me."

A sob echoed eerily from the depths of the cave. A black shape stumbled around an outcropping. "Brian!" she cried.

He rushed forward, crushing her against his chest.

Thirty-five. Thirty-four.

"We've got to get out of here," they both said simultaneously.

He released her and whirled, grabbing her hand and taking off running for the exit. "Why?" he grunted.

"Nuke bomb…armed…at the bottom…of this tunnel… shock wave…"

Oh, damn. They burst out into the open air. He looked around frantically. The shock wave would come straight out of the cave, then spread in a cone. He leaped to the south, curving back west toward the Sollem compound.

Twenty-two. Twenty-one.

"Run!" he urged Sophie.

They scrambled wildly over the rocks, stumbling and clawing, as he cast around frantically for a hiding spot.

There. A low, deep pocket at ground level with a heavy boulder stretching across its top. He dragged Sophie toward it. "Hurry!"

Nine. Eight.

They dived for the opening.

Six. Five.

He grabbed her and rolled, as far back into the crevice as he could wedge them.

Three. Two.

The first blast was muffled, more felt than heard. Or maybe it was just that his ears were ringing so badly with panic that he didn't really hear the noise. The scream of jets overhead came next. A second blast—a cluster of blasts, actually, followed the first one. It was much louder. The ground shook, showering them with dirt and bits of shale.

The first bomb must have been the bunker buster. The second attack was the big munitions, designed to destroy everything inside the newly opened can of sardines.

"Was that the nuke going off?" Sophie asked fearfully.

"I don't think so. I think the ground would have shaken a lot harder."

"I armed it and then broke the computer so it couldn't be turned off. It'll explode any second," she said urgently.

"The targeting computers are fairly fragile. If an armed one was destroyed, the instructions for the bomb to activate shouldn't get transmitted. Who knows? Maybe someone down there disarmed it anyway."

Sophie sagged in relief in his arms.

Brian continued grimly, "However, if our bombs breached the containment chambers on the weapons, there could still be a radiation release. I want us to get the hell away from here, now. Can you run some more?"

"Do I have any choice?"

He replied with a smile in his voice, "Not really."

They crawled out from under their hiding place. A bright orange glow lit up the night. The Sollem compound, the remains of it at any rate, was on fire.

He pressed his radio button. "I've got Sophie. Everyone pull back. There may be a nuclear radiation release. Acknowledge."

Jack acknowledged immediately by ordering sharply, "Everyone, back off now. Full speed retreat. No covering fire. Just run like hell. You too, Ripper."

Vanessa transmitted, "Rendezvous on me. I'll have the Teddy R. send in a chopper for immediate evacuation."

Brian took off running. "Shed your gear," he called out, dropping his rifle and backpack as he went. He reached over and helped Sophie wrestle out of her flapping robe and tossed it aside. He grabbed her elbow and propelled her along beside him, sharing his strength and stamina with her as they fled across the desert.

Thank God for all the running on the beach he'd done with her back in San Diego. Both of them were conditioned for the most important run of their lives. Side-by-side they raced toward the ridge ahead of them.

Sophie spotted the rest of the Medusas fleeing roughly south across the sand, too. Their paths converged, and as one they all burst over the top of the ridge.

One of the prettiest sights she had ever seen stretched out below her. A big, twin-rotor rescue helicopter squatted at the bottom of the dune, its side door open and Vanessa and Isabella standing in it, waving them forward.

Slip-sliding a good six feet down the loose sand slope with every running step, Sophie called on the last reserves of will she could muster. Almost there. They'd almost made it. And then they tumbled inside the chopper, its rotor blades biting into the air before the door was closed, lifting them off the ground. The aircraft veered hard and picked up speed fast, racing low across the desert.

Sophie collapsed on the cold metal flooring, her chest

heaving. Thankfully, Brian was breathing about as hard as she was. He made eye contact with her, and nodded his approval, apparently too winded to talk. But she'd kept up with him. He'd boosted her along with him, and she'd done it. She'd kept going. No matter what. Pride welled up inside her.

Jack huffed between hard breaths, "Any radiation being picked up?"

Vanessa nodded. "There's been a release. But not from a full-blown detonation. One or more of the bombs must have been compromised in the attack."

"How bad?" Brian panted.

"Bad enough. Thankfully, this is a sparsely populated part of the world. There are no major cities for several hundred miles east of here. That's where most of the radiation cloud will be blown."

"How about us?" Sophie asked grimly.

"They'll have to test us when we get back to the ship. But our exposure should be minimal. Dirt and rocks stop most radiation. If everyone was behind some sort of rock structure at the time of the blasts, most of the initial radiation wave should have missed us."

Sophie looked over at Brian. She saw in his eyes that he was remembering the crevice they'd dived into at the last moment. He smiled reassuringly at her.

She looked back at Vanessa. "What about the people in the compound?"

Vanessa threw her a regretful glance. "The first bomb damage assessment won't be done until daylight. But I expect anyone who survived the air strike won't survive the radiation."

The interior of the helicopter went silent for a moment. They took no pleasure in having killed the entire Sollem clan. Sophie thought of Grandma Sollem and Freddie's wives and children. They'd known the risks. They knew who and what

Freddie was, and they'd known they were protecting him. It was a tragic loss. But at the end of the day, it had been their choice to share his fate.

Brian leaned against the front bulkhead and held out an arm to her. She cuddled up against his big, warm body, as he drew her close.

"We did it," she murmured in awe.

"No, *you* did it," he replied. "You saved thousands or maybe even millions of lives tonight."

"I wasn't talking about that, silly."

He craned his head to look down at her questioningly.

She answered slowly. "You turned a legal secretary from Utah into a commando. I lived through the mission that was supposed to kill me. You didn't lose your job. We stopped a terrorist. And despite it all—maybe because of it all—we found each other."

A smile spread slowly across his face, gathering momentum and turning into a full-blown laugh.

A cheer went up around them and Jack slapped Brian on the shoulder. "Congratulations, buddy. You're now an official member of the Frazzled Significant Others of Medusas Club."

Sophie frowned. "But I'm not a Medusa."

Vanessa leaned forward. "Do you want to be? After the way you conducted yourself tonight, I'd be happy to continue your training and bring you on board when you're ready."

Sophie blinked. Looked around in shock. Everyone was smiling and nodding at her. It wasn't a joke! She glanced up at Brian. "Do you think your nerves could take it?"

He rolled his eyes. "As long as you swear never to go on anymore solo suicide missions."

Sophie looked over at Vanessa, who was grinning. The Medusa team leader answered for her. "I think that could be arranged. We Medusas generally prefer to work as a team."

Sophie met Vanessa's gaze. "I would be honored to be given a chance to join your team. But I don't want any free rides. I want to earn my way on to the team fair and square."

Vanessa laughed. "You can count on that."

"Do I get to pick my trainer?"

Jack spoke up. "As long as it's Brian Riley, you do."

Sophie grinned. "Then we have a deal."

Brian's arm tightened around her and he smiled down at her in joy so bright it nearly blinded her. "And to think," he murmured. "I was satisfied with a single perfect moment before. But now I have an entire perfect life to look forward to. *We* have it to look forward to!"

She stared up at him. "Really?" she breathed. "Do you mean that?"

He gazed deep into her eyes and said soberly, "Yes, I do. There's something I wanted to say to you before you went out on the op—"

She interrupted, "There's something I wanted to tell you, too—"

Simultaneously, they declared, "I love you."

They stared at each other in shock. Then laughed. Then everyone in the chopper was laughing.

She wrapped her arms around him and held on tight. Tight enough to get through the rest of the helicopter ride out of the desert. Tight enough to get through continuing to train with him until she could join him in his work. Tight enough to stick beside him, through thick and thin, for the rest of their lives.

They really had done it. She'd been sure she'd fail in her training, but with Brian's help, she hadn't. She'd been just as sure she was going to die on the mission, but she'd lived. And there was no way an exciting, dangerous, sexy man was going to burst into her quiet boring life, sweep her off her feet, and fall madly in love with her, either. But he had. Oh, how he had.

Maybe Brian was right. Maybe nothing was impossible, after all.

* * * * *

Don't miss Always Look Twice,
by Sheri WhiteFeather, the next BOMBSHELL
*title available from Mills & Boon® Intrigue
in November 2008.*

Mills & Boon® Intrigue
brings you a sneak preview of…

Karen Whiddon's Bulletproof Marriage.

After two years of thinking her Lazlo Group
spy husband Sean McGregor is dead, SIS agent
Natalie Major is stunned when she calls for
help from a mission gone bad – she's trapped
by enemy fire – and out of the smoking ruins
her husband strides towards her, back from the
dead…to avenge his own "murder" and to
win back the woman he loves!

Don't miss this thrilling new story in the
MISSION: IMPASSIONED series, available
next month in Mills & Boon® Intrigue!

Bulletproof Marriage

by

Karen Whiddon

If reinforcements didn't show up soon, Natalie Major thought grimly, she might as well paint a target on her chest and leap into the open. The unknown assassin— or assassins—were that close. The decaying concrete warehouse she'd holed up in only had two ways out—and one of them had been blown to rubble.

She needed help. Corbett Lazlo, her father's oldest friend and owner of one of the top private investigative agencies in the world, had promised to send someone. She'd asked for the best.

Now she wished she'd asked for the most prompt.

Gallows humor. She'd never been particularly good at it before, though she'd grown more proficient.

Her husband wouldn't even recognize her now if he were still alive. Once, he'd been Lazlo's top agent. She'd married a Lazlo Group spook, just like her own father had been. Retired now, and in a wheelchair, her father lived in relative seclusion. Her beloved husband, Sean, hadn't been so lucky. He'd been killed two years ago this week. Lazlo's group seemed to be the ruin of everyone she loved, so in honor of her dead husband and disabled father, and in defiance of the Lazlo legacy she could easily have embraced, she'd worked her way to the top of SIS, the British Secret Intelligence Service. There was no job too difficult, no task too dangerous for Sean McGregor's widow.

Until now.

She scouted the area. Trapped inside the abandoned warehouse, she was fast running out of options. The concrete walls made a good shield against bullets, but she needed to see her enemies. Right now, she could only hear them. And it was hard to fight when you had no idea who the enemy might be. Or where they were hiding.

Plus, cement was cold and hard and reminded her too damn much of a tomb.

The shooters fired off another round of shots. AK-47s. Random bullets ricocheted crazily and dangerously off the cement walls and floors. She couldn't even dodge them, having no idea where they'd go.

She'd found the abandoned warehouse two days

ago. A concrete bunker in a run-down area of Glasgow had seemed relatively safe. Not wanting to endanger others by staying at a B and B or hotel, she'd used the concrete warehouse as her base, returning to sleep and regroup while attempting to gather information on whoever had sold out her team. Since Millaflora—a low-down, no-good mole operating as a double agent inside the SIS—had already been caught, she had no idea who she was looking for.

Officially, she was on administrative leave, supposedly holed up, incognito in an unknown luxury hotel on the French Riviera. No one in her office knew she'd come to Glasgow, not even her supervisor.

And though she'd tried to take extraordinary precautions similar to those she used when deep undercover, her enemy had found her.

Whoever "they" were.

She supposed the whys and the hows didn't matter. Not now. All that mattered was that if help didn't arrive soon, she was dead.

Her ammo nearly gone, no backup, and no alternative plan—pretty shoddy situation for an undercover agent who'd recently been promoted to team leader.

It had to have something to do with the code. Natalie was sure of it. She'd been so close to cracking it. She and her team.

Now they all were dead and she was on the run.

And she had only herself to rely on. In seven years of service, she'd never had a single casualty. Until now. Now she'd lost her entire team. They'd been eliminated, killed in a way that left no doubt she was next. All the codes they'd been working on had disappeared, at least as far as anyone knew. She'd told no one that she'd made her own private copy.

Not knowing who was on her side, she hadn't dared to contact SIS. She'd called her father, knowing he'd contact Corbett, knowing Lazlo would help.

"Come on, reinforcements," she muttered. Her father'd told her Corbett had promised to send help. The head of the Lazlo Group never went back on his word.

A movement across the alley caught her attention. Finally! Someone had arrived to help her out of this hellhole.

She took another look and blinked, wondering if the stress had finally claimed her mind.

Out of the mist and smoke, a dead man strode toward her, keeping close to the wall, staying in the shadows, but coming. For her.

Natalie began to shake.

Shots rang out. Crouching, the man began to run. More shots. So far, he hadn't been hit. He'd always been lucky that way.

At least, until the day he'd died.

Dead. He was dead and buried.

Rocking back onto her heels, she rubbed her eyes and took another look.

She hadn't been wrong. The man she'd loved more than any other, her soul mate, her husband, the man she'd mourned, the man she'd never thought to see again, kept moving toward her.

Frozen, she watched as he continued, his low crouch purposeful and unafraid. Or maybe he didn't care. After all, a man couldn't die twice, right?

Her heart drummed in her ears. Sean. Her husband, Sean. This couldn't be real, couldn't be happening.

She wasn't the type to faint—not anymore. Too many hard lessons learned. Instead, she'd taught herself to push back, to fight.

But how did one battle a ghost?

From the smoke and the grave, against the periodic bursts of gunfire, he continued to come toward her. He moved exactly the way she remembered—purposeful and bold, dodging bullets as though he were untouchable. She'd often thought that very arrogance had been what had gotten him killed.

Killed.

Yet here he was, ducking under the concrete overhang into her shadowed hiding place, solid and real and alive.

When he reached her, he stopped, his dark gaze intense. She couldn't move. He was still beautiful, even in the dust and the dirt and the danger. She caught her breath, unable to speak.

"I'm here," he said, his voice husky, as though too long unused, a hint of wariness in his gaze.

"I…" She moved toward him, inspecting him, still unable to believe what the fates had just returned to her.

"Get down," he snarled, yanking her behind the concrete wall with him as the shooters let loose with several rounds of shots.

"What the—" he cursed, letting her go. "They've got AK-47s. You must have royally pissed someone off. Why are they trying to kill you?"

She still couldn't find her voice. Unable to help herself, she let her gaze roam hungrily over his muscular body—the way her hands used to.

"Either I'm dead, dying or you're not dead," she said, feeling like an idiot, still not sure what to think.

"No." His dark gaze locked with hers, daring her wrath. "I'm not dead."

TWO SPARKLING CHRISTMAS ROMANCES...

Karen Rose Smith
Melissa McClone

Christmas Together

...full of the joys and warmth of the season

Twelfth Night Proposal
by Karen Rose Smith

Rescued by the Magic of Christmas
by Melissa McClone

Available 7th November 2008

Celebrate 100 years of pure reading pleasure with Mills & Boon®

To mark our centenary, each month we're publishing a special 100th Birthday Edition. These celebratory editions are packed with extra features and include a FREE bonus story.

Plus, you have the chance to enter a fabulous monthly prize draw. See 100th Birthday Edition books for details.

Now that's worth celebrating!

September 2008

Crazy about her Spanish Boss by Rebecca Winters
Includes FREE bonus story
Rafael's Convenient Proposal

November 2008

**The Rancher's Christmas Baby
by Cathy Gillen Thacker**
Includes FREE bonus story *Baby's First Christmas*

December 2008

One Magical Christmas by Carol Marinelli
Includes FREE bonus story *Emergency at Bayside*

Look for Mills & Boon® 100th Birthday Editions at your favourite bookseller or visit
www.millsandboon.co.uk

4 FREE

BOOKS AND A SURPRISE GIFT!

We would like to take this opportunity to thank you for reading this Mills & Boon® book by offering you the chance to take FOUR more specially selected titles from the Intrigue series absolutely FREE! We're also making this offer to introduce you to the benefits of the Mills & Boon® Book Club—

★ FREE home delivery
★ FREE gifts and competitions
★ FREE monthly Newsletter
★ Exclusive Mills & Boon® Book Club offers
★ Books available before they're in the shops

Accepting these FREE books and gift places you under no obligation to buy, you may cancel at any time, even after receiving your free shipment. Simply complete your details below and return the entire page to the address below. You don't even need a stamp!

YES! Please send me 4 free Intrigue books and a surprise gift. I understand that unless you hear from me, I will receive 6 superb new titles every month for just £3.15 each, postage and packing free. I am under no obligation to purchase any books and may cancel my subscription at any time. The free books and gift will be mine to keep in any case.

18ZED

Ms/Mrs/Miss/Mr ....Initials ....
BLOCK CAPITALS PLEASE

Surname ....

Address ....

....

....Postcode..........................

Send this whole page to:
UK: FREEPOST CN81, Croydon, CR9 3WZ